AF439211

CROSSMATCH

CROSSMATCH

CROSSMATCH

a novel

Carmel Miranda

Copyright © 2020 Carmel Miranda

All rights reserved. This book or any part of it may not be reproduced or used in any manner whatsoever without prior written permission of the author, except for the use of brief quotations in a book review.

Crossmatch is a work of fiction. All characters and events in this book are a product of the author's imagination. Any resemblance to real persons, living or dead, is purely coincidental.

First published in Sri Lanka by Katha Publishers in December 2020

Cover design and digital art by Carmel Miranda, Anya Wikramanayake and Nelun Harasgama

Illustrations by Carmel Miranda

Crossmatch

1. To match (related items from two or more lists or groups)
2. *(Medical)* To test the compatibility of a donor's and recipient's blood or tissue prior to blood transfusion or organ transplantation

For

A, A and A

CONTENTS

Part I

1

I start to daydream during the second stage.

There's not been much progress in the last half-hour despite much coaxing and repeated cries of 'Push!'

I'm told there is no cause for alarm – yet. This could go on for another hour or so.

I think about the baby, and wonder what it will be named. I know the naming process is likely to be involved. The parents might consult an astrologer, who will be informed of the date, place and precise time of birth. Using this information, he will draw up an astrological chart – the horoscope: a map of the heavens at the particular moment in time the child was born. He will then pick a set of auspicious letters, or sounds, from which the parents will choose one to be the first part of their offspring's name. If the child is lucky, it will escape relatively unscathed, with a name that is short, simple, and easy-to-pronounce. But more often than not, it would be long and unwieldy, a slew of syllables strung together.

Or, they might simply name the child after a popular cricketer, or film star, or worse – a politician.

Even so, it would be better off than me. For I had been named after something dull and unexciting.

An institution.

A hospital, actually.

The story that I had been told went something like this: after years of trying to have a baby, my parents had consulted a string of the best specialists in the country, only to be told that my mother would never be able to conceive. But then, a well-known doctor – the owner of an establishment called the Lotus Nursing Home – had treated her and achieved the impossible, and in gratitude, my mother had bestowed on her miracle baby (me) the name 'Lotus'.

Why do parents burden their offspring with names that they misguidedly think would make them (the offspring) special? Okay - I know the lotus is a beautiful flower, sacred to many religions and all that, but it's just not me. When I hear the name, I picture a super-fast sports car. Or the love-child of dreamy, *ganja*-smoking parents. As far as I knew, my parents had been fairly ordinary, hard-working doctors at the time of my birth. So couldn't they have picked an ordinary, simple name for me? For the billionth time I wonder, why name me after a hospital?

A high-pitched scream pierces the air and snaps me out of my reverie. I freeze, gloved hands clasped in front of me, forgetting for an instant where I am. There is a gush of blood – it forms a crimson pool on the polythene sheet, then wells up and breaks up into rivulets that zig-zag their way to the edge of the bed and drip into a cracked white enamel pail, each successive drop taking longer to trickle down as the blood slowly thickens into dark, glistening, jelly-like clots. The space I am standing in feels cramped and claustrophobic; there are three of us in the cubicle and the bed occupies most of it. Faded mustard-coloured curtains which had probably once been a bright yellow are drawn snugly around us, and above, a ceiling fan rotates slowly, circulating eddies of warm, humid air.

The apron tied around me envelopes me from neck to ankle and tickles my chin irritatingly. It is made of a stiff green waterproof material and rustles loudly like a *siri-siri* bag with the slightest move I make. Not that I can move much in these cumbersome white rubber boots, which bear some suspicious-looking stains and are several sizes too large for me.

The midwife, oblivious to my catatonic state, performs a quick manoeuvre and looks up beaming, holding something in her hands. Something pink and shiny and wriggly…

…and alive.

'It's a girl!'

She makes the announcement triumphantly, as if she personally arranged for this to happen.

As three miraculously becomes four, the warm, musty smell of fresh blood mingled with the rank odour of sweat concentrated in the enclosed space hits me like a punch, and a black wave of dizziness threatens to engulf me. I will myself not to faint, desperately trying to keep my blood circulating by flexing my knees and ankles.

Oh, yes.

Reality check.

I am in Labour Ward, or the 'Birthing Centre' as it is now fashionably called, witnessing my first delivery and trying to stop myself from passing out on the floor.

Nothing I had seen or read had prepared me for this. The attending midwife had asked me to glove up and assist her, but during the monotony of the preceding hour my thoughts had drifted. I remember now what led to my daydream: it was the thought of the emerging baby and the names it might be saddled with.

The mother – who is lying on the bed with her thighs splayed out and her feet hooked up in stirrups – seems as shell-shocked as me, but at the sight of her bloody offspring, manages to produce a tremulous smile and then collapses back on the pillow, losing further interest in the proceedings. Her long black hair is damp and matted, and beads of sweat dot her forehead and the skin above her lips. She looks young – no more than nineteen or twenty. A colourful 'friendship' bracelet with threads of red, yellow and blue braided in an intricate design is knotted about her slender wrist. There is no sign of the father. He is redundant at this moment anyway. And this is not one of those modern units that welcome fathers into the birthing process, thank you very much. I concentrate on staying upright, resisting the urge to escape from the stuffy cubicle, and thankfully, the dizziness passes.

The baby immediately proceeds to thrash its limbs about and set up a clamour - a series of high-pitched, reedy wails, plaintive and persistent. Its wide open mouth dominates the wrinkled contorted face like a big 'O', and its body is covered with flecks of blood, mucus and *vernix* - the greasy cheese-like substance that coats a baby's skin in the last few months of pregnancy.

Whoever said babies are beautiful? This one looks like something out of a horror movie.

'Come, come,' the midwife says to me cordially, as if she were inviting me to have a cup of tea. She is one of the senior ones, a witch-like crone with a bushy unibrow, protruding incisors and a voice like an ambulance siren. 'Are you going to cut this today or tomorrow?'

She cackles loudly and hands me a peculiar pair of scissors with blades that look like a parrot's beak, saying, 'Cut here,' pointing, of course, to the umbilical cord. I fumble with the instrument and then clumsily position it between the two plastic clips that are clamped on the cord a few inches apart. As I hesitantly press the handles together, she clicks her tongue and exclaims impatiently, '*Aiyo*, not like *that!* Harder!'

With trembling fingers I squeeze the handles, slicing through the translucent milky-grey cord. It is soft and gelatinous, like the tentacle of a giant squid (minus the suckers), and is surprisingly easy to cut. I expect bleeding, but only a few drops of dark blood ooze from the cut ends.

As soon as the baby's tie to its mother is severed, the paediatric registrar appears as if by magic - a petite girl with short straight hair cut in a bob who looks barely more than a child herself. A bright pink stethoscope is slung around her neck and a miniature koala bear clings to the lapel of her white coat. The clip-on bear wears a red shirt with the words 'I ♥ *Australia*' printed on the back in tiny white lettering. She sweeps her straightened hair behind her ears, snaps on a pair of gloves in a business-like manner and swoops down on the baby, deftly bundling it up in a towel and rubbing it vigorously. It seems to object to this rough treatment, screwing up its little red face and screaming angrily, its wails punctuated by little sobs.

Who could blame it? It has just been rudely evicted from its warm and comfortable home of nine months, squeezed through a narrow tunnel into an alien world of bright lights and loud noises. But of course its vocal efforts are achieving their purpose – expanding its compressed lungs and filling them with air. The tips of the delicate fingers and toes which had been tinged with blue turn a healthy pink within a few seconds.

The registrar gives the baby a quick once-over, listens to its heart beat with the pink stethoscope, and after a final vigorous rub, places it on the mother's chest. The wailing stops instantly and it lies there contentedly, seeming to sense that this was the body that had sheltered it these past few months.

I gaze at the mother and baby, entranced.

So there's something to this mother-newborn bonding business, after all.

I am transported to another place, another time, and I picture another mother and baby, lying in a different room – this mother not smiling but lying unconscious, the baby small and weak. Was that baby placed at its mother's breast like this? Or was it whisked away in an incubator while its mother haemorrhaged uncontrollably?

My thoughts are interrupted once again, this time by the paediatric registrar's crisp pronouncement: 'Baby's fine!' With a swish of the faded yellow curtains she disappears as suddenly as she had arrived.

The midwife acknowledges the registrar's words with a nod. I start to peel my gloves off but the midwife stops me.

'No, no, not finished! What about third stage? You forgot?' That witch-like cackle again.

Oh… yes. Had completely forgotten about the third stage of labour: the delivery of the placenta.

She places one hand firmly on the mother's belly, and, with her other, gently tugs the cut end of the cord which is dangling from the birth canal. With a further gush of blood, the placenta – a fleshy, floppy disc about the size of a plate - comes tumbling out and lands heavily with a soft plop into a steel dish, wobbling like a jelly and dripping blood. On one side, its surface is dusky red and raw, and on the other is a thin white membrane covering thick tortuous worm-like blood vessels. The young mother utters a soft moan, but is soon distracted by the little mite who has now latched on to a nipple and is sucking away, noisily and contentedly. It has been cleaned up somewhat, and with most of the muck on its face wiped away, looks fairly presentable.

'Right!' the witch says, beaming at me. 'Next time, you will do the delivery.'

2

It is an explosive start to my first rotation in 'gyn and obs' (short for gynaecology and obstetrics, and pronounced *gin* and obs, which sounds to me like something you'd order in a bar). This morning, my 'Clinical group', comprising Harsha, Tara, Dinesh, Devika, Rehan and myself – a motley crew of six united by the alphabetical arrangement of our surnames – had assembled in the Maternity block across from the main hospital, where we were introduced to the consultant we had been assigned to for the rest of the month.

Harsha is a chubby, cheerful boy from a village near Kandy, who's dreamed of becoming a doctor ever since he was a little boy. Tara is the daughter of a wealthy businessman who owns a chain of furniture stores. Like me, she grew up in Colombo, but there, the resemblance ends. She's pretty and popular, has six ear piercings and changes hairstyles more frequently than she changes her toothbrush. Dinesh is a short, shy boy from Trinco who is afflicted with a severe stutter but is the smartest in the group and is a whiz at cricket. Devika is studious and smug, the 'goody-goody' of the group. Pretty in an anaemic kind of way, she wears her long hair neatly centre-parted in a geometrically straight line and hanging in a snake-like plait down to her buttocks. Rehan is lanky and laconic, almost surgically attached to his beloved motor-bike. He hardly ever turns up for lectures but has an incredible memory which sees him through exams.

The consultant, Dr Henry Fernando, is a stooped elderly gentleman with fluffy silvery-white hair and gold-rimmed spectacles, and looks like somebody's kind old grandfather. He mumbled a few words of greeting to us, rubbing his fingers and thumb together in a peculiar manner, and then shuffled off leaving us in the hands of his super-efficient senior registrar, a gruff, statuesque female called Dr Indira Costa.

Henry is close to retirement and we found out that he suffers from Parkinson's disease – which explained the mask-like facial expression, the strange finger tremor and the shuffling gait. The disease appears to restrict him severely, and now he hardly performs any operations, only conducting the occasional clinic and ward round. His senior registrar Indira – soon to be a consultant – handles most of his workload and would be in charge of us. She is as fast as he is slow, and, in an emergency, could whip a baby out of a uterus with her powerful arms faster than you could say 'Lower Segment Caesarean Section'.

We were informed that we had to each conduct three normal deliveries and assist in three C-sections before getting signed up at the end of the month. After a lightning-quick ward round, we had all been assigned tasks, mine being to report to Labour Ward, which is how I ended up in these ill-fitting boots, swathed in polythene, standing in a puddle of blood and various other body fluids.

Feel all tingly and pumped-up when I leave Labour Ward. Is this what they call an adrenaline rush? Had not been looking forward to starting obstetrics this morning but can't wait to return tomorrow.

For me, this is a novel feeling indeed. You see, unlike most of my fellow-students who embraced their medical studies with fervour and enthusiasm, I had never harboured a burning desire to be a doctor. I can't count the number of times I had been tempted to chuck the whole thing up and switch to something else. Like maybe accountancy, or IT. Or even join a bank or a travel agency – things that my school friends had ended up doing. But, being something of a plodder, I resisted temptation and simply carried on. And so, I am now in the fourth year of the medical course, studying at the Colombo Medical College, a prestigious institution that has been churning out doctors for almost a hundred years, and one I'm told (frequently) I'm privileged to attend.

So how had I ended up here? Being the only child of two doctors (my parents had met while studying at the same Medical College) and fairly studious in school, it had been a surprisingly easy path. My father had been so pleased when I was selected for the medical course that I didn't have the heart to tell him that really, it was the last thing I wanted.

I made it through the first two years in a daze (anatomy and biochemistry can have that effect on you; physiology had been the saving grace). The third-year subjects microbiology and parasitology hadn't been much better. Learning the names and habits of hundreds of disease-causing bugs and microorganisms had been mind-numbingly boring. The low point of the third year had been the parasitology practical in which I had to fish through a small jar of liquidized human faecal matter with a toothpick *(seriously)* and prepare a slide so that I could spot, under a microscope, the eggs of a worm that inhabited the digestive tract of the unfortunate person who had donated the specimen.

Still, the third year hadn't been a total disaster.

That was the year we started 'Clinicals'.

That is, we were let loose on the hospital wards and got to meet *Real Patients*. After a year and a half of pottering around cold dissecting rooms, dusty labs and lecture halls, the medical course suddenly came to life, and in spite of myself, a flicker of interest started developing inside me. On the wards, I was amazed to find that total strangers opened their entire lives to us. They confided in us their most intimate secrets, and allowed us to prod and to poke them – all because we were in this unique profession, albeit on the lowermost rung.

That first year on the wards was meant to inculcate in us the principles of 'taking a history': gathering information from the patient. We were taught that many medical conditions could be diagnosed just by taking a good history. We had to learn exactly what questions to ask in order to elicit the information required to make a diagnosis, much like Sherlock Holmes solving one of his famed mysteries by asking just a single question.

We were also taught how to examine patients methodically and systematically, and we spent hours tramping up and down the wards until our feet ached, practicing our newly acquired skills on hapless patients.

'Inspection! Palpation! Percussion! Auscultation! In that order!' Dr Nadaraja would thunder these words at us at regular intervals during our first ever stint on the wards, two months of general medicine. 'Some diagnoses can be made from the foot of the bed. Look before you touch!' Woe betide the student who picked up a stethoscope to listen to a patient's heart or lungs bypassing the first three steps.

Inspection, palpation, percussion, auscultation.

It was a mantra we would never forget. Nada was an irascible old-school physician who believed that medicine was an art rather than a science, and despised the use of electronic devices and other modern gadgets. Sadly, he dropped dead of a heart attack in the hospital car park in the middle of our rotation, but fortunately not before he had drilled into us most of the third-year basics.

Speaking of electronic devices, there goes mine again. I feel a vibration against my hip and fish out my mobile phone from the pocket of my white coat. It had buzzed several times during the morning but I had ignored it, because although some consultants encourage googling during ward rounds, others are quite strict about the use of mobile phones during clinicals. Hence, whenever I am on the wards, I keep my phone - an embarrassingly large smartphone which was a birthday gift from my father - carefully hidden and in silent mode.

There is a string of messages on the phone: they are mostly from other students - members of study groups or tutorial groups - informing me about timings of classes and tutorials. The last three messages make me frown. Aunty Christine - my father's oldest and bossiest sister - is constantly pestering me about something or other.   I try to avoid her as much as possible, but ever since she learned to text, I am never out of reach, and I usually receive a daily barrage of messages from her. And she has this annoying habit of texting in capitals, which makes it seem like she is shouting at me.

The first message read: CALL ME

Then: WHERE ARE U? CALL ME

And finally: PLS CALL ME ITS URGENT

I am tempted to ignore her messages, but I know she will continue bombarding me with them until I respond. I dial her number reluctantly, and she answers immediately.

'I've been texting you from morning, child!' Her speech is rapid and staccato, like the sound of a machine-gun firing.

'I've been in hospital all morning, Aunty. You know I don't answer my phone when I am on the wards.'

Of course she knows.

'Yes, yes, but this is really important.'

It always is, with her.

She goes on briskly, 'I want you to do me a favour.'

'Okay,' I say resignedly. 'What is it?'

'There's this boy,' she begins. 'Leela's sister's son. You know Leela, no? Our driver Tissa's wife? The one with the goitre? She now comes to clean for me three times a week, ever since Prema had her womb operation. You remember the sister? She comes here occasionally to help out when we have a party? She works in some factory now—'

I interrupt her impatiently. I am in no mood to listen to the convoluted social and medical histories of her domestic staff. 'No, I don't remember her. So what do you want me to do?'

'I'm trying to tell you, child. Let me explain, will you!' She sounds offended and I bite back a retort.

She resumes. 'So, this boy - the son, has met with an accident. He was knocked down by a car or something. They said he's quite serious. Leela is *really* upset. And the mother also, naturally! That poor woman has so many problems. Leela's sister,

I mean, not Leela. Useless drunkard of a husband and another child at home to look after. She had been worried about the boy these last two weeks because he had left home. It seems he got a new job or something… but then he went missing… and now this!' She races on at full speed. I wait a few moments till she pauses for a breath.

'So…the favour?' I prompt her gently.

'Wait. I'm just coming to that. He was admitted to the Accident Ward last night. So, could you check on him? You're still somewhere there anyway, aren't you? They're really worried. The doctors are keeping them in the dark – you know – the usual story…'

'Yes, yes,' I find myself saying. Anything to stop that verbal torrent. 'I'll go and see him.'

I should have guessed. This is a regular habit of hers, asking me to visit every Tom, Dick and Harin she knew who was admitted to the hospital, some of whom had a very tenuous connection to her. 'What's his name?'

'Thank you, dear. His name is Anil…'

'Anil? Right. I'll see what I can find out,' I say reluctantly.

'Thanks, dear,' she says again. 'I'll tell Leela you'll check on him. She'll be very grateful.' She hangs up and I grit my teeth.

Does she not realise how much work and how little spare time I have?

I know that, despite my reluctance, I will do what she asks me to. She sounds concerned about this young fellow, anyway, whoever he is. Beneath her super-annoying autocratic exterior, my aunt is a good-hearted woman.

Anyway, shouldn't take me more than ten minutes to pop in to the Trauma Unit and check on him. After all, it's on my way home.

In a few minutes, I reach the hospital gates. On my left, the Trauma Unit looms tall. The temptation to head straight home is very strong. The adrenaline surge has ebbed away leaving me drained and tired. The hours of standing in Labour Ward have left my feet throbbing and there is a gnawing emptiness in my stomach. It's been a busy day and I have a mountain of reading to get through when I get home. I hesitate for a few moments, torn by indecision, and then, I hear my aunt's words echoing in my head like the spitting of a distant machine-gun. *'Thanks, dear, I'll tell Leela you'll check on him.'*

With a resigned sigh, I head towards the Trauma Unit.

3

If you are a fan of modern architecture, the newly built Trauma Unit - a gift to the country from some benevolent foreign government - will impress you with its sweeping curves and sharp angles. If you are not, you might consider it something of an eyesore - a ten-storeyed monstrosity made of glass and steel rising up in the midst of traditional colonial buildings. It replaced a small building called the Accident Ward which had become hopelessly inadequate to deal with the ever-increasing amount of trauma in the city. Old-timers like Aunty Christine still referred to it by the old name.

Outside the entrance, beneath the massive portico which is a clear dome supported by gleaming chrome pillars, an ambulance flashing blue lights is in the process of disgorging a stretcher holding an unfortunate accident victim. I pass the crowded reception desk, manned by a nurse and a clerk. In the doorway ahead I see a tall, gawky figure approach, hands in the pockets of a short white coat, cropped hair framing a square serious face. The figure vanishes suddenly and I realise it's my reflection in the glass doors that slide apart silently as I approach.

Inside, it's busier than the Pettah Bus Stand at rush hour. Not surprising, considering it's the biggest unit of its kind in the country. As I enter the huge foyer with its gleaming marble floor, I narrowly miss collision with a trolley bearing a dazed-looking man sitting up, clutching a bloodstained white towel to his nose. The trolley whizzes past me like a Formula One car and is manoeuvred expertly into one of many cubicles which line one side of the huge space, where its occupant would await the arrival of an emergency doctor. The more urgent cases are wheeled straight in through the swinging red double doors marked 'RESUSCITATION ROOM', called 'Resus Room' for short. Rows of identical grey plastic chairs bolted to the floor are occupied by an assortment of people who stare, glassy-eyed, at a large television screen mounted high on the opposite wall, which is tuned to a news channel showing images of the aftermath of an earthquake in another part of the world. More trolleys bearing patients flash past. A policeman in uniform stands discreetly nearby, walkie-talkie in hand, and a phone rings incessantly, its shrill tone heightening the feeling of chaos.

I hurry through the crowded foyer and make my way to Ward 72, the male Trauma Ward, on the first floor. I know my way around the place, having completed a month-long stint in orthopaedics and trauma just a few weeks ago.

The pungent smell of antiseptic that pervades the entire hospital seems stronger here. Surgical wards are generally cleaner than medical wards as surgeons are obsessive about germs and infection, and orthopaedic surgeons even more so. In response to my query, the young nurse who mans the nurses' station opens the admission register, a large book which records the names of all the patients admitted to the ward. Even in the twenty-first century, everything that goes on in this hospital is recorded by hand painstakingly on paper. She checks the previous day's entries and shakes her head.

'No, we don't have anyone by that name here. But there was a patient who went straight to theatre from Emergency, and to ICU after that. That could be him.'

If she is referring to the boy, he must be more seriously injured than I thought. I thank her and trudge to the lift which takes me to the Trauma Intensive Care Unit – or TICU – on the fifth floor.

In the waiting room outside the TICU, a handful of people sit listlessly on the ubiquitous grey chairs which line the walls.

In one corner, a bespectacled, grave-faced, white-coated young male doctor with dishevelled hair sits talking quietly to a thin woman dressed in a drab blue blouse and long black skirt. The lid of a vacuum flask peeps from the top of an oversize shopping bag that the woman clutches in her lap. The doctor has obviously just delivered some bad news to her, for she is sobbing silently, her thin body shuddering and heaving with each breath, a crumpled handkerchief balled up in her hand. A wizened grey-haired woman in a shabby green nylon saree sits hunched next to her, gnarled hands clasped tightly in her lap and tears trickling down her wrinkled cheeks. The doctor fiddles awkwardly with the stethoscope around his neck and says a few words more before leaving the pair. I avert my eyes as I pass them, not wanting to intrude on their grief. Such scenes are common in the Trauma Unit, where tragedy befalls families daily. I am learning to deal with such situations by cultivating a kind of detached empathy, but I cannot help the sharp wrench that goes through me when I see the woman weeping. I wonder who her tears are for. Her husband perhaps, or a parent, lying within, probably the victim of a careless accident.

Even though medical students have the run of the hospital, protocol dictates that I get the permission of someone in authority before I visit a patient. I enter the ICU and look around for a nurse. Its design is typical – rows of beds in spacious cubicles on either side of a central aisle, with the nurses' station in the centre, commanding a view of the entire unit. Deep green curtains separate each cubicle from its neighbour. A small whiteboard hanging on the wall at the entrance tells me that all of the ten beds are occupied. The names of the occupants of the beds are written in small letters, and I spot 'Anil' scrawled against Bed Six.

That must be him.

The nurses' station is unmanned, and I soon see why. There is a commotion around one of the beds, which is concealed behind drawn curtains. One of the patients must be in need of their attention. I catch up with the doctor who is hurrying back up the aisle. I glimpse his name printed on the badge which is clipped onto the pocket of his coat: Dr Janaka Something-or-other. He pauses as I quickly introduce myself and inquire about the patient I have come to see. I don't want to take up too much of his time. He is obviously busy with a 'bad' patient. Hopefully, this shouldn't take long. Such visits usually take the following pattern: a minute to get a quick summary of the patient's condition from the medical officer, and then a few minutes - not more than five - to say a polite hello to the patient, introduce myself as the medical student niece of my aunt, inquire into their well-being, promise to look in again *(I'll try, but my schedule is so hectic)* and then I would be off.

'Bed Six?' He stares at me, eyebrows shooting up, pushing his spectacles up the bridge of his nose.

Surprised by his reaction, I reply, 'Yes, Bed Six.'

Shaking his head, he says, 'Ah - you're too late.' He runs his hands through his hair, which remains dishevelled, sticking up in little spikes that would look comic were it not for the despondent expression on his face.

Too late?

'He's gone.'

I try to hide my annoyance.

Gone? Gone where? Transferred to a ward, I suppose. Which means I'll have to traipse all around the hospital to find him again.

Still, it's good news. If he's been shipped out of the TICU it means his condition must have improved.

He looks around distractedly.

'Which ward was he transferred to?' I ask quickly, wondering what was wrong with the patient behind the green curtain. 'He's not in Ward 72.'

He gives me an odd look. 'No - he's still *here*——'

'But you said——'

Then, he drops his bombshell.

'I mean - he's - he had an arrest...'

I gape at him and ask stupidly, 'An arrest?'

'Yes. A cardiac arrest.'

'You mean...?'

He nods again and says flatly. 'Yes.' He jabs his thumb towards the curtained cubicle behind him. 'This is Bed Six. Resus is still going on…but it looks hopeless.'

'But how? When?' My voice comes out in a squeak.

'Little while ago.' He sounds tired. He pulls up the sleeve of his coat and looks at his watch. 'Thirty-four minutes, to be exact.'

There must be some mistake. Maybe I got the number of the bed wrong.

He is still talking. '… they're still doing CPR. We shocked him, he's had adrenaline, the works, but we couldn't get him back.'

I am still gaping at him in disbelief. Behind him, a nurse emerges through the curtains and runs back to the desk.

This could be a mix-up. It's probably a different patient.

'What's his name?' I ask urgently.

'Anil. Anil Kumara.'

My heart sinks. *Yes, that's the name she mentioned.*

'You know him?' he asks curiously.

'Er, no… not personally. Just the family… they work for my aunt.' I mutter. 'She asked me to look in on him. Said he had been involved in an accident…'

Aunty Christine! I'll have to tell her!

'Yes, he was hit by an SUV. Last night. Multiple trauma.'

'But what happened now?'

'It's probably the head injury,' he says tiredly. 'It was quite bad. Increased intracranial pressure. There was massive brain swelling. He must have coned.'

He is referring to the deadly side effect of very high pressure within the skull, where the lower part of the brain is squeezed downwards through the hole in the base of the skull through which it connects with the spinal cord.

He continues, 'He was in a pretty bad way when he came in to Emergency. Head injury with deteriorating GCS. On top of that, maxillo-facial injuries, rib fractures, and a femoral fracture also. The neurosurgical team took him to theatre first, because he developed a subdural haemorrhage…' he keeps talking but I barely take in his words. I still can't believe that the person I popped in to see has just had a cardiac arrest.

'…the orthopaedic team were waiting till he stabilised – they wanted to take him back to theatre to fix the femur. But he started to deteriorate – we were going to take him to CT scan, but he arrested before we could get him there.' He shakes his head, looking distressed. 'I've just told the consultants involved. Neuro and Ortho. It's been more than half an hour so I'm going to stop the resus.' He turns and dives through the curtains.

I linger outside the curtain, wondering what to do next. I should just leave now. There's nothing I can do here.

I follow him into the cubicle.

I don't see the body of the boy at first – only a glimpse of his head and chest through gaps between the people crowded around the bed. His head is swathed in white bandages, and what is visible of the left side of his face is swollen and distorted. A burly male nurse leans over the bed, performing cardiac compressions, droplets of sweat dripping down his face. The thrusts are rapid and powerful, each one depressing the chest wall two inches or more and causing the head and limbs to jerk spasmodically. The silent movement of his lips looks like he is praying but I know he is counting down the thrusts, pausing when he gets to thirty, allowing two breaths to be delivered to the lungs through the tube which protrudes from the boy's mouth. The airway is controlled by an anaesthetist dressed in green scrubs, a red stethoscope around her neck. With gloved hands she squeezes a breathing bag – the Ambu bag – gently and firmly each time the nurse stops his compressions. The only sounds in the cubicle are a rhythmic whoosh from the mattress which accompanies each compression and the hiss of the bag as it empties and refills with oxygen.

The anaesthetist looks up. 'Both pupils are dilated and nonreactive.'

'Wait! Let's stop for a rhythm check.' Janaka holds his hand up, signalling for the compressions to halt, and they all turn and stare at the monitor. I crane my neck and see only an ominous flat green line moving across the screen.

'Nothing.' He checks his watch, looking distraught. 'Thirty-six minutes since we started.' The male nurse resumes chest compressions determinedly.

'Any more ideas?' He looks at the anaesthetist, a gleam of hope in his eyes, but she shakes her head.

'Right, then. We're going to stop now. Is everybody okay with that?'

From the glum expressions on the faces surrounding the bed, I can see that everyone is not okay with it, but no one says anything.

'Thanks, everyone,' he mutters. The nurse reluctantly halts the compressions and the crowd disperses, leaving the cubicle in silence one by one. The anaesthetist disconnects the Ambu bag from the tracheal tube and places it gently on the bed.

She says to him, 'You did your best. His management so far seems to have been absolutely correct. You've looked for all the treatable causes. The head injury must have been pretty bad.'

He doesn't look convinced, but nods and mumbles, 'Right. I suppose I'd better confirm it and get on with the paperwork. Anyway, thanks.'

She smiles in acknowledgement, turns the wall oxygen off and leaves the cubicle.

4

I've seen dead bodies before, of course.

Lots of them.

On the busy, congested wards of a government hospital, death is commonplace.

In the overcrowded medical block, for instance, at least half a dozen deaths occur daily, mostly those of elderly people who are brought to hospital *in extremis*. Instead of being allowed to end their lives peacefully at home, they are rushed to hospital by well-meaning, panic-stricken relatives at the eleventh hour and are subjected to all manner of medical torture as doctors and students perform resuscitation techniques in last-ditch efforts to revive them before finally giving up.

Deaths on surgical wards are less common, but I had seen a few. The memory of the last one I witnessed is still etched vividly in my mind: that of a tragic burn victim, a thirty-five-year old woman who had set herself alight after pouring kerosene over her body. The Burns Unit had been full that day and she had been admitted to the Trauma Ward instead.   Not that the Burns specialists could have helped her much, anyway. With more than eighty percent of her body covered with burns, she had almost no hope of surviving. My skin still crawls when I recall her pitiful screams and the horribly disfigured skin, blackened and blistered in some parts and pink and raw in others. And   of course, the acrid smell of kerosene that hung around her like a cloud. One day, she had torn all tubes and dressings from her body and staggered out of bed, moaning and wandering around the ward like a doomed soul, until she was captured and led back to her bed. The end, when it came two days later, was a merciful release, and the generous doses of morphine administered to her only subdued her fitfully. I never found out what drove her to do what she did.

And then, there were those dead bodies I faced in the dissecting rooms of the Anatomy Block. Dissection of a human body is a rite of passage for new medical students. On the very first day of medical school I had faced a roomful of naked dead bodies, laid out on rows of cold dissecting slabs. My senses had been overwhelmed by that sight and the unpleasant smell: a pungent, rancid, oily odour – the smell of human flesh pickled in formaldehyde. That day marked the first step of the change from being a normal teenager to someone who would never look at a human body the same way again.

A group of us students – a 'Body Group' – gathered round each body, laughing and joking to hide our discomfiture. We began dissecting: tentative stabs at first, but soon, confident sweeping cuts deep into the flesh. We started with the upper limb that day, teasing out nerves, ligaments, muscles and tendons. Over the next few months we moved on to the abdomen and pelvis, chest, lower limb, and finally the head, neck and brain. Heart, lungs, kidneys and liver were plucked out and studied, till all that was left was a hollow torso. By the end of the course we were intimately associated with the body, or what was left of it.

But this is different.

The dead bodies on the slabs weren't even called that; we referred to them as cadavers. Only at the first unnerving encounter did they even bear any resemblance to a human form. And the moribund old patients who ended their lives on the medical wards too were anonymous, nothing more than mannequins to be used by us to hone our medical skills.

And they had all been older, and they had lived their lives. They probably had married, had children, grandchildren, travelled the country and maybe the world too. But this – this is the first time I have seen the dead body of such a young person, someone around my age, who would never have a chance to do any of these things.

I had never known this boy but when I look down at his lifeless body, a mix of emotions sweeps through me: pity, sadness, anger. Pity for the boy, sadness for his family, and anger that he had ended up here, like this. I wonder what events had led to the accident. Had it been carelessness on his part, or had the driver of the vehicle been at fault? I picture his mother - Leela's sister - receiving the news of her son's death. Would she react like the woman I had seen outside, sobbing silently? Or would she beat her breast and howl and wail like a banshee? Did he have brothers and sisters who would mourn for him?

I step closer and gaze down at the body spread-eagled on the narrow hospital bed, surrounded by debris that is evidence of the vigorous efforts that had been made to resuscitate him. His head lolls to one side, one eye closed by the swelling around it, the other open and staring sightlessly at a point somewhere beyond me. A rumpled white sheet partially covers his trunk, leaving the abdomen, chest and arms bare. The Ambu bag, plastic syringes of varying sizes, an oxygen mask and other medical flotsam and jetsam lie scattered on the bed and floor around. A limp pillow cloaked in a crumpled white pillow-case lies on the floor, pushed to a corner of the cubicle. The 'crash' trolley bearing the defibrillator and emergency drugs is parked at a crazy angle next to the bed, its drawers gaping open and contents spilling out. Red, green and yellow wires snake across the body connecting it to the machine which is still switched on, the flat emerald-green line moving relentlessly across the little black screen.

One other person remains by the bed, a burly man wearing a white apron over a white shirt and sarong, the attire of male nursing attendants in the hospital. His shiny bald head and luxuriant bristling moustache with twirly ends makes him look like a villain in a local teledrama. The impression is strengthened by the thick rope-like gold chain he wears around his neck and the chunky gold bracelets on his wrists, a legacy from his years of working as a cleaner in a hospital in Dubai. Dias is the head attendant in the Trauma Unit and is the man who, I suspect, really runs the place. His villainous appearance belies a genial nature, and although tough on his minions, he is well liked. He potters around the bed tidying up, and for once, he is subdued and simply nods at me in acknowledgement instead of his customary exuberant greeting.

The doctor leans over the boy's body, checks for a carotid pulse at the side of the neck, and then switches the defibrillator off. The flat green line on the monitor contracts into a dot which vanishes with a soft beep, leaving the screen completely black. Then, using the stethoscope, he listens carefully over the heart and both sides of the chest. Thus begins the formal process of confirming death, a ritual which is becoming increasingly familiar to me.

'No breath sounds or heart sounds,' he intones solemnly.

Next, he produces a slim silver torch from the pocket of his white coat, switches it on with a click and shines the beam into the dead boy's eyes. He directs the light into each eye, lifting each eyelid in turn as he does so, the left eye being more difficult to expose because the lid is puffy and bruised.

'Both pupils dilated and not reacting to light.'

As he completes the process of confirming death, I take a closer look at the dead boy. He looks about twenty or so, his body thin, almost emaciated. Impossible to say what his face normally looks like because it is distorted by the swelling over his left cheek and eye. The thick stubble on his cheeks and jaw looks a few days old, and the hair that escapes from the bulky bandage around his head is straggly and unkempt. His fingernails have thick black lines of dirt underneath them and the soles of his feet are calloused and dirty. Surprising, this scruffy, bedraggled look, for his aunt is a hard-working woman who, despite poverty, is always clean and well groomed. But this boy looks like a vagrant. Didn't Aunty C mention something about him being missing from home? Had he been in some kind of trouble? Drugs, perhaps? I look for tell-tale puncture marks on his arms, but there are none. In addition to the swollen cheek, there is evidence of other injuries he had sustained in the accident – some bluish bruises on his chest and his right leg in traction, with a swelling around the thigh.

Janaka straightens up, switches the torch off with a click and looks at his wristwatch. He pronounces, 'Death confirmed at four twenty-two p.m.'

He turns away, shoulders slumped. 'I'll arrange the inquest.'

I try to recall a forensic medicine lecture on the subject of inquests I'd attended at the beginning of the term. Snatches of words in the lecturer's high-pitched voice come back to me now. 'An inquest is a fact-finding inquiry about a death,' I remember her saying. She had reeled off a string of situations in which a doctor was required to order an inquest. 'Remember, when you are junior doctors, you will be faced with this situation,' she had squeaked. 'You can forget everything else in this lecture but you can't forget this.' I had, of course, forgotten most of the lecture but I did remember that an inquest was required in all deaths due to RTAs – road traffic accidents.

'I'll get the paperwork done. There'll probably be a post-mortem.' He disappears through the curtains.

Dias clicks his tongue and speaks for the first time, shaking his head sadly.

'Very sad, no? I feel sorry for this boy and his family.'

He unclips the wires from the pads which are stuck on the chest, disconnecting the body from the heart monitor. 'People should be more careful when they are driving.' As he peels the circular adhesive patches off, I notice a faint scar in the lower abdomen, on the right side. About two inches long and horizontally placed, it looks like an appendicectomy scar.

I murmur in agreement, not knowing what to say. He straightens both legs, removing the heavy weight attached to the right leg and I see another scar that snakes across the boy's left flank, dark and projecting slightly from the skin surface. I wonder where he got that from. It looks recent, but certainly not from Thursday's incident. A previous accident or skirmish perhaps.

'You know him, madam?' Dias treats us medical students with respect and usually speaks to us in English, another legacy of his years working overseas. He looks at me curiously, coiling up the wires neatly before replacing them on the crash trolley. He seems to sense that my presence is due to more than a medical student's interest in an unusual 'case'.

He pulls the sheet up, hiding the scars and ugly bruises and the injured leg. I shake my head, reluctant to explain the connection again. 'Er... I know the family.'

I step aside to allow him to pick a syringe from the floor and wince as something hard strikes my hip. It is the partially-open drawer of the bedside locker, which seems to be stuck and refuses to close. Trying to loosen it, I jiggle the drawer and pull it open and discover some clothes stuffed in the shallow space. Pulling them out, I examine them curiously – presumably they are the clothes the boy was wearing when he was brought in. There is a grubby blue cotton shirt, spattered with caked bloodstains down the front, and a pair of shorts in a green and brown camouflage print – the long, baggy kind with oversized pockets on each side. It is slashed and ripped in a couple of places. The shorts would have been cut away from his body after he was brought to the Trauma Unit. As I stuff the pathetic bundle of garments back and try to shut the drawer, my fingers encounter something hard within them which is preventing the drawer from closing completely. Reopening the drawer, I pull the clothes out again and discover a small grey mobile phone wrapped in a sheet of newspaper in one of the pockets of the shorts. I am about to replace it when Dias stops me. 'Madam, you said you know the family, no?'

I nod, turning the phone around in my hands. It is an old-fashioned one, with a small screen and buttons for a keypad. It is switched off.

'Then you can return the phone to them, no?'

I frown and shake my head. 'No, all his belongings will be returned to the family, once the inquest is over.'

'Better if you can give it to them, madam, since you know them.'

How to explain that I had not known this boy when he was alive, and that I will probably never meet his family? 'No, I can't take the phone,' I say firmly. 'It will be returned with all other property through the official channels.'

He shakes his head. 'There's no other property, only these torn, dirty clothes. No shoes or slippers even. Before it can be returned, somebody will steal the phone. If not here, in mortuary. Those fellows are always waiting for a chance like this. This way you can be sure the family will get it back.' He speaks persuasively, and I find myself wavering. I suppose I could hand the phone over to my aunt – she would make sure it was returned to the boy's family. It didn't look valuable, but I am sure his mother would be glad to have it back. But I hesitate and wrap the phone up, deciding to replace it. It doesn't feel right somehow, walking away with a dead person's property. It's really none of my business anyway.

We hear heavy footsteps and deep voices outside the cubicle, and the curtains part.

OMG. It's the boss of the Trauma Ward himself, aka King of Orthopaedics.

Dr R. M. B. Perera, MBBS, MS, FRCS – better known to us students by his nickname Rambo – is the surgeon in charge of the Trauma ward. He is a highly respected orthopaedic surgeon who possesses some classic 'surgeon characteristics': impatience, perfectionism, and a quick temper. And of course, an ego the size of this building. He is followed by his senior registrar and Janaka, who looks even more distressed than he did before.

The cubicle seems to shrink and looks like it would burst at the seams as the three men enter and stand around the bed, along with the burly Dias. I step back to make room for them, considering slipping out before I am noticed, but my escape route is solidly blocked by the newcomers. Rambo is a big man, broad and muscular – hence his nickname. I'd heard that he had been a star rugby player when he was younger. The senior registrar Dr

Jayasinghe - nicknamed Jay - is also large, but in his case it is due to an abundance of adipose tissue, rather than muscle. They are both dressed in green surgical scrubs and have surgical caps on, with masks pulled carelessly around their necks.

'I was in the middle of a hip replacement when you called,' he says to Janaka in his deep booming voice. 'Tell me what happened.'

'Sir, he was brought back from Neuro theatre early this morning—'

'Yes, yes, I know that,' he interrupts. 'What happened now?'

'Their instructions were to keep him sedated and on the ventilator for twenty-four hours. Around noon he started to deteriorate... we were about to move him to the scan room when he arrested...' his voice trails off and he does that thing with his hair again - running his fingers through it and making it stand on end.

Rambo interrupts, 'And he'd been stable till then?'

'No, sir, not entirely. A few ups and downs. I called the Neuro team earlier on to let them know. They did say that there was quite bad brain swelling. They were thinking of taking him back to theatre if he didn't improve. He was due for a scan today anyway...'

We gaze down at the body and Jay breaks the silence. 'What do you think happened, sir?'

Rambo strokes his chin thoughtfully with chunky, sausage-like fingers. It's a myth that surgeons have long, delicate fingers. Thick black chest hair peeps from the top of the 'V' neck of his scrub top, which is stretched tightly across his broad chest. 'Mmm... most probably the head injury. Subdurals are associated with more brain injury. But something as sudden as this - we mustn't forget embolism. Fat embolism or even pulmonary embolism from DVT. Or could be a cardiac event. I know he's a bit young for an MI, but it's possible. There'll be a p.m., I'm sure.'

His gaze settles on me, noticing me for the first time. I try to shrink into a corner of the cubicle. 'Medical student?' He frowns. 'You're not with my present lot, no? You were in the previous group. One of the de Silvas, right?'

I'm surprised that he remembers. I'd kept a low profile during my month in the Trauma Unit, trying to stay under the radar as much as possible. Although it's not such a feat of memory remembering my name, I suppose. Four of the six members of my clinical group share this fairly common surname.

Flustered at being the focus of attention, I mumble that I had just been visiting the patient.

'You know him?' He raises an eyebrow. 'Really? He looks like a beggar, no!'

I explain the connection once again.

'Ah, I see. Poor bugger. I don't know why these fellows can't be more careful when they cross the road. These pedestrians! They have this habit of just jumping out in front of your vehicle, no?'

His forehead furrows again. 'So, you were in my group last month?'

'No sir, the month before that.'

'Ah, yes. What de Silva are you?'

'L, sir,' I mutter.

'L? Ah, yes, Lotus! I remember.' He chuckles and the faithful sidekick sniggers annoyingly. I remember the first time Rambo heard my name, he made a crack about a fast car. 'So what are you doing now?'

'Gyn and obs, sir.'

'Gyn and obs!' He snorts derisively. 'Utter waste of time! Those jokers aren't proper surgeons even! And not much to learn, no? Only three bloody organs—'

Jay starts to giggle like a schoolgirl in anticipation, his paunch jiggling under his scrub top.

'...and two of them are identical!' He delivers the punch line triumphantly and Jay guffaws loudly while I 'Ha-ha' politely. I've heard this derogatory joke about gynaecology so many times, it's not funny anymore. It is customary, almost compulsory, for each medical speciality to make fun of others. He is blissfully unaware that orthopaedic surgeons are very often the butt of these jokes, which emphasise them being known for their brawn rather than their brains.

Rambo says, 'Well, I have to get back to the list—' he looks at me and addresses me directly. 'De Silva, I think you should check on this fellow's post-mortem and report back to me. If it's fat embolism I'd like to know. We haven't had a case for years…'

Great.

Another assignment!

On top of all the reading I have to do and trying to get some deliveries in, this is all I need. Work just keeps piling up…

He exits the cubicle and almost bumps into someone about to enter it. It is the neurosurgery registrar, an earnest, good-looking young man with rosy-pink lips whom half the female medical students (and some of the male ones) have a crush on. I myself don't have any strong feelings for him but ever since I witnessed my first neurosurgical operation - a marathon ten-hour procedure performed to remove a large brain tumour - I have nothing but a healthy respect for neurosurgeons, who can stand and operate for hours on end without any need to eat or drink, or more importantly, go to the toilet. The registrar greets Rambo respectfully with a 'Good afternoon, sir,' and expresses his regret about the boy's death.

'Although I'm not totally surprised, sir. He had a very severe head injury. We were expecting some more brain swelling.' He launches into a detailed description of the head injury and the findings at surgery. I am able to follow some of it but not all. He mentions the subdural haemorrhage, which Janaka had also talked about, and throws in phrases like 'cerebral contusions', 'cerebral oedema' and 'midline shift'. From the expression on Rambo's face, I could see that he too is not following the conversation entirely.

'Yes, yes,' he interjects. 'But we should have operated straight away, no? Then maybe we could have prevented this.'

'Definitely not, sir. He was in no condition for such a major operation,' the registrar asserts.

Rambo doesn't look convinced, but is not up to facing an argument with the articulate young doctor.

He mumbles, 'Right. Anyway, let's wait for the post-mortem and see. This girl here is going to check on it and enlighten us.'

So saying, he strides away, followed by the other doctors, leaving 'this girl' standing alone in the middle of the aisle.

Back at the desk, Janaka is completing the documentation on the boy's death. I pick up the file which is bulging with papers and X-rays and settle down at the desk opposite him. The letters 'MLC' are stamped across the front of the file in smudged purple ink. 'MLC' stands for 'medico-legal case', and all cases of accident, assault and poisoning are stamped thus as soon as they enter the Emergency Unit. The Judicial Medical Officer, or JMO - a doctor who specialises in Forensic Medicine, the field that links medicine with the law - is notified in all such cases, and he would interview and examine the victim, documenting all injuries for the purpose of criminal trial.

I open the file and begin to read.

5

Finally leave the hospital at six in the evening.

What a roller-coaster of a day! Birth and death, within a few hours of each other.

It's later than usual. The setting sun has transformed the bright blue sky into a palette of fiery oranges tinged with hues of pink and purple. The trees lining Hospital Road are filled with the raucous chorus of crows settling in for the night. I walk slowly, trying to dodge the bird-droppings which shoot down from above like small damp missiles, spotting the road with white blotches like a tie-and-dye print.

The aroma of freshly-baked bread wafts through my nostrils as I pass a bakery, reminding me that I have eaten nothing since breakfast, which was a hasty slice of toast with jam. The only thing that has prevented me from slipping into a hypoglycaemic coma is probably the very sweet cup of plain tea that the midwife insisted on serving me after the delivery. I pop into the bakery and emerge a few minutes later munching a hot fish-bun and carrying a few more in a brown-paper bag.

Home is just a ten-minute walk away, a house down a quiet lane at the end of Kynsey Road in which I live with my aunt Sherine, my father's younger sister. Traumatised by my mother's death from cancer fifteen years ago, my father chose to deal with his grief by looking for a complete change of scene. He took a job with the WHO, but the nature of his work - which involved travelling all over the world - made his three sisters advise him that it was better for me to stay behind in their charge.

I was installed with my youngest aunt - a lawyer by profession who had recently married - and I foolishly believed that I would be gaining a set of surrogate parents to replace my dead mother and absent father. But the 'nice boy' my aunt married - a handsome, charming businessman from a prominent Colombo Seven family - turned out to be a serial adulterer and the marriage ended messily, leaving her with the large crumbling mansion as part of the divorce settlement. My aunt sold part of the enormous garden for a fortune and now devotes herself to fighting for the rights of abused women, tortured prisoners and other downtrodden groups. Which is all very well, but it left me mostly on my own knocking about the sprawling empty house, which is not what I had bargained for. My father - bereft of his family - threw himself into his work. He travels extensively and I see him only two or three times a year but we speak frequently on the telephone and he Skype-calls dutifully once a month, usually from some impoverished or war-torn third-world nation.

I let myself in, noticing with a pang that the garage is empty. The house is dark and silent, and the only greeting I get is from the black-and-white cat from next door who gets up from the front steps and stretches, yawning lazily. It would be nice to have someone open the door for me and welcome me in for a change. The daily, who is not really a daily (more of a twice- or thrice-weekly), disappears at about three in the afternoon after cleaning up and rustling up a few curries.

After a quick shower to rid myself of the smell of the hospital (a strong odour of antiseptic that clings to one's body and clothes for hours after leaving the place) I call Aunty Christine and break the news to her. The call lasts several minutes as she expresses her shock and demands all the details.

'I can't believe it, child. *Dead?*'

'Yes - it seems to have been a horrific accident.'

'That poor mother. I must call Leela now. Anyway, thanks, dear, for seeing him.'

'That's alright.' I pause and ask, 'Aunty, do you know what the boy was up to?'

'What do you mean?'

'You implied he was in some kind of trouble? What did you mean?'

'I'm not really sure,' she replies vaguely. 'He had always been a steady boy, working and supporting the family. But he had left his job recently and hadn't been home for some days, and the mother had been worried about him. Why do you ask?'

'Well, he looked like, down and out. Long hair, unshaven, dirty, like he had been living rough.'

'Really? Poor boy. Anyway, dear, I need to call Leela now, I don't know if she has heard the news yet. And thanks for letting me know.'

She hangs up.

I open my obstetric textbook and turn to the chapter on labour. I start to read about the first stage of labour, but my thoughts keep flitting back to the dead boy. I picture his scrawny chest being compressed by the beefy hands of the male nurse, his limbs jerking with each thrust... the flat green line on the monitor... the pupils of his eyes, huge and dark, not reacting to the light from the torch...

Closing the textbook with a snap, I connect my mobile phone to my laptop. I hadn't had enough time to read through all of the pages of the boy's case notes as the file needed to be dispatched to the JMO's office, so I had taken photographs of every page and all his scans and X-rays, which were now being uploaded onto the computer. Once the upload is complete I start reading.

I skip the first page which contains his name and hospital number and start with the notes made by the doctor who saw him when he was brought in. The words are written in thick black ink, in a sloping, barely legible script.

Pedestrian in RTA - hit by SUV

Had he been careless in crossing the road, or had the SUV driver been speeding - drunk, perhaps? Had the driver stopped, or had it been a hit-and-run? My last question is answered as I read the next line.

Brought in by driver of SUV

And then, scribbled on the side of the page:

?assault

Why had the doctor queried assault? Doesn't fit in with the rest of the story somehow.

The next few lines describe the boy's medical condition when he was brought in, and the initial part of his treatment. He was described as being drowsy and restless, with a score of 12 on the Glasgow Coma Scale. His arrival had set into motion the usual Trauma protocol which is documented in the next few lines.

I scroll to the next page where his injuries are listed in medical shorthand.

1. Depressed skull # R parietal area

2. # L maxilla

3. # ribs 4, 5, 6 L side

4. #R femur (mid-shaft)

Pretty nasty. He had broken an assortment of bones in his body: his skull, his left cheekbone, several ribs and his right thigh bone.

Next come the images of his CT scans and X-ray films. The scans of the head and neck are confusing: two or three pages of what look like a series of cross-sections - or 'cuts' - through his head from top to bottom. I'm not quite sure how to read them but I can see the sharp break in the smooth contour of the skull on the right side, and a segment of the skull pushed inwards. I wonder what he had hit his head against. It had certainly been one hard knock, pushing the broken segment of skull inwards like a dent in an eggshell. A slim white crescent shape lies between the skull and the brain - the classic scan appearance of a subdural haemorrhage, a collection of blood beneath the dura mater, the tough membrane that clothes the brain.

Next, I zoom in on the picture of the X-ray of his thigh. It is spectacular: the longest and strongest bone in the body, the femur or thigh bone – in this case the right one – had snapped in two like a twig from the force of the impact it had received. I know that fractures of the femoral shaft – the long narrow midsection of the bone – didn't occur easily and were usually caused only by major force. The X-ray showed the two broken segments – stark white against the black background of the film – overlapping, pulled towards each other by the powerful quadriceps muscles of the thigh. It would have taken a lot of muscle power to pull them apart and align them. No coincidence that most orthopaedic surgeons I had encountered were on the brawny side.

I hear the front door open and a few moments later, a short, plump woman walks into the kitchen carrying a laptop and a huge bag stuffed with papers which she deposits on the table. Aunty Sherine is dressed, as usual, in a baggy cotton top and loose linen trousers. Her prematurely greying hair - which she refuses to colour - is cut extremely short and envelopes her scalp like a close-fitting cap.

As is usual when we meet each evening, we swap stories. She tells me about a woman she has been counselling who is trying to find refuge from an abusive husband. I offer her the bag of fish-buns and tell her about the events of my day. She is fascinated by my account of labour and childbirth and saddened by the death of the young man.

'I'm sure I've met this boy. His aunt used to bring him to Christine's place when he was younger.'

'Could be. She said that the mother too, has worked for her on and off.'

She rummages in the bakery bag and pulls out a bun. 'He was a quiet boy, as I remember. But that was many years ago. I'm glad you managed to see him – at least now the family will know what happened.'

'Yes, I'm glad I went.' I pause and then say, 'It's a bit fishy, you know.'

'What, this?' she says, looking at the bun. 'Well, isn't it a maalu paan?'

I frown at her, but she is not trying to be funny. She has just bitten into the fish-bun and is munching contentedly.

'No. I meant, what happened to the boy seems a bit fishy.'

'Ah…what do you mean, fishy?'

'Well, he's supposed to have been hit by a car. But…I wonder whether there's more to it.'

'Really? Like what?'

'He may have been… assaulted.'

'Assaulted? Why do you think that?'

'I had a look through his case notes. The doctor who saw him initially had queried assault.'

'Mmm…but I suppose the police will look into all that, no?'

'I suppose so. There must be witnesses. Somebody must have seen what happened, no.'

I help myself to another fish-bun. 'I wonder what will happen to the man who knocked him down…'

'Well, he'll be remanded. There'll be a hearing, and then he'll be released. Depending on the circumstances of accident, of course.'

We munch in silence for a few moments and then she asks, 'Doesn't the family live in Wanathamulla?'

'Do they? I don't know.'

'I think they do. That place! It's a hotbed of crime. Drug dealing and all kinds of illegal activities. I've done some work there on and off.'

'But Aunty Christine says he was a very hard-working boy, not the type to get involved in anything dodgy.'

'How would *she* know? I suppose that's what the aunt says. Anyway, that's what people always say when someone dies. No one will say anything bad. You'd better speak to the aunt yourself. That is, if you really want to get involved.'

She's right. I hardly know these people.

No need to get involved.

I switch the laptop off and turn back to my textbooks.

Lots of reading to catch up on. Back to the first stage of labour.

I start reading. *'Labour can be defined as the presence of regular painful uterine contractions which produce progressive effacement and dilatation of the cervix and descent of the presenting part, ultimately leading to expulsion of the fetus, placenta and membranes…'*

Whoa…who writes this stuff?

Before I can make it to the second sentence a gigantic yawn overtakes me. My eyelids feel like they are stitched together, and I crawl upstairs into bed and fall asleep.

6

The next morning there seems to be no opportunity to check on the post-mortem for I am assigned to a gynaecology list which is scheduled to start at eight and I am to 'scrub up' and assist in the first case, which is a hysterectomy. I arrive at the theatre by seven-thirty; Harsha and Tara arrive a few minutes later. The other half of our group is assigned to Labour Ward today.

I've scrubbed up before, of course, in general surgery and orthopaedics, but this is my first gynae operation.

Under the hawk-eyed gaze of the theatre sister, Sister Chithra, I scrub diligently, using a small bristly brush to scrub between my fingers and under my fingernails, the dark brown antiseptic solution frothing into a satisfying yellow lather by the end of the required five minutes. Next, a quick rinse, keeping hands high, being careful not to touch anything. I dry my hands, don a long green gown and squeeze my hands into tight-fitting surgical gloves.

Keeping hands clasped in front of me as if in prayer, I take my place on the left side of the anaesthetised patient, whose abdomen has already been cleaned and 'prepped'. In response to a nod from the anaesthetist, Indira, who is also scrubbed up, picks up a scalpel and proceeds to make the first incision: *'knife to skin'*.

The slightly curved cut just above the pubis - the 'bikini' incision - is standard for many gynae operations. The cut skin edges gape open, revealing yellow globules of subcutaneous fat.

The scrub nurse mops the bright red blood that wells up in the wound, and the operation is under way.

My role turns out be to pull back on the lips of the surgical wound with a retractor - a curved metal instrument rather like a giant shoe-horn - the idea being to provide the surgeon with a good view of the operating field. This seemingly simple task is harder than it appears to be. I am required to maintain a steady traction on the handle of the retractor, holding it at just the right angle. The heat from the too-bright theatre lamps which are suspended above the operating table like twin suns blazes down on us and soon makes me break out into a sweat, and I feel droplets trickle uncomfortably down my forehead and neck.

I can only relax my hold once the uterus is lifted out of the pelvic cavity. I feel the blood flowing back into my arm as I marvel at the size of the organ lying in the tray. It is as big as a king coconut, enlarged to about ten times its usual size by the presence of multiple fibroids.

The consultant, Dr Henry Fernando suddenly makes an unexpected appearance in theatre. The Parkinson's appears to be well controlled today, for he is perky and talkative, and proposes that he scrubs for the next case - another hysterectomy. I see Indira and Sister Chithra exchange looks - there is no mistaking the meaning of that shared glance. He is going to slow things down considerably. Sure enough, the list proceeds, but at a much slower pace. This time the troublesome organ is small and shrunken, being removed because of menorrhagia - excessive menstrual bleeding.

The operation seems to be doomed to delays right from the start. I realise with a sinking feeling that the list is probably going to overrun. Tara, who is asked to assist, has her scrubbing interrupted when Sister spots the rings on her fingers (all six of them) and asks her to remove them and start again.

The operation begins with Henry at the helm, but comes to a complete halt a few minutes later as he creates a *ha-ho* after the unthinkable happens - a fly has somehow entered the hallowed premises of the theatre complex and is seen buzzing about inside the theatre. He folds his arms adamantly, refusing to proceed until the fly has been eliminated or removed. It's not a common-or-garden housefly, but one of its larger cousins, the kind with huge red eyes and a shiny metallic blue body, and it darts around the theatre making whirring noises like a miniature helicopter. The next few minutes reminds me of one of those old slapstick comedy movies, with everyone who isn't scrubbed rushing about with rolled-up newspapers, falling over each other in their efforts to get rid of the unwelcome visitor. Only the anaesthetist remains unperturbed, ignoring the fly and taking the opportunity to finish off the Sudoku puzzle in the daily newspaper.

I glance at the clock; it's almost eleven. 'I'm supposed to check a post-mortem report,' I whisper in Harsha's ear. 'I was hoping to do it after the list but at this rate we won't be finished till after the lunch break.'

He whispers back, 'Why don't you do it now? I don't think anyone will notice. You won't take long, no?'

'No. I'll be back as soon as I can. Cover for me, okay?'

In the chaos, no one else notices me slipping away.

7

I find the mortuary with difficulty, tucked away in a corner of the hospital. It is a dreary grey four-storey block annexed to the Pathology Department, shared by that department and the JMO's office. Above the entrance I see a sign - the words don't make any sense to me at first.

TACEANT COLLOQUIA; EFFUGIAT RISUS. HIC LOCUS EST UBI MORS GAUDET SUCCURRERE VITAE.

It's Latin, of course. I don't know many Latin words but you can't be a student of medicine without picking up a smattering. Most of the old names given to medical conditions have Ancient Greek and Latin roots: elegant double-barrelled names which roll euphoniously off the tongue, such as *angina pectoris* and *diabetes mellitus*. These long, unfamiliar terms often discouraged new medical students but I had always found them fascinating. Modern medical terms which are derived from English words don't sound half as nice.

I wonder what the phrase means. I know *risus* means laughter, from *risus sardonicus*, the name given to the grinning expression produced by spasm of the facial muscles in tetanus. *Locus* means place, of course, and *mors* must refer to death. The other words are unfamiliar but all is revealed when I spot the English translation written in small letters below:

Let conversation cease. Let laughter be banished. Here is the place where death delights to help the living.

The translation is familiar; I've heard that this inscription is commonly found at the entrances of mortuaries all over the world. So this is the original Latin version of that phrase.

A receptionist who seems to be taking this instruction to heart sits behind a large desk inside the entrance - a thin morose-looking woman with a downturned mouth and a large hairy naevus on her chin. A large black tray labelled 'Specimens' stands next to a smaller one labelled 'Reports' on one side of the desk. A row of people stand silently in line before her as she shuffles through the 'Reports' tray.

The receptionist glances up at me briefly and waves me through the lobby towards a doorway. Stepping through, I find myself in a large room with wooden shelves lining every wall. The stale smell that envelopes me - a mixture of dust and formalin - evokes memories of the anatomy dissecting rooms. I seem to be in some kind of museum, but the exhibits are unusual.

I stand stock-still, staring at the objects on the shelves: dozens of liquid-filled glass jars of every conceivable shape and size, containing a bizarre collection of human organs and parts. I recognise a liver, mottled and grey, riddled with multiple darker spherical shapes that look like tumour deposits, and a kidney cut open to display a large oddly-shaped stone - a 'staghorn' calculus. Both share a shelf with a grisly specimen of a fetus with a perfectly formed face, missing the top of its head and most of its brain. A human skull with a jagged crack above gaping eye sockets disregards the instructions at the entrance and grins down at me from a higher shelf. One wall is lined with wooden shelves filled with textbooks and journals.

'If you're here for the pathology tutorial you're way too early.' I hear a voice behind me and tear my gaze away from the fetus to see an attractive young woman with highlighted brown hair dressed in a pink shirt and narrow black trousers looking inquiringly at me, holding a box of slides in her hands.

'Er… no. I'm here to check on a post-mortem.'

'Ah, you're in the wrong place!' She smiles sweetly. 'This is the pathology museum, and through this door is the histopathology lab. You need to go to the basement - that's where the mortuary is.'

'Ah... okay.' I turn to leave the room, uncertain where to go.

'Here, I'll show you.'

'Thanks.' I follow her out of the room and down a flight of stairs, thinking to myself, *what's a nice girl like her doing in a place like this?* I wonder if she is a doctor. She's not wearing a white coat. Apart from the grinning skull, she is the most cheerful thing I have encountered here so far.

She chats as we walk, striding ahead on three-inch heels. Her name is Renuka, and she is indeed a doctor, a pathologist in training. She tells me that the mortuary clerk who usually files the post-mortem reports is away on sick leave.

'Dengue. Won't be back for at least another week,' she confides. 'She's still in hospital, platelets down to forty thousand yesterday. But don't worry, we'll get you sorted.'

Down in the basement, the air is cold and dank and I shiver involuntarily. We pass through a narrow corridor with doorways on either side. No daylight ever reaches here; the only lighting comes from old-fashioned fluorescent lights fixed onto the ceiling - the type that makes a humming noise when switched on. The smell of formalin from the lab upstairs is replaced by a more unpleasant odour, a sweet fetid smell which I realise could only be that of decomposing human flesh. My skin prickles with goose bumps - not only because of the cold.

My guide chatters on, unaffected by the ambience. She halts suddenly and startles me by yelling loudly, *'Lionel!'*

There is an answering shout from one of the rooms. She pops her head through a set of swinging doors, beckoning to me. Beyond the doors is a curtain made of wide strips of thick polythene, once transparent but now yellowed and grimy. I follow her gingerly through the curtain, trying not to touch the strips. Looking around, I realise with a heart-lurching shock that she has brought me right into one of the post-mortem rooms.

It is the first time I have been in one. It is large and cold. Very cold. An ancient but powerful air-conditioning unit fixed high on to one wall blows what feels like Arctic air directly at me in noisy blasts. The walls and floor are covered in cracked and chipped pale green ceramic tiles, discoloured and outlined by blackened, grimy grout. Under the harsh glare of several fluorescent lamps, four stainless-steel tables lie in a row, two of them occupied, each by a naked corpse. A sinister-looking masked figure wearing a long white plastic apron, gloves and black rubber boots is hunched over one of the corpses, looking for all the world like a modern-day Frankenstein. From the dark blue uniform the man wears under the apron, I assume he is a technician or something like that. He looks up, lifts his right hand up in a brief salutation and resumes his task.

I catch a glimpse of his eyes when he glances up – there is something odd about them. One eye had looked straight at us and the other seemed to gaze in a different direction altogether.

He is busy with one of the corpses, that of an emaciated old woman with sparse silvery-grey hair, whose loose skin hangs from its skeletal frame like a wrinkled garment that is several sizes too large. Using a long curved needle expertly held in his fingers, he is suturing closed a long incision which stretches from the Adam's apple to the pubic bone. The needle is larger than anything I had ever seen used in surgery and is attached to a thick white thread.

His movements are quick and sure, with the ease born out of years of practice. On a tray next to him are scattered a variety of instruments: a broad saw, scalpels, several pairs of scissors, forceps, cutters shaped like pliers and a long knife with a serrated blade that looks uncomfortably like a bread knife.

Renuka introduces me and explains my mission to him.

'This is Lionel – he's our mortuary assistant, he helps the pathologists with the post-mortems,' she tells me. 'He knows everything that goes on around here. If you tell him the details of your patient he'll be able to track down the p.m. report. I'll leave

you here – let me know if you run into any problems, okay? I'll be
in the Histopath lab.'

I thank her and she disappears through the grungy curtain,
leaving me with my new acquaintances – Lionel and the two
corpses.

Lionel nods and says, 'I will be finished in five minutes,
madam, then I can help you. Please take a seat.'

I inspect the only chair in the room – a black metal chair
encrusted with rust – and decide to remain standing, pulling my
white coat tighter around my body. Lionel continues to work in
silence. While he is working, I sneak a glance at the second corpse,
that of an obese man with a huge belly. Heavy jowls and rolls of
fat obscure his neck; even his genitals are completely hidden by
an overhanging fatty apron. A similar long incision has been
made in his body and loops of gas-filled intestine protrude from
the belly and spill out on to the metal table, giving the startling
appearance of a gigantic, glistening pink snake escaping from his
body. The rib cage has been wrenched apart and the breast bone
lifted up to reveal the lungs – two smooth pinky-grey spongy bags
sitting in the chest cavity – with the heart nestling between them,
covered in more fat, bright yellow blobs spread over the dull red
heart muscle.

Gross.

*Wonder what made him kick the bucket. Looks like a prime
candidate for a coronary.*

I know that later on in the fourth year, I would be required
to perform two post-mortems myself, under the supervision of a
pathologist. I try to visualise myself plunging my hands into that
enormous abdomen and feeling my way through those slippery
loops of bowel. At the thought, I suddenly exhale, long and deep,
and I realise that, all this while, I have been holding my breath to
avoid the unpleasant smell that surrounds me. I try breathing
through my mouth; that is much better, although difficult to
maintain for a more than a few minutes. Lionel doesn't seem to
be affected by it; his sense of smell would have adapted so that
he wasn't bothered by it anymore. I had observed the same

phenomenon during anatomy dissections when the initial unbearable stench of the formalin surrounding the cadavers became unnoticeable after a few hours.

When his task is finished, the mortuary assistant sheds the apron, mask and gloves, revealing a neat, straight moustache which gives him a military air. He limps across the room to a large stainless-steel sink to wash his hands, soaping them vigorously before rinsing and drying them. The strong smell of Sunlight soap mixed with that of the dead bodies doesn't improve the air in the room. Slipping out of the boots, he puts on a pair of rubber slippers, replacing the boots neatly on a rack.   I can see the necessity for the thick rubber boots - the floor below the post-mortem tables is wet and sloshy. There is a long rubber hose attached to a tap on the wall - it is probably used to hose down the tables after a post-mortem.

'Come, madam, we have to go the office,' he says, leading the way out of the room, his limp quite pronounced. In contrast to his slightly spooky appearance, he is soft-spoken and polite. Once again, I sidle through the curtain of polythene strips carefully, trying to avoid touching it. We move to another room across the passage, an office with desk and chair, filing cabinets, a computer, and metal bookshelves stacked with files and papers.

He checks the number that I give him against those listed in a big book and says, 'This p.m. was done yesterday, ma'am. The young boy who had the accident, no?'

'Yes,' I say looking at each of his eyes in turn, not knowing which one to focus on. 'It's done already?'

'Yes, yesterday evening.' He must notice me looking at his eyes for he raises his hand up to his left eye and then holds it out, saying, 'Glass.'

I stare at the glistening white orb which has appeared on his palm. It looks like - *it is* - an eyeball!

I look at his face. His left eye socket is sunken and empty, the eyelids puckered like the lips of a toothless old woman. *A glass eye! That explains the squint.*

He casually pops the eye back into its socket and tells me he lost the eye in an explosion when he was in the army. The limp is also due to a war injury. As a result of his injuries, he says, he left the army and took this job ten years ago.

'Could I see a copy of the report?' I ask.

Soon I have the report in my hands. I start reading: it begins the usual way such reports do, with a description of the external appearance of the body. *The body is that of a male, poorly nourished, aged between twenty and twenty-five…*

I hurriedly glance through the first few pages, turn to the last page, and drop my eyes right to the bottom where the conclusion is typed neatly under the heading 'Cause of death':

Cardiovascular failure secondary to traumatic brain injury.

An illegible signature follows, accompanied by a stamped seal.

So Rambo was wrong. It was the head injury that had killed the boy, not fat embolism (which even I knew was pretty rare anyway). I wonder what he had hit his head against, to cause such severe damage to his brain. The primary impact from the vehicle must have been on his thigh – to cause the fracture – so there must have been a secondary impact with his head hitting some other object or hard surface.

Lionel is still talking. I shake myself and look at him questioningly.

He repeats, 'Body was collected by funeral parlour this morning.'

I say, 'That's okay, I only wanted to see the report. I have to tell his consultant about it. I'll quickly read this, and then leave.'

I wasn't sure how much detail of the post-mortem Rambo would want to know. Surely just the cause of death would be sufficient? Or would he want to know more? I sit at the desk and start speed-reading, hardly taking anything in. I skim through the first page. 'Right parietal depressed skull fracture…' *yes, I'd spotted that fracture in his CT scan* '…cerebral oedema… cerebral contusion… compression of ventricles… facial swelling on left side and fracture of left maxillary bone.'

More medical jargon on the next page: 'No cardiac valvular lesions… normal coronary arteries… no evidence of myocardial infarction' … *so it wasn't a heart attack… too young for that, anyway* '…trachea, bronchi and lungs normal… single kidney on right side… liver normal… no evidence of emboli in lungs, kidney, and brain… no venous thrombosis in leg veins…' *so that's another of Rambo's theories down the drain* '… cut injury right loin…'

A cut injury? Wonder what caused that…

The entire report runs into four pages – too much to take in at one go. I pull out my phone and quickly snap photographs of all the pages. I return the report to Lionel and rise to leave, marvelling at the amount of damage inflicted on the boy's body by a single impact, which must have taken just a split second.

'Professor Pathirana will be coming in for a post-mortem soon,' he says, interrupting my thoughts. 'You can speak to him about it.'

'Professor Pathirana?'

He points to the signature and seal on the last page of the report. 'Pathologist. That's his signature. He did this p.m.'

'Oh... I see. No, I have to get back. Thanks for your help.'

8

On leaving the mortuary I make a detour to the Trauma Unit. The person I am looking for is seated at a desk, busily scribbling in a patient's file. Dr Rohan Cooray is the doctor whose characteristic black-inked scrawl I had recognised in the notes of the dead boy. Tall, gangly and hyperactive, he is popular with medical students because he loves to teach. I learnt to suture a cut under local anaesthesia for the first time under his tutelage.

Several textbooks are piled in an untidy heap next to him on the desk. He often dipped into the books during lulls in his shift, revising for his primary examination in surgery. Rumour has it that in his previous post, working under a surgeon with dubious surgical skills, he had advised a patient against going under the knife, warning him that he would very likely die as a result of the operation. The patient had promptly checked himself out of the ward and consulted a different surgeon. The first surgeon had found out, blown a fuse, and immediately got Rohan transferred out of the unit, which is how he ended up working in the Trauma Unit. Soon afterwards, he had faced the same surgeon at the surgery examination and unsurprisingly, he had been failed – not once but in two successive attempts. Undeterred, he was preparing for the examination for the third time now.

He looks up and greets me cheerily. 'Ah… hullo! What's up? Want to do some suturing?'

I shake my head and drop into the chair opposite him.

'No, I can't. I'm supposed to be in gynae theatre right now. I'll have to get back soon.'

'Too bad. I have a chap who's just come in with three self-inflicted cuts on his forearm. He's a drug addict – high as a kite, won't need much anaesthetic. So, what can I do for you today?'

'Want to ask you about a patient you saw on Thursday night.'

He puts his pen down and rocks back in his chair. 'Which one? That night was busy as hell.'

'A boy named Anil Kumara. Do you remember him?'

He shakes his head, frowning.

'Young boy, after an RTA. Head injury, fractured femur.'

'Ah yes.' His face clears. 'I remember. What about him?'

'He died, did you know?'

His chair hits the floor with a thud. 'No!'

'Yes. Yesterday, in the TICU.'

'What happened? I mean, what was the cause of death?'

'The head injury. I've just had a look at the p.m. report.'

He clicks his tongue and says, 'He had some serious injuries alright, but I never thought they would turn out to be fatal. I mean, the guy was like, talking to me when he first came in. But he did have a nasty head injury.'

'Yes. A depressed skull fracture and subdural haemorrhage.'

'There you are. Traumatic subdurals are bad news, no? Usually associated with concomitant brain injury.'

'Did he say anything to you? About what happened?'

'Nothing that made any sense. He was just about conscious, but pretty confused. He was brought in by the guy driving the SUV. Apparently this young fellow just ran across the road smack into his vehicle. Nowhere near a pedestrian crossing.'

'Are you sure? That it was an accident?'

'What do you mean? Yes, it seemed pretty straightforward. The SUV driver described it to me. It happened on Havelock Road, near that junction with the red colour Chinese restaurant and that row of shops. There's a barber salon also – the guy who owns the salon had helped him to put the boy into the vehicle. The driver was absolutely shattered. But it's funny you should ask...' his voice trails off and he looks thoughtful.

'What?'

'Actually, at first I thought he had been beaten up. His face was a real mess. But according to the SUV driver, it was definitely an RTA.'

'But you queried assault. I saw your notes.'

'Yes, you're right. When I first saw him, he mumbled something about someone attacking him. That's why I made a note of that. But then the driver came in and told us a different story, and he seemed to be more credible. The young guy was not coherent. GCS was ten, eleven - something like that.'

'What was he like? The driver, I mean.'

'Oh, he looked like a decent chap. Middle aged, well dressed. He works for a tea company or something.' He pauses. 'My God, he must be devastated.'

'Will he be arrested now?'

'I suppose he'll be remanded... but if it wasn't his fault, it should be alright.'

I am silent, thinking about what he has told me.

'What's your interest in that case, anyway?' he asks curiously. 'I thought you're doing gynae now, not trauma?'

'I know the family. His uncle is my aunt's driver.'

'Ah. Well, if you want to know what happened, you could ask that other guy.'

'Other guy?' I look up, surprised. 'What other guy?'

'Why - there was someone else with him.'

'Someone else? Who?'

'A friend of his, I assumed. He corroborated the driver's story.'

A student nurse rushes up to us and presents him with an X-ray which he holds up and studies with a frown.

'What did he look like?'

'Looked a bit older than the boy. About thirty or so. Well-built fellow. Pumped-up muscles. Long hair, tied back. Dressed fully in black. And tattoos. All over his arms.' He hesitates and then says, 'Looked a bit of a thug, to tell you the truth.'

It is the first I hear of a friend being there.

He slips the X-ray film in the viewer and switches it on. 'Go on, then. Tell me what you see.' It shows two views of a forearm, wrist and hand. I spot the abnormality right away. The hand awkwardly displaced backwards, in profile resembling a fork. And there's the fracture, a crack across the lower end of the radius.

'Colles' fracture?'

'Correct! You haven't forgotten your trauma.' He takes the X-ray down, switching the viewer off. 'Anyway, the police will sort all that out. I'm sure they must have taken statements from everyone involved.'

He's right, of course. I thank him and get up to leave, and then stop as I remember something.

'There's just one more thing ...'

'Yup? What's that?'

'In the p.m. report they mentioned a cut injury...' I describe what I remembered reading.

'Yes, I noticed that. It was on the back – in the loin area. I spotted it when we log-rolled him.' He is referring to the procedure where a trauma victim is turned to one side and then the other to examine the back for injuries. I had seen it done a couple of times. The victim is rolled with his spine aligned in a straight line – like a 'log' – in order to prevent exacerbation of a possible spinal injury.

'What was that due to?'

'Don't know. I assumed a piece of glass or something sharp. It looked superficial – wasn't bleeding or anything. His GCS started to deteriorate soon after that and the Neuro team took over.'

Back in theatre, I start to change back into surgical scrubs and then I notice that my phone is missing.

After a frantic fruitless search I realise I must have left it in the office at the mortuary where I had snapped pictures of the post-mortem report. The fly that had caused such a disturbance in theatre must have been banished or exterminated because when I peep in, the operation is under way and no one seems to have noticed my absence. I decide to return to the mortuary to retrieve the phone.

For the second time that day, I enter the mortuary. This time I walk boldly past the unsmiling receptionist straight down to the basement. The post-mortem room is empty of any living beings and I find Lionel taking his tea break, sitting in a tiny windowless room equipped only with a table, chair and kettle. He is sipping from a steaming mug of plain tea and munching a Marie biscuit when I knock on the open door. He jumps up at the sight of me, scattering crumbs and almost spilling his tea.

'Sorry to disturb your break, Lionel. I've misplaced my phone and I think I must have left it here,' I say. 'I'll have a look in the office, right?'

'I'll help you look, madam.' He brushes crumbs from his shirt front. I follow him down the corridor.

There is no sign of my phone in the office.

'We can dial your number from my phone, then it will ring and we can find it,' Lionel suggests, taking his own phone out of his pocket and offering it to me. I take the phone, key in the digits of my phone number and we wait, listening. To my relief, a few seconds later I hear the familiar ring-tone of my phone, muffled and faint but getting gradually louder until it appears in the doorway, ringing merrily, with lights flashing, held in the hand of a strange-looking man.

'What's this?' the stranger snaps irritably, holding the ringing phone up. This had to be the pathologist Lionel had mentioned, Professor Pathirana. I hastily end the call and stop the strident ringing.

'It's my phone, sir. I left it behind when I was here earlier.'

He glowers at me, still holding the phone up as if it were a pathology specimen.

He looks rather like a specimen himself. And not a very healthy one at that. Gaunt and cadaverous, much like one of the bodies in the adjoining rooms, his white shirt hangs on his bony frame as if it has been placed on a coat-hanger. The sleeves, rolled carelessly up to the elbows, reveal skinny arms, and the loose, crumpled grey trousers sit low on his hips, held up by a frayed leather belt. The sharp rectangular outline of a pack of cigarettes is visible in his shirt pocket.

I had seen this look before - in countless patients. The thin, wasted frame, the puffy eyelids, the dark-ringed, muddy eyes and the unhealthy, sallow complexion all hinted at some underlying illness. And what's with the cigarettes? Aren't doctors supposed to set an example to their patients? But then, being a forensic pathologist, I suppose many of his patients must be dead already.

He doesn't ask who I am or what I am doing there, but grunts and hands the phone to me. I approach him and take the proffered phone, concealing my surprise. The man smells like an ashtray. And I get a whiff of something else mingled with the stale smell of tobacco - a sharp, sweet smell that reminds me of nail-polish remover or surgical spirit. I thank him politely and he turns and walks away without comment.

Lionel whispers, 'If you want to find out more about that p.m., you can ask him.'

I shake my head vehemently. I have no wish to confront the grumpy professor again.

'He's not so bad - you can talk to him,' he urges.

Okay. What the hell. I trot behind the professor, saying, 'Excuse me, sir.'

He stops, turns and growls, 'Now what?' He sways for a second and holds on to the wall.

I swallow nervously. 'I wanted to ask you about a post-mortem you did yesterday. The boy with a head injury and fractured femur from TICU.'

'Ah, yes.' He clears his throat and seems to make an attempt to sound almost civil. 'That one. And who are you?'

'Medical student, sir—'

A grunt. 'What do you want to know?'

'About his injuries….' I begin hesitantly.

'Multiple trauma. Brain injury. It's in the report.'

'He was hit by a car…'

'Yes, he was.'

'So, being hit by a car could have caused the femoral fracture and the head injury also?'

'What are you getting at?' His right hand drifts to his pocket, and he fiddles with the pack of cigarettes restlessly with long thin fingers whose tips are stained brown with nicotine.

'I mean, could the head injury have been caused by assault?'

He stares at me in astonishment.

'Why are you asking me this?'

'Er-er—' I stammer.

He continues without waiting for a reply. 'Was there anything in the history to indicate otherwise?'

I am beginning to regret starting this conversation. 'Yes, he claimed he had been assaulted.'

'When?'

'Uh…I'm not sure, sir,' I gulp. 'Possibly just before the accident?'

'So you don't know.' He glares at me. 'Look, Miss Whoever-you-are. This is not how things work around here. The Coroner is supposed to collect all the relevant information and I make my report based on the post-mortem and all other facts available, including what the doctors report. There was nothing to indicate that this was anything but the result of an RTA. Nobody said anything about assault! You can't just turn up and spout some nonsense about something that might have happened.'

After that outburst there is nothing I can say except 'Yes, sir,' meekly.

He turns to leave and I say impulsively, 'There's just one more thing, sir.'

'What?' He snaps, turning back, positively glowering now.

'Dr Rambo—'

'What?'

'No - I mean - Dr Perera, the orthopaedic consultant,' I say, flustered now. 'He was wondering if fat embolism could have played a part. Because it was a femoral fracture…' I am babbling now but I see that he has calmed down somewhat at the mention of Rambo's name.

'I didn't find any evidence of fat embolism. You can tell him that. Has the body been released to the family?'

I nod, relieved that he has stopped snapping at me.

'Well, that means that the Coroner was satisfied. Understood?'

He stomps off without waiting for a reply, stumbling into a chair. He almost falls, but rights himself and walks away, leaving the chair askew.

What a grumpuss.

And what's that smell? Is it what I think it is?

I hastily check for messages on my phone and sure enough, there is one from Harsha.

Where R U? Op almost over

I check the time - it has been almost an hour since I left the theatre. I hurry back with my phone safely tucked in my pocket and change quickly, slipping in as quietly as I had left. I am just in time. Dr F has scrubbed out and is washing his hands at the tap. The shrivelled uterus lies forlornly in a dish, never to haemorrhage again. Indira is closing the surgical incision, assisted by Tara, who rolls her eyes at me expressively over her mask, indicating that she, at least, had noticed my absence.

'*Cut!*' Indira barks at her and Tara jumps to attention, snipping a suture hurriedly.

'*Where were you?*' Harsha hisses, under his breath.

'I told you. At the mortuary. To check that p.m. report.' I whisper back to him.

'But you took so long!'

'Yes, I know. I left my phone there and had to go back for it. Did anyone notice?'

'No - she was busy keeping him out of trouble.' Lowering his voice further, he describes how, while operating, Dr Fernando had encountered a troublesome 'bleeder', but fortunately Indira had come to his rescue and helped him gain control of it before the bleeding became excessive.

We watch Indira start suturing the skin edges together. I whisper, 'By the way, you'll never guess what! I met Prof Pathirana the pathologist.'

'And?'

I lower my voice. 'He's a strange-looking fellow. I think he had been drinking.'

'*What?* No way!' He almost shouts in his surprise.

'*Shhh!*' I hiss. Indira raises her head and gives us a look.

We are silent for a few moments and when she resumes suturing I whisper, 'Yes. I smelled it on his breath.'

'Are you sure?' he whispers back.

'Yes. It was unmistakable. And not only that – he didn't look well at all. Thin and wasted like those chronic alkies we see in the medical wards.'

He shakes his head. 'That's unbelievable. You mean he turns up to work drunk?'

'Yes! And you know what? He was due to do a post-mortem.'

Even with the mask covering the lower half of his face, I can see his jaw drop. The thought of the professor carrying out his duties while under the influence of alcohol is quite shocking to me as well. Another thought strikes me. If this was a regular occurrence, how accurate were his post-mortem findings? Could he have overlooked something in the boy's post-mortem?

Walking back to College after the list, I tell him more about the visit to the mortuary. A group of students overtakes us and one of them comes over to me.

'Hey! Message for you from Rambo. He wants you to get permission from your consultant and attend the grand ward round on Wednesday morning. He said something about a p.m. report?'

So he had remembered. It's a good thing I made that trip to the mortuary today.

9

Nowhere is the medical hierarchy more evident than on ward rounds.

Ward rounds take place daily, or sometimes twice a day. On the 'grand' round, which usually takes place once a week, the consultant and his entourage review every patient in the ward in more detail than usual, discussing cases, sorting out problems, and, of course, teaching students. The grand ward round is a tradition that is conducted with pomp and ceremony, and reminds me of some archaic rite, almost religious in its solemnity.

Each participant has their particular role to play in this ritual. The consultant - today, Rambo - could be likened to the high priest presiding over the ceremony. Fussing around him like a stout elderly priestess would be Matron Rani, the senior matron of the Trauma Unit, in her navy blue uniform, white stockings and gleaming black patent leather shoes. With her elaborate starched white cap and huge pointy bosom, she looks like a ship in full sail. The young nurses would flutter around like vestal virgins, eager to please, ready to give the high priest whatever he needed - a stethoscope at this bed, a file or a torch at the next. The orderlies and attendants are the acolytes, carrying the paraphernalia needed for the ceremony and assisting whenever a patient needed to be examined: whipping off a sheet here, unbuttoning a shirt there. The younger doctors are the novitiates - the smug senior registrar with his beefy arms folded across his broad chest; he will soon be appointed consultant and would then play the main role himself. The new registrar, fresh from the Part 1 qualifying exam, full of knowledge but with little experience. The overworked house officer – shirt crumpled and tie a little crooked – looking harassed and sleep-deprived, but in fact, the only one who has any idea as to what is going on.

And then, of course, there's us, the lowly medical students: lowest in the pecking order, bottom of the food chain. We are neophytes; postulants newly admitted into the sacred order. Even our attire marks us out – the white coats we wear are shorter than the doctors' coats, denoting our lesser status.

It had proved surprisingly easy to get myself excused from the obstetric clinic this morning. When I arrived at seven-thirty, the waiting room was already beginning to fill up with expectant mothers. Indira was seated at her desk, getting ready to start the clinic, looking smart and unusually feminine in a yellow saree, her hair tied up in a yellow scrunchie. And was that actually a touch of make-up on her face? She excused me readily, asking me to come straight back once the ward round was over. The others in my group were envious of me because they would have the dullest jobs in the clinic – to check blood pressure and fetal heart sounds in all the pregnant mothers who would attend.

I was quite glad to get away, and arrived at the entrance of ward 72 at ten minutes to eight to find Matron, the nurses, doctors and students gathered there. Dias, the head attendant, clad in a spotless white uniform, was bustling about, peering into corners to ensure that every last speck of dust had been swept away before the arrival of the consultant. Even his gleaming pate seemed to be shinier than usual.

Rambo arrives at ten minutes past eight, and, after a cheery 'Good morning,' apologises for his tardiness.

'Traffic was hellish this morning. Some road diversion that I didn't know about.'

Matron utters some soothing noises. 'Yes, yes. I think it's due to the new pavements being made on Horton Place. The road is all broken up there.' They chat for a few minutes about the traffic and the state of the roads, Jay chipping in with his two cents' worth.

Rambo is always impeccably groomed for the ward round and today is no exception. With his hair slicked back and gelled into place, perfectly ironed salmon-pink shirt, grey trousers with a knife-like crease, designer belt and glossy silk tie, he looks like he has stepped right out of the fashion pages of the Sunday newspapers.

Matron, in true priestess mode, holds out a freshly laundered white doctor's coat to him, and turning round, he slips his arms into its sleeves elegantly. After adjusting the lapels, he starts the ward round with us in tow, stopping at each bed to deal with its occupant. I hover on the fringe, wondering whether I would get an opportunity to speak. Today the crowd on the round is ridiculously large. I count *fifteen* people following him (Matron, three nurses, three doctors, one attendant and seven medical students). I am so far away from the consultant, I can barely see the top of his head, and his voice is just an indistinguishable rumble.

When the *perahera* reaches the mid-point of the ward, Rambo suddenly stops and I hear him say loudly, 'Ah, I almost forgot – where's that de Silva girl?'

All heads swivel toward me and I wriggle through the throng and say, 'Here, sir.'

'Ah, good.' He looks pleased. He leans against a bed, folding his chunky arms. 'You managed to get away from the baby-doctors. So – tell us about the post-mortem.'

From my pocket, I pull out a sheaf of papers from the pocket of my white coat – printouts of the report – and start to read aloud.

'Stop, stop!' he interrupts. 'We don't have all day. Tell us the findings. Summarise.'

I stuff the papers back and take a deep breath. 'The pathologist's conclusion was that death was due to traumatic brain injury.'

'*What!* Not fat embolism?' He looks devastated that his pet diagnosis hasn't been verified. 'But it's classic, no! Sudden deterioration and death after fractured femur! Jay, I think you should write this case up for the journals.'

He seems bent on pursuing his theory, in spite of evidence to the contrary.

Jay pipes in. 'In any case, it'll have to be presented at the M and M meeting. She can present it, no, sir.' He nods towards me.

I glare at him. The M and M meeting *(M and M stands for Morbidity and Mortality - nothing to do with chocolates)* is a monthly event in which all the surgical or medical units get together over short-eats and iced-coffee to discuss cases which have ended up in major complications or death. Hindsight is twenty-twenty, they say, and this is never truer than at an M and M conference. The entertainment is provided during question time, when the person presenting the particular case usually is the target of a volley of questions and criticisms about its management.

I continue as if he had not spoken. 'He said that he didn't find any evidence of fat embolism, sir. And the boy had a fairly severe head injury. Depressed skull fracture and a subdural haemorrhage, associated with some brain contusions.'

'So did he actually look for fat emboli? Who was the pathologist? Did you ask him?'

'Yes, sir. I did speak to him. It was Professor Pathirana,' I say, thankful that Lionel had pushed me into a conversation with the pathologist.

'Hmmm… bloody pathologists! What do they know about real patients anyway,' he grumbles. 'They only mess about with dead bodies and bits of tissue...' He looks sulky, like a child whose favourite toy has been taken away from him.

'I'm sure that Pathirana chap could have made a mistake, Jay,' he continues. 'He may be a professor and all that, but it's a textbook case. Maybe he missed something.'

Jay nods vigorously, sycophant that he is.

'Now, let's get on with this round. We've wasted enough time.'

He seems to have had enough of me. I ask to be excused, saying I am expected back at the clinic.

The waiting room is teeming with women in various stages of pregnancy. Who would have thought you get so many pregnant women into a small room like this? Unlike rooms in other clinics, which are joyless places filled with mournful-looking sick people, this one is buzzing with animated conversation as the women compare swollen ankles and give each other bits of advice about heartburn and stretch marks.

I start off diligently, greeting my first lady with a bright smile and a polite 'Good morning.' She waddles in ponderously and sits heavily on the chair, taking a few moments to catch her breath. I check her blood pressure and then ask her to lie down on the examination couch. She pulls her voluminous gown up and her underskirt down, exposing her belly, which is swollen by her gravid uterus.

Inspection, first.

Eyeballing the upper edge of the bump I estimate the period of gestation – the POG – to be thirty weeks.

Next, palpation.

With the tips of my fingers, I palpate the lower end of the bump, looking for the hard, spherical head of the baby. I can't feel the head!

A headless baby? Impossible!

A vision of the grotesque fetus I had seen preserved in the Path museum floats through my mind and I panic.

No, not impossible.

I frantically dig deeper, causing the woman to wince, and to my profound relief, I locate the head, round and hard, like a coconut. As I poke it, it bounces back like a rubber ball and hits my fingers reassuringly.

Next, I check the FHS – the fetal heart sounds – using a Pinard, an old-fashioned instrument shaped like a trumpet which picks up the baby's heart beat and transmits it, amplified, much like an ear trumpet does, to the listener's ear. Mastering the technique of using it requires some practice and I fumble with it for a few moments before I hear the baby's heartbeat racing away somewhere in the middle of the abdomen.

The second woman walks in in a cloud of mentholated vapour. When she lies on the couch and exposes her belly, the sharp pungent smell almost overpowers me. She seems to have smeared Siddhalepa all over her abdomen, and some of it rubs off on my fingers. After I finish with her, I spend a good five minutes scrubbing my hands with soap and water trying to get rid of it but the distinctive smell lingers on my fingers for the rest of the day.

The next one takes a few minutes to unveil herself and unwrap the black garment that covers her like a tent. Beneath the abaya she wears a long-sleeved, knee-length loose garment and a pair of baggy white pyjamas. I wait patiently until she unpeels each layer and exposes her abdomen for examination. It is her fourth pregnancy and her abdominal skin is like parchment, slack and thin, and marked by numerous stretch marks.

After the first ten patients or so, the smile becomes fixed on my face and my questions are getting terse.

Who would have thought that there are so many pregnant women in this city? Did these people never hear of family planning?

I sigh and greet the next woman, my smile frozen and insincere.

Part II

10

It feels like I'm sitting in a sauna. It's a hot, humid afternoon and the air-conditioners inside the lecture theatre aren't coping. To make it worse, I'm surrounded by the warm bodies of about a hundred of my fellow-students.

The dimmed lights, the humming of the air-conditioners and the drone of the lecturer's voice provide ideal conditions for a postprandial afternoon nap.

Professor Balasuriya, the pathology lecturer, is a brilliant academic, but sadly, not a gifted speaker, being cursed with a dull, monotonous voice. I catch a few of the words he drones out: *fibroadenosis…fibroadenoma…metastases…carcinoma.*
Incomprehensible swirls and whorls in hues of pink, purple and red, looking like giant abstract paintings, flash up on the screen as he talks.

The topic is diseases of the breast, and the pictures on the screen are slides of breast tissue stained with H&E stain, which colours tissues making it possible for them to be studied under a microscope.

The room lights suddenly come on, signifying the end of the lecture. I awake with a start, blinking in surprise at the last picture he has put up, which is not a slide of tissue but a colour photograph of a popular Hollywood actress. It shows her simpering on a red carpet dressed in a low-cut long white evening dress studded with sequins, her cleavage exposed.

Everyone is wide awake now - especially the boys, who ogle the picture and snigger. I hear curious murmurs around me.

'… and as she's tested positive for the breast cancer gene she decides to get her breasts removed surgically rather than face the risk of getting cancer - which is almost ninety percent in her case.' He has been talking about the genetics of breast cancer, but I seemed to have slept through most of it.

With a click the last slide flashes up on the screen: a photograph of a news article about the actress and her decision to have a double-mastectomy.

He concludes the lecture, picks up his laptop and leaves the podium, while we remain in the lecture theatre waiting for the next lecturer to appear.

The next lecture is on statistics and is pure torture. *Do we really need to know all this? What on earth is a student's tea test?*

I sit through the lecture obsessing about Bala's concluding words, which have touched a chord in me. So - this celebrity deliberately mutilates her stunning body and has her two major assets removed rather than risk developing cancer?

Interesting. I wonder what other cancers are carried in the genes. I knew that some cancers have an inherited component but this is the first time I have heard about detecting a cancer gene by testing.

There's a reason for my concern. I lost my mother to cancer when I was just seven years old. Paranoid thoughts start racing through my mind. *What if* the cancer she had suffered from was one that was genetically determined? And *what if* - like the actress - I had inherited a 'cancer gene'? *What if*, already, a nidus of tumour cells has begun to multiply somewhere deep within my body?

What if….?

I possess enough insight to realise that I am showing classic signs of the condition sometimes known as 'Medical Students' Syndrome': a bizarre affliction affecting those studying medicine, where the student is gripped by the conviction that he or she is suffering from the very ailment that is being studied.

Anyone who has ever studied medicine will tell you that this is a real condition which has affected them at least once in their career.

The incidence of this condition peaks in the third year when the student starts to learn about scary diseases. To the sufferer, a headache signifies a rapidly expanding brain tumour, and an innocent pain in the abdomen can only be due to an acutely inflamed appendix (about to rupture, of course). I myself have, at different times in the last two years, been convinced that I have had the following diseases: Hodgkin's lymphoma (after discovering some enlarged lymph nodes in the side of my neck), malignant melanoma (that oddly-shaped birthmark on my forearm), and AIDS (*seriously*) following an accidental needle-prick while drawing blood from a patient.

When I get back home that evening Aunty Sherine is already home. I find her sitting at the dining table tap-tapping away at her laptop.

'Ah, it's you,' she says. 'I just spoke to Christine. She had gone for that funeral.'

'Oh! That boy's funeral?'

'Yes. Her driver's nephew.'

'Ah, okay.' I say this absently, my mind still on the pathology lecture.

She looks at me curiously. 'I thought you'd want to know about it, since you were so interested in what happened to him. You can call her and speak to her about it if you like.'

'Yes, yes. I'll do that. Thanks.'

After a pause I say, 'Aunty Sherine, didn't my father leave all his old documents and other stuff here in boxes?'

She looks surprised. 'Yes, some old papers and things. Why?'

'I was wondering if my mother's medical files would be there.'

'Why?' she asks again.

'Umm, I just wanted to look through them.'

Her forehead furrows as she stares at me. 'Yes, they're lying around in the spare room somewhere.'

'Thanks, Aunty.' I turn to leave the room.

'Oh, Lotus.'

'Mmm?'

'I think you should get your father's permission before you start digging through his things.'

'Yes, sure. I'll do that.'

I go straight to my room, lock myself in the bathroom and examine both breasts thoroughly for any untoward lumps and bumps, and emerge five minutes later, satisfied and tumour-free (for the moment).

11

The suction machine makes a gurgling sound, rather like that of
water gushing down a sink when the plug is removed. But it is
bright red blood, not water, that rushes down the clear plastic
tubing and cascades into the bottle with a whoosh. Glancing up,
I am surprised to see that the large glass bottle is almost full.
There has been almost two litres of blood sloshing about inside
the girl's abdominal cavity. That's more than a quarter of all the
blood circulating in her!

She has made it to the theatre in the nick of time.

The girl lying on the operating table is a nineteen-year-old
who had been brought to the Emergency Unit by her mother
earlier tonight complaining of dizziness, and had fainted while
waiting to be seen by a doctor. The alert Emergency doctor had
picked up the rapid, thready pulse, the cold, clammy hands and
the pale, almost white tongue, and correctly diagnosed that she
was bleeding internally.

'In medicine, common things are common!' Going by this
oft-repeated maxim, he suspected that it was likely to be bleeding
from a ruptured ectopic pregnancy. Even though both the girl
and her mother had denied the possibility of a pregnancy, our unit
was notified. The mother had been appalled and blackguarded the
doctor for even suggesting such a thing *(how dare you, she's not
married, doesn't have a boyfriend even)*.

It is gynae 'Casualty' night and a few of us have decided to
spend it in the unit. Till the call came from the Emergency Unit
at about eleven, all we had done was sit around having cups of

plain tea in the nurses' tea room. There were four of us: Harsha, Tara, Rehan and myself.

When the girl was wheeled into the operation theatre, the deathly pallor was evident on her lips and tongue. She lay quite still, eyes closed, her breathing shallow and rapid. Just before the anaesthetist administered the anaesthetic medication she had opened her eyes and murmured a few words. Twenty minutes later, the bleeding has been arrested and Indira holds the culprit up between her gloved thumb and index finger - a tiny fetus which had implanted itself in the right Fallopian tube. Of course, the narrow tube could not accommodate the growing fetus and had ruptured, causing catastrophic haemorrhage. We crowd around the dish in which the fetus has been placed. It is less than an inch in length but already bears a faint resemblance to the baby it would have grown to be. I see large eyes in an oversized head and can even make out digits on the ends of the little limbs. The minute its journey down the tube to the womb was interrupted it was doomed; it could never have survived.

When I get back home, it is one in the morning. The adrenaline is at work again, coursing through my system, and I am too wired up to sleep. I lie in bed, thinking about the girl with the ectopic pregnancy. If she had not come into hospital when she did, she would be dead by now. And what if the little embryo had been carried down an inch or so further into the womb, resulting in a normal pregnancy? How would her mother take the news of her diagnosis? And did the father of the baby even know what had transpired tonight? What was the story there? Forty-five minutes later I am still awake, tossing and turning. Finally I give up the attempt and get out of bed.

I tiptoe into the spare room, careful not to make a sound that might awaken my aunt, asleep in the next room. I stifle sneezes as clouds of dust rise like smoke-signals from dusty old box-files which I retrieve from top of the old almirah. There's a pile of them, together with some heavy framed photographs which are also coated in dust. I place the framed photographs carefully on the floor, upright and leaning against the wall, settle cross-legged on the floor, and open the boxes one by one.

The first one is crammed with old photographs - pictures of my parents and their friends, and some of me taken in infancy and childhood. My first birthday, my second birthday… I pick one up. *Cringe.* There I am, in a flouncy white dress with a pink sash, wearing a tiara, standing by a huge cake which looks like a castle, surrounded by my parents, aunts and uncles. My mother stands next to me laughing, knife in hand, a pink ribbon tied around its handle. She had been a petite woman, with a dark complexion and sharp, exquisite features. I turned out to be quite unlike her in appearance. In the photograph, I am about to blow out the candles and everyone's eyes are on me. My father stands behind her and an older man with backswept grey hair and bushy eyebrows whom I don't recognise is on the other side of her, looking at us and smiling. Some long-forgotten uncle, I suppose. I sigh wistfully and put the photograph down. I can't remember the last time I celebrated my birthday with a party. Memories of happier times, carefully filed away in my mind, threaten to come crowding back and I blink back unexpected tears. I resist the temptation to sift through the rest of the photographs, and move on to the next box, remembering what I am here for.

This one is filled with papers and certificates: medical courses and conferences attended by my parents. Nothing interesting there.

The next one looks promising - my mother's name is written across the front of the box in big letters.

They never told me what my mother died of and I never asked. A few months after I was born, she had started working at the Lotus Nursing Home - the very institution that had been instrumental in fulfilling her dream of becoming a mother. Alas, she had not been there for more than a few years when the illness struck. I was only seven, but I recollect the word 'cancer' being whispered in hushed tones by relatives and friends. I remember her growing progressively thinner month by month, until she was nothing but skin and bone at the end - except for her belly. I have a vivid memory of her abdomen growing larger as the rest of her body shrank. I imagined that there was a baby inside, because, in my childish mind, that was the only reason that a belly would enlarge so rapidly in the space of a few months.

I remember her collar-bones jutting out like two door handles, and the skin on her abdomen becoming tense and shiny as it expanded, until ugly *striae* - stretch marks of pale wrinkled skin - appeared in several places. When the end came, my first emotion was regret that I was never going to have that little brother or sister. I'm not sure I even knew that she was dead. Some well-meaning relative told me she had 'gone away'. I remember her lying in the living room in a funny kind of bed with frilled white satin sheets and shiny brass handles; I had never seen a coffin before. In the next few months, I kept expecting her to come back. I remember keeping watch on the front gate through the large window in the sitting room, pricking my ears up each time I heard the gate creak.

A year or two later, I realised that she was never coming back, and that what was in her enlarging belly was actually the cancer that they had been murmuring about.

Until now, I had never wanted to find out for myself what form of the dreaded disease she had suffered from. I hold her file in my hands now, realising that I was about to find out. A picture of the Hollywood actress flashes in my mind and I open the box.

The grey cover of the thick file is inscribed with her name, hospital number, date of birth and blood group. I open it and leaf through it; it's one of those folders where the documents are slotted into pockets made of clear polythene. Everything is arranged neatly, in chronological order. There is evidence of many hospital admissions. *Admitted for CT scan, admitted for chemotherapy, admitted for fever.*

And then I see a large card with the words '*Diagnosis: Carcinoma of the stomach*' written in large letters.

There it is, then. I feel the tension leave my body.

Stomach cancer is nasty. But it wasn't breast cancer. So, then I can't have that sinister breast cancer gene Prof Bala was talking about, can I?

One less thing to worry about.

I don't want to read anymore, and quickly replace the boxes.

Now I realise that her increasing girth was caused by the rapid outpouring of fluid from the cancer deposits that would have studded the lining of her abdominal cavity. I had seen many patients with this malignant condition, their bellies huge and glistening like my mother's had been.

Back in my bed, there is something that keeps niggling at the back of my mind. I am sure that it's something that I had seen in one of the boxes, but I can't quite pin it down. I keep trying to catch the elusive thought, but it keeps slipping further and further away. Finally I give up and surrender myself to sleep, and this time I fall asleep quickly and easily.

12

My nocturnal activities have taken their toll, for the next morning I drag myself out of bed with difficulty. I am tempted to sleep in, but attendance at the monthly ward class is compulsory. This term we are assigned to a very unpleasant physician called Dr Ramanayake, and I am not looking forward to the class at all.

Some students find the whole 'Teaching by Humiliation' thing a huge laugh, but for me, there is nothing more embarrassing than being ridiculed in front of my student colleagues, patients, patients' relatives, nurses, attendants, cleaners and random lookers-on. Somehow, the notion that students learn best when publicly embarrassed and humiliated has become firmly entrenched in medical education.

Dr Ramanayake in particular takes the belittling further than necessary, seeming to derive sadistic pleasure in the confusion and distress he evoked. I had taken an instant dislike to him the minute I laid eyes on him. With his jet-black *(definitely dyed),* well-oiled hair smoothed down and combed back from his sloping forehead, beady eyes, hook-like nose and skinny neck with folds of redundant skin, he reminded me of a bird of prey.

Like all predators, he chose his victims carefully, going first for what he assumed to be the weak and helpless. In my group, his favourite prey was Dinesh, whose nervous stutter made him fair game.

'Right, let's start with you,' he would say, pointing a knee hammer at his chosen victim, eyes glittering with anticipation. We were each required to prepare a case history and he would choose one of us at random to present their case to the class. I can't decide which feeling is worse - the agonising suspense of wondering whether you would be chosen to be the unlucky victim for the day, or the terror that floods through you when you are actually picked.

I see Aunty Sherine pottering around in her kitchen garden as I down a cup of coffee hoping it will revive me. She has obviously been up early, because I see a dish of steaming *kiribath* on the table, with the table laid for two.

'What's this doing here with my stuff?' I call out, picking up the object which has been placed next to my plate. I turn the mobile phone over in my hands. It looks familiar but it's certainly not mine.

'What?' she yells.

'This phone? What's it doing here?'

'Isn't it yours?' She enters the kitchen and washes her hands at the sink.

'No. This is my phone.' I hold my phone up for her to see. 'Where'd you find it?'

'In your pocket.'

'What?'

'Yes, the pocket of your white coat. I gave it to the laundry. The other one's back, by the way.'

I remember now.

I stare at the phone in dismay. I remember holding it in my hands, meaning to replace it in the drawer. But at that moment Rambo and Jay had burst in and I must have slipped it into the pocket of my coat. It is the phone I had discovered in the drawer of Anil's bedside table in the TICU.

I had inadvertently walked away with the dead boy's phone.

'What's wrong?' Aunty Sherine asks, seeing the expression on my face.

I explain to her. 'What shall I do now? I never meant to take it.'

'It's alright, you can return it to his family.'

'But how?'

'Christine, of course. Leave it here, I'll ask her driver to pick it up. He can give it to his sister-in law. He's the boy's uncle, remember?'

'Okay, will do,' I say, relieved, and help myself to a rhomboid-shaped piece of *kiribath* cautiously. My aunt is many things but a good cook she is not. Surprisingly, it tastes quite good despite breaking up into small pieces before it could reach my mouth. 'Wasn't it wrapped in a piece of paper?'

'Yes, an old newspaper. I threw it in the bin. There's some nice clean bags in that bottom drawer, you can put it in one of those.'

I'm not sure what makes me rummage in the bin and look for the piece of newspaper, but I find it, fortunately right at the top. I retrieve it and inspect it. It is crumpled and stained at one corner. I take my aunt's advice and place the phone, together with the sheet of newspaper, in a clean plastic bag.

The ward class starts out well but turns out to be a disaster. Dr R surveys the group and chooses Devika who has 'Pick me' written all over her eager face. The others breathe sighs of relief and we troop to the bedside of her patient, a thirty-year-old bank clerk with a history of being unwell for one month, with weight loss and bouts of fever.

It is a classic clinical problem known by the old-fashioned term 'Pyrexia of unknown origin' or 'PUO': fever of more than three weeks duration with no apparent cause. The possible causes are numerous and varied, and so it is a favourite teaching topic with physicians.

Devika does a pretty good job with the history, telling the story well. In fact, it is such a good history Dr Ramanayake doesn't get an opportunity to pick any holes in it at all.

I can see he is getting bored, and his beady eyes start roving over us like an armed drone seeking its target. His gaze locks on a victim, and he fires, interrupting Devika's narrative.

'So… what are the causes of PUO?' He has picked on Rehan, who is lolling against the neighbouring bed.

'Er... what, sir?'

'I said, what are the causes of PUO?'

Rehan looks flummoxed.

'Get on with it now!' Dr Ramanayake barks impatiently. 'We don't have all day.'

Rehan is silent, frowning ferociously as though trying to formulate an answer, but I am sure he has no idea what the letters stand for.

After a few seconds of agonising silence, Dr Ramanayake snaps at Dinesh, 'You! Tell this moron what PUO stands for!'

'Pie-pie-pie—' stammers poor Dinesh, his tongue betraying him in the stress of the moment.

'Pah!' he snorts impatiently. 'Anyone?'

Before anyone else can answer, Devika chirps, 'Pyrexia of unknown origin, sir.'

'Yes, quite right,' he says grudgingly. 'So, you—' He points the knee hammer at Rehan. 'What are the causes?'

Rehan says innocently, 'Sir, if we knew the causes, then we can't call it pyrexia of unknown origin, sir.'

There is a silence.

He continues, 'Then it would be pyrexia of known origin, sir.'

I can't believe my ears. Is he trying to be funny with Dr R? I hear a stifled snort of laughter from one of the students as I wait for the explosion.

It follows in a few seconds. Dr Ramanayake goes ballistic. He accuses Rehan of being a smart-ass and trying to waste his (Dr R's) time, and rants and raves for several minutes. The patient, a mild-looking man in spectacles, looks shocked at the onset of the tirade and then sympathetic, his illness forgotten momentarily. Dr R finally evicts us from the ward unceremoniously, calling us all 'useless fellows' and refusing to sign us up.

In the corridor outside the ward, the group exhibits mixed reactions. Devika is miffed that she hasn't been able to complete her presentation.

The others are thrilled at being let off early but my feelings are mixed; although pleased to have a free hour that morning, I know that we would have to repeat the class with the hated physician later this term.

Harsha and I walk towards the surgical block. He is obsessed with surgery and spends every free minute he has hanging around the surgical wards and operation theatres.

We halt outside the vascular unit. 'There's an interesting patient here,' he says enthusiastically. 'He's got a triple A, and he's being worked up for surgery. Do you want to see him?'

I can understand his excitement. Surgery to repair an abdominal aortic aneurysm - triple A for short - is a major operation guaranteed to satisfy any budding surgeon's thirst for blood and excitement.

I decline the offer. 'No, thanks. I'm off to see the girl from last night, the one who had the ectopic.'

'Okay. I'll catch up with you later.'

In the gynae ward, the girl is sitting up in bed, propped up on two pillows, looking surprisingly well, considering that she had almost bled to death less than twelve hours ago. She looks at me curiously as I approach her. She doesn't recognise me, of course. I was just one of a group of masked strangers who surrounded her last night before she went under the effect of the anaesthetic.

I tell her that I was present at her operation last night. Her face breaks out into a smile, which transforms her rather ordinary face.

'Thank you, doctor. I feel much, much better now.'

I tell her I'm not a doctor, but a medical student. We are commonly mistaken for doctors, and are frequently addressed as such by patients, even if they know we are students.

Her name is Ashani and she tells me that she has completed her A' Levels and hopes to enter university.

'My mother thinks it's a waste of time, university students going on strike and protesting all the time. She wants me to do accountancy. But I really want to go to campus.'

I want to talk about the pregnancy but can't bring myself to broach the subject. We talk about the issues of university students and I then say goodbye, promising to look in on her the next day.

I find Indira and Dr Henry Fernando in the side room of the ward, having tea. Indira sees me and waves me in.

'What are you doing here? Have you cut the ward class?'

I tell her about Dr Ramanayake, Rehan and the ward class and she bursts out laughing. Even Henry manages to arrange his frozen features into a semblance of a smile and emits a soft chuckle. This is a new side to Indira, one I haven't seen before. She is usually quite brusque with us students.

'He's a real rascal, that Rehan! Come, sit down and have a cup of tea with us.'

I sit awkwardly and pour myself some tea from a chipped grey teapot. It feels strange to be sitting around the same table as the consultant and senior registrar. I almost gag when I sip the tepid milky-brown liquid. Like all tea that is made in the hospital wards, it tastes like someone has emptied the contents of the sugar bottle into it.

She says, 'Dr Fernando and I were just talking about the ectopic.'

'Oh, you mean, Ashani?'

She gazes at me blankly. 'Who?'

'Her name is Ashani.'

'Oh… yes. Have you seen her?'

I nod. I don't expect her to know the girl by name. It's typical practice amongst doctors to depersonalise patients and refer to them by their illness rather than by name. For example, they may talk about the haemorrhoid in Bed Ten, or the septic foot that needs to go to theatre.

'We haven't told the mother yet. I was planning to talk to her today but Dr Fernando thinks we should talk to the girl first and see what her wishes are, since she's not a minor.'

I blurt out, 'She doesn't want the mother to know.'

They look at me in surprise. 'How do you know? Did she tell you that?' asks Indira.

I tell them the words she had uttered on the operating table before she lost consciousness. She had whispered softly, 'Please don't tell my mother what's wrong with me.'

'See?' says Henry, quietly. 'Our first duty is to our patient. We must respect her wishes.'

'But she still lives with her parents,' objects Indira. 'They have a right to know.'

'No. She's nineteen – you must get her consent first,' he says firmly. 'Let's have a chat with the girl first, what's her name—' he looks at me.

'Ashani,' I say.

'Let's talk to Ashani and see what she what she has to say to us.'

'The mother is coming in at twelve, so we must decide before that,' she says. 'I'll talk to her and see if I can change her mind.'

I leave them arguing about the matter and slip away.

The package is still sitting on the kitchen table when I get back home. I pick up my phone to call Aunty Christine and remind her to send her driver to pick it up, but I pause as I have an idea. I dial Harsha's number instead.

'No, Lotus, sorry, I really can't,' he says, in response to my request. 'The triple A is going to theatre at one and I'm planning to be there.' His voice bubbles with excitement. 'I might even get a chance to scrub!'

My heart sinks. If he does go in to theatre with the triple A, he could be out of action for hours.

I try Tara next, but her phone is switched off.

I stare at the phone, and then take it out of the bag and press the power button, but, as expected, nothing happens. The phone is dead. Rummaging through the bottom drawer of the kitchen cupboard I find what I am looking for, among a tangle of wires and plugs and other bits of electrical junk: three old phone chargers, no longer used, but hopefully, still working. I connect each in turn to the phone.

Yes. The third one fits.

When I plug it into the electrical wall socket a green light comes on, telling me there is life inside it. While I wait for the phone to charge, I pick up the sheet of newspaper that the phone had been wrapped in and glance through it idly. It is dated two months earlier. On one side is the Vacancies section. I wonder whether the boy had been looking for a job, and that was why he had saved that particular page. I turn it over. On the other side is a half-page advertisement for brand-new apartments in a condominium called Seaview City. The rest of the page is filled with news articles. None of them look particularly interesting. There is one about the president opening a new bus stand in some faraway town that I have never heard of, and another about a well-known philanthropist donating some money to a charity for the deaf and dumb. Another short article describes a prize-giving ceremony in a school where the minister of education was the chief guest.

After allowing the phone to charge for about ten minutes, I press the power button once again, feeling a little guilty at being so nosy. With a musical beep, the phone whirs to life. The screen lights up and the first thing that appears is the home screen with a photograph in the background – that of a young boy and a little girl. The boy must be Anil, of course, although his face looks nothing like the swollen distorted face of the dead boy I had seen in the TICU. The boy in the picture has a thin face with sharp features, eyes set a little too close together, and hair cut short. He wears a red T-shirt and denim jeans, with a backpack on his shoulders. The girl looks about five or six years old, hair braided in two long plaits which are tied at the end with blue ribbons, and wears a simple dress with puffed sleeves in a blue floral print. They are seated on a bench, his arm around her shoulders, both smiling broadly at the camera. In the background are smooth green lawns, flower beds and a see-saw: it looks like a park of some kind.

I wonder who the girl is - probably his little sister, although the age gap seems quite large. I recall Aunty Christine mentioning another child in the family.

Feeling less guilty now, I look through the contents of the phone. A list of names have been saved in the 'Phone book'. The first name listed is *Amma* - Mother. I scroll through the list and stop in surprise when I come across a familiar name.

Lotus.

Another Lotus? Strange… it's not a common name. I click on the name and an unfamiliar number appears - it looks like a land line number and it ends in a series of 4s. *So this boy knew someone else called Lotus?* That's quite a coincidence. I wonder who this other Lotus person could be.

I can't explain the curiosity that I have now begun to feel about the boy. Next, I look through the call log. There are a few numbers - Amma, and a few other unfamiliar names. The most recently dialled number is a mobile number with no name attached, and before that: *Lotus,* again.

There is one more photograph, that of two laughing boys looking into the camera, one of them being the same boy as in the first photograph.

Two more calls to make. The first is to Aunty Christine. Fortunately she is at home and is able to speak to Leela, her maid, who gives her the information I need, which I scribble in my notebook. She starts to ask me why I need it but I cut her off in mid-sentence. I jot down the numbers from the boy's call log in my notebook and then switch the phone off.

I dial another number and hear the ring-tone, a high-pitched, lilting female voice belting out a Hindi song. I hold the phone a few inches from my ear and wait for the owner of the phone to answer.

Five minutes later I hear a familiar racket outside the front gate in response to my phone summons - a loud spluttering accompanied by a throaty bleating sound, rather like a sheep with laryngitis. I grab my bag and the phone and leave the house, locking the front door behind me.

'*Kohatadha*, miss?' *Where to?* Sunil turns and beams at me as I climb into the back seat of his red tuk-tuk, which shudders and shakes like a live thing. Sunil is one of the neighbourhood tuk-tuk drivers, a cheerful young fellow with coal-black skin, an ear-stud in one earlobe, and shoulder-length hair tied back in a pony-tail.

I read out the address I had written down and ask him, 'Do you know this place?'

'Yes, miss. I know it very well.'

'Let's go, then!'

The tuk-tuk takes off with a mighty roar and further spluttering. A few minutes later I am bouncing in the back seat while Sunil speeds along, sounding the bleating horn indiscriminately and completely disregarding the condition of the roads.

'Miss, why do you want to go there?' he yells over his shoulder. 'Better not to go there alone.'

I too shout at the top of my voice to make myself heard above the din of the engine. I tell him briefly about the accident. 'I want to visit the boy's mother and return this phone to her.'

'Okay, miss, I will come with you!' He revs the engine happily and we are on our way.

13

The bunch of purple plastic grapes dangling behind the windscreen dances madly as street signs whizz past. Then Baseline Road, Canal Road, and now a road alongside a long narrow serpentine canal which twists and turns amidst clusters of shabby dwellings. Wide, smoothly-tarred roads give way to narrow streets and rough gravelly lanes littered with garbage and lined by small shanties. We cross a railway line and I see more shacks on both sides of the track, just a few feet away from the sleepers. People walk up and down the railway track as if it were a path and a child scampers across, ball in hand. Sunil tells me that we are now in the heart of Wanathamulla. I have never been here before but I know that it is one of the city's most populous slums, which has mushroomed on the banks of the old Dutch canal that winds through this area – once an important route for transporting people and goods. He points out a tall narrow three-storey building painted in a deep pink and white that towers over its neighbours and seems to lean precariously over the canal bank.

'That's Wanatha Wimal's house,' he shouts.

I have no idea who that is. He informs me that Wanatha Wimal is the alias of a notorious drug-dealer. As we pass the building, which looks like a three-tiered wedding cake, I peer out at it cautiously, and he says cheerfully, 'Not to worry, he is not there now, miss.'

'Then where is he?'

He bellows over his shoulder. *'Hiray!' In prison!*

I spot a bump coming up on the road ahead and brace myself, hanging on to the sides of the seat. Sure enough, after we hit it I become airborne and then return to earth, wincing as my bottom hits the lumpy rexine-covered seat with a bone-shaking thud.

We turn into a narrow crowded lane and the little vehicle swerves crazily to avoid colliding with a brown cow which is standing in the middle of the street, stolidly chewing its cud. In spite of loud honking it ignores us, refusing to budge even an inch. Sunil manoeuvres the tuk-tuk slowly and carefully around the animal and we continue down this street, avoiding a gunny bag strewn with bright red chillies drying in the sun. We careen to the end of this street and lurch to a sudden stop. Two men seated on plastic chairs outside a doorway with a cardboard box between them look up at us briefly and go back to their game of chess.

We have arrived at our destination, Ambawatte, which seems to be a sub-slum on the fringe of the main slum. Ambawatte Lane is little more than an alley, barely wide enough to let a three-wheeler pass through, so Sunil switches the engine off and hops out, saying, 'Wait here, miss, I'll find the house and come.'

I remain in the back seat, attracting wary stares from some of the inhabitants of the lane who pass by. A mangy brown mongrel with engorged teats noses hopefully around a pile of garbage heaped nearby. The vehicle is parked close to the canal bank and as I watch the murky green water flow sluggishly past me, I wonder what it would be like to live a few feet away from this polluted waterway. The canal is fed by huge sewage pipes that disgorge their dubious contents through large circular openings set into its walls - they look like mouths fixed open in permanent yawns. A yoghurt cup and some drinking straws entangled in a plastic shopping bag drift slowly past. I see two urchins squatting close to the water's edge, casting makeshift fishing rods into the water. Rows of washing are hung out to dry on the barbed-wire fence lining the narrow gravel path; well-worn once-white school uniforms, threadbare denim jeans, and six yards of a saree in a faded blue-and-green mango design flap sadly in the breeze close to me. An old man clad only in a sarong snoozes on a ramshackle bench, chin resting on his bare chest. A row of neat flower beds filled with red, yellow and orange cannas is a surprising sight, adding a welcome splash of colour to the dreary surroundings.

I feel a sharp sting like the prick of a needle on my elbow, and slap at it reflexly with my other hand. Lying in the palm of my hand is a dead mosquito. I recognise the species by the white bands on its legs: it is that vicious day-biter, *Aedes aegypti*. Not surprising, for I had spotted plenty of breeding places for the insect - the carrier of dengue and a host of other nasty diseases - empty tins, coconut shells and old tyres that could collect water.

Sunil's face appears suddenly. 'Come, miss, I found the house.' I dismount and he wheels the tuk-tuk to the side of the path.

We make our way down the narrow passage which is lined by more shanties. I am surprised to see that many of them are made of brick and concrete and some are even two-storeyed. The government's new urban development plan for Colombo which called for relocation of the city's slum-dwellers had already taken effect in places like Slave Island but obviously hadn't been implemented here yet. Some of the doorways are open and I can see right into the dwellings. In almost every front room a television set is visible, and atop one roof, a satellite dish.

Two half-naked children stop their play to stare at me curiously, one with creamy yellow snot trickling from a nostril. A buxom woman wearing nothing but a red and yellow *cheeththa* with the knot tucked into her cleavage squats comfortably by a wayside tap, washing a bucketful of clothes. There is no drain to receive the excess water and a frothy rivulet flows down the passage towards the canal. I step over the soapy stream and we soon arrive at our destination, a small shanty with unplastered brick walls and a door made of rough wooden planks nailed together. A small window to the left of the door is boarded up with pieces of thick cardboard. Compared to some of the other structures down the lane, it looks dilapidated.

Seeing me hesitate, Sunil raps sharply on the door, but there is no answer. Instead, a woman appears in the doorway of the shack opposite and looks us up and down. She is plump and blowsy, dressed in a stained white sleeveless blouse and a long, shapeless faded blue skirt. She catches my eye and smiles, revealing misshapen teeth stained with betel. I look away, not wanting to start a conversation. She has other ideas.

'They are inside. Just knock again.'

I give her a reluctant half-smile, not wanting to appear rude. In this place, it seems normal to mind your neighbour's business.

'They are still in mourning.'

I turn my back on her and knock on the door. The rhythmic pounding of pestle on mortar resonates from a hut nearby, causing the ground to vibrate with each thud.

The lack of response from me doesn't deter the woman. 'The whole *watte* is mourning,' she continues, eyeing us curiously. 'Two funerals in such a short time.'

There is still no sound from within the shack. A small child, naked except for a pair of faded red knickers and a gold talisman strung on to a thick black cord around its neck, appears at the woman's side and tugs at her skirt. She picks the child up and swings it onto her hip. The child is scrawny, with stick-like limbs, big bright eyes and a mop of unruly curls. To my horror, it dives into the woman's blouse, yanks out her left breast and fastens its lips firmly around the nipple. I am taken back but the woman seems quite unconcerned about the activities of the child who sucks at the nipple and gazes at me unblinkingly. Sunil gazes fixedly at some point in the opposite direction.

The woman continues to talk. '…and they hardly come out after the funeral.' I find it difficult to concentrate on her words. The child tosses the breast aside and decides to try the other one. The breast flops down limply, the nipple dark and proud against the huge chocolate-brown areola. The woman slaps the child's hands away, sets it down and casually stuffs her breast back into the blouse as if she were stuffing a pillow into its case. The child immediately starts to whimper.

'Two funerals?' I ask, trying to avoid staring at her breast, which seems to be in danger of escaping from the blouse again.

'Yes, the other one just one month ago. Very sad, no? And such friends also.'

Just then we hear the squeak of a latch and the door opens a crack. Sunil – who seems to have taken charge of the situation – thrusts his head in and I hear the words *'ispirithala'* and *'dosthara'*. *Hospital. Doctor.*

The door opens wider and a woman peers out at me. I recognise her instantly. She is the woman I had seen in the waiting room outside the Trauma Intensive Care Unit – the one whom Janaka, the ICU doctor was speaking to when I entered.

She looks frightened, her left hand gripping the door tightly.

'Kawdha?' *Who are you?*

'Can we come in? I want to talk about your son.'

'I don't want any trouble,' she says, attempting to shut the door.

'I'm from the hospital,' I say, holding the door open with my hand. 'I want to give you something that belonged to him.'

There is a silence, then the door swings wide open and she ushers me in. 'Sorry. I didn't know who you were. I thought you were someone else.'

Thinking it would be wise to take Sunil in with me, I gesture to him to follow me. The neighbour cranes her neck and looks on inquisitively, but the woman shuts the door firmly in her face.

She invites me to sit on a low worn-out settee. Sunil takes up a position by the door, standing with feet apart and arms folded, looking rather like my personal bodyguard.

There is an awkward silence while I look around and wonder what to say. The room is small and dark. The only light comes from a glass skylight set into corrugated zinc roofing sheets and from a surprisingly large flat-screen television that sits atop a wooden cabinet which is filled with plates, glasses and small ornaments. The television is switched on but muted and tuned to a children's cartoon show. The moving pictures on the television screen cast a flickering light over the room.

A child of about six or seven sits cross-legged on the rough cement floor facing the television set, her eyes glued to the silent screen. After an initial glance at me, she turns her attention back to the television and takes no further notice of us. I recognise her – she is the little girl in the photograph in the boy's phone. On the cabinet, next to the television, propped against the wall is a framed photograph of the dead boy, encircled by a thick garland of jasmine flowers. It seems to be an enlarged version of a studio photograph that has been taken for an identity badge or a passport, for the background is a bleak grey screen, and the boy stares fiercely at the photographer, unsmiling, hair neatly side-parted and plastered onto his scalp. We all gaze in silence at the photograph, and the atmosphere in the small room becomes charged, as if a cloud of grief had suddenly appeared, blocking out the sun.

There are two green plastic chairs facing the television but the woman remains standing near a narrow doorway covered by a thin curtain which seems to have been fashioned out of the remnants of an old saree. She is slim and wiry, dressed in a simple white blouse and skirt which are crumpled but clean. A white *pirith* thread is tied around one wrist. She smooths down the skirt with her hands, no longer looking frightened, and looks at me expectantly, a hopeful smile on her face. When I glance from the photograph to her face, I see a strong resemblance between her face and that of the boy. They both have the same thin narrow face and close-set eyes, but her face is more angular and gaunt, with dark shadows under the eyes.

She finally breaks the silence. 'Have you come about the money?'

My surprised expression must have told her that she is on the wrong track. Her smile disappears and her shoulders slump in disappointment.

'Er... no. I came to return this.' I hold out my hand. She gazes at the phone blankly.

'It's your son's phone,' I say. 'It was left in the hospital, by his bed.'

She takes it automatically and places it on the cabinet. Then, tears begin to flow down her cheeks. Sunil and I exchange glances.

'I'm very sorry about what happened to Anil,' I say awkwardly.

She wipes her damp cheeks with the palm of her hand and asks, 'Were you his doctor? A different doctor spoke to me there.'

'No, I'm not a doctor. I'm studying to be one. I went to see him because I know Leela. She works for my aunty, Christine.'

'Ah, Christine *Nona*!' She starts weeping again, telling me how kind Christine has been to her family.

'Why did you ask me whether I have come about the money?' I ask her curiously. 'What money?'

Her manner changes immediately and her face becomes guarded. She shakes her head. 'No, no, I was mistaken. It's nothing.'

'Please tell me. I'll try to help if I can.'

She tucks a stray strand of hair behind her ear and stares down at the floor. 'No one can help us now, doctor.'

'Was he involved in something illegal?'

She looks up, scandalised. 'No! My son would not do anything like that. He is – he was a good boy.'

But of course she would say that; she is his mother. I'm sure that even Wanatha Wimal's mother believes that he is a 'good boy'.

'Where was he working?'

'He was working in a supermarket but two weeks ago he had taken some leave – I don't know why, he never told us this. They said he never came back to work. But then he came home and told me he had got something new. They were going to pay well. He said our money problems would be over soon.'

'What was this new job?'

She shakes her head. 'I don't know, he didn't say. They gave him an advance. But then the last time he came back he said that they owed him some money. He said they were trying to cheat him but he was determined to get what was due to him.'

'When did you see him last?'

'About ten days ago - Tuesday last week. He must have been working very hard because he was looking very tired. He had lost some weight too.'

'Do you know how much money?'

She shakes her head. 'He never told me details. But we were trying to save some money for the new flat, so I think he wanted to use the money for that.'

'What new flat?' I ask.

She spreads her hands. 'We have to leave this place. The government is going to destroy all these houses and take the land. They have built brand new flats for us.' She raises her right hand high. 'Very tall buildings. Fifteen, twenty floors high. But we have to pay fifty thousand rupees.'

'Fifty thousand?' I echo. 'That's a lot of money.'

She nods. 'And after that, every month, four thousand rupees. For twenty years. If we don't get a flat, we have nowhere to go. I have lived here all my life.'

It is quite a sad story. It seems that the shanties are due to be demolished in five months. She has reserved a flat in the new housing development by paying a ten thousand rupee deposit, but unless the balance was paid within three months, they would lose it.

'What about the advance payment he got?'

'He wanted to get something special for his little sister.' She looks at the little girl with tears glistening in her eyes. 'He bought this TV for us with that money. We didn't have a TV before. But he said he would be getting more - much more.'

So the little girl is his sister. But the whole story sounds questionable to me. I find it hard to believe that somebody would be legitimately willing to pay 'much more' money to a twenty-year-old with no qualifications to speak off. Her next sentence strengthens my suspicions.

'Last week – he came home and said someone might come looking for him, and if they did, I was to say I didn't know his whereabouts.'

'And did someone come?'

She hesitates. 'Yes. Two men came. On a motor cycle. One of them told us that Anil was in trouble. They said something about money...'

'Do you know who they were?'

'One of them – he's from this area. The other one I haven't seen before.'

'What exactly did they say?'

'They were very angry and said that he would be paid what he was due, but they said he was trying to demand more. They threatened us and broke that window.' She points to the boarded-up space and then bursts out, 'It's not true of course. I don't believe it. He was a good, honest boy.'

She shakes her head. 'Now we will never get the money.'

There is another awkward silence as she wipes fresh tears away.

In an attempt to change the subject, I say, 'Your neighbour in the house opposite – she said that there had been another funeral in the neighbourhood recently.'

Her face crumples. 'Yes it's true.' She fingers the thin white thread tied around her wrist. 'It's a bad time for us.'

'Who was the other person who died?'

'A boy called Manoj. He was friends with my son. It was such a shock to everyone.'

Manoj. I'm sure that name was listed in the boy's phone contacts.

'How did he die?' I ask only to distract her, but to my dismay, she starts crying again.

'It was terrible, what happened to him! He was attacked –
stabbed and beaten up.'

'But why? And by whom?'

'Nobody knows. He was a very simple boy. The police said
it was one of those beggar killings, but he was not a beggar.'

'Beggar killings?'

'Haven't you heard?' She looks surprised. 'Somebody has
been killing beggars all over Colombo. It has been in the news.
But Manoj was not a beggar. He was crippled in one leg because
of polio, and had a bad limp, but he did not beg. He was trying to
make a living selling lottery-tickets, and had just bought a small
cart for that purpose.'

I recall reading something about a series of deaths of
beggars in the city which had made headlines a few weeks ago.

Just then, I hear a wheezy cough from beyond the curtain
and a feeble voice quavers from the next room. 'Daughter, who
is it? Who's there?'

'It's nothing, mother,' she calls out. 'Some visitors.'

To me, she says, 'That's my mother. She's... not been very
well.'

Standing up, I say, 'We must leave now. I am sorry if we
troubled you.'

'No, no. No trouble. Thank you for returning the phone.
But I could not give you anything to drink. Please have a cup of
tea before you go.'

I decline the offer and say we have to leave.

'There's just a couple more things I wanted to ask...' I
hesitate near the door.

'Yes?'

'Anil met with the accident on Havelock Road—'

She looks puzzled. 'Havelock Road?'

'Do you know what he was doing in that area? Did he
know someone there?'

She shakes her head. 'I don't know what he was doing
there.'

'And what about his friend who went with him to hospital?'

She stares blankly at me. 'Which friend?'

'There was someone with him in hospital. When he was brought in.'

She shakes her head. 'Not a friend. That was the gentleman who was driving the jeep. He took Anil to hospital.'

'No, there was another person.' I give her the description that Rohan the Emergency doctor had given me. Tall, muscular, long hair tied back.

She looks puzzled, shaking her head. 'I don't know any friend of his who looks like that. If there was someone, he would have come forward and spoken to me, no? Or come to the funeral?'

I have no answer to give her.

'The two men who came - one of them had long hair—' she points at Sunil's hair. 'Tied like that. He was tall. And had tattoos. All over his arms.'

Tattoos all over his arms? I'm sure Rohan had mentioned tattooed arms too. 'Someone from his workplace?' I suggest. 'Do you think he was the one who was at the hospital?'

She shakes her head. 'I don't know. But I don't think he could be a friend.' She shudders. 'The way he spoke! It was scary.'

Before we leave I write my phone number on a scrap of paper and hand it to her.

'Please call if you need anything. I'd like to help if I can.'

14

We walk back down the narrow alley towards the canal.

'Miss,' says Sunil, 'You know that television set?'

'Yes, what about it?' I say, stepping over a pile of rubbish heaped by the side of a doorway.

'Latest model. Flat screen, LED. Very expensive.'

'How do you know?'

'I was checking prices recently. Wife wants to buy new TV.'

'Wife!' I exclaim. 'Sunil, I never knew you were married!'

He blushes. 'Married twelve years, miss. Three children.'

'Three children? Really?'

He tells me the ages of the children – ten, eight and five.

'So how expensive do you think that TV was?'

'At least seventy or eighty.'

I stop and gape at him. 'What! Seventy or eighty thousand rupees?'

'Yes, I am sure. I checked same model TV.'

I shake my head in disbelief. 'That's a lot of money to spend on a television set!'

'Yes, miss, he could have easily paid the deposit for their new flat with that money.'

'Unless he was absolutely sure of getting more money.' Once again, I wonder where he got the money from. What kind of job would pay that kind of money before even starting?

'She could always sell the TV,' he offers. 'But you can't get much for a second-hand set.'

We reach the tuk-tuk and Sunil exclaims in annoyance.

'What is it, Sunil?'

He squats down and inspects his rear left tyre. 'Flat!'

'Flat tyre? Oh no! How did that happen?'

I see it too now, completely deflated, with the rim almost touching the ground.

'What shall we do?'

He remains squatting, inspecting it from all angles. When he straightens up his face is grim and set. He looks around us but the place is now deserted. There is no sign of the chess-players, the children or the old man.

'I can get it fixed, miss. But you should go back. I will find another three-wheel for you.'

'No, I can stay till you get it fixed.'

He is firm. 'No, miss. Let's go. Better not to stay here.'

He is insistent, so I agree to leave. We walk along the canal till we come to the main road.

'There's plenty of tuks passing. I'll get into one of those.'

'Sorry for the trouble, miss.'

'It's okay Sunil, it's not your fault.'

I hail a passing tuk-tuk and am home in ten minutes.

A dark blue jeep with white lettering stencilled on the side is parked outside the house, blocking the driveway. In the driver's seat is a young chap with a crew cut in a khaki uniform. He smiles at me politely as I squeeze past the vehicle and enter the house.

'Aunty Sherine, why is there a police jeep parked outside—' I stop abruptly. Sitting on one of the living room chairs is a big man wearing a red T-shirt, grey track pants and running shoes. He gets on his feet lightly when he sees me and says pleasantly, 'Ah. You must be the niece.'

Taken aback, I mutter, 'Yes, I am the niece. And you are?'

'Ah, you're back!' Aunty Sherine enters the room carrying a glass of water, which she hands him. 'Let me introduce you. Lotus, meet SP Boteju—'

He extends his hand, saying, 'Pleased to meet you.' He has a strong, firm grip. 'You're Chubby's girl.'

'Chubby?'

He chuckles. 'That's what we called him in school – your father. He was a little bit on the plump side then, you know.'

'You know my father?'

'We were classmates,' he says, smiling. 'I must say it's a good thing you don't take after him. You must look like your mother.'

Before I could respond to this, he turns to my aunt and says, 'I'll make a move, then. Don't forget the meeting on Wednesday.' He empties the glass with a gulp, places it on the coffee table and leaves.

'Who was *that*?' I say, drawing back the curtain framing the front window, watching him as he springs lightly into the passenger seat of the jeep. It takes off with a roar.

'I told you,' she says. 'He's a policeman. Very high up.'

'But why was he here?'

'He's helping with some work we are doing with prisoners.'

'Hmm... didn't seem like an official visit. Looked like he was jogging or something.'

'He just dropped by to give me some papers.' She picks up the empty glass and disappears into the kitchen.

I follow her. 'Aunty Sherine, do you know anything about these beggar killings?'

She looks at me in surprise. 'Why do you ask?'

'I heard someone talking about it,' I say evasively. 'I was curious.'

'I only know what has been in the papers,' she says. 'And I know it has caused a stir in the beggar community. They feel they are being targeted for some unknown reason.'

The laptop whirrs into action with a beep as I switch it on. The sleek silver machine was a gift from my father, presented to me in my first year of medical school. As I wait for it to boot up I try to recall what I had heard about the so-called beggar killings of a few weeks ago. When the search page appears I type in 'Beggar killings in Colombo', click on 'SEARCH' and sit back. A list of results appears in a few seconds. I click on the first one. It is a news article from *The Reader*, a popular newspaper which is known for its melodramatic headlines and anti-government stance.

'BEGGARS BEING TARGETED BY KILLER!!' the headline screams in large, bold type. A colour photograph of a man with both legs amputated above the knee sitting in a wheelchair on a street corner accompanies the article. I read on:

'The beggar community in Colombo lives in terror, wondering when the killer stalking them will strike again. Just when they thought they could go back to sleeping on the streets in peace following a lull in the shocking killings, the serial beggar-killer strikes again!'

It goes on to describe the latest in a series of mysterious murders of beggars or homeless people – some of them disabled – which had occurred in Colombo over the past few months. I'd read about them in the papers and heard about them on the news, but hadn't given too much attention to them before this.

I scroll down to the next headline: 'COLOMBO BEGGARS ON HIT LIST'. This is an editorial hinting that beggars are being targeted by a government-sponsored hit-squad who are trying to clean up the city of Colombo. 'Is it coincidence that the spate of killings started along with the recent beautification of the city of Colombo?' the editor daringly questions.

An article in another newspaper claims that the murdered beggars were victims of the beggar king, in retaliation for failing to give part of their earnings to him. The so-called 'king of beggars' controlled the activity of beggars in a certain geographical area and demanded part of their earnings in return. A serial killer targeting beggars is a theory put forward again by another journalist in *Lanka Today*. Even the foreign news channels have covered the killings. A BBC headline declares 'HOMELESS KILLINGS STRIKE FEAR IN COLOMBO' and emphasises the violent nature of the killings. Some of the killings are described in gruesome detail, especially the most recent one, the murder of a disabled lottery-ticket seller who had been stabbed and bludgeoned to death. An interview with his grief-stricken mother - along with photographs of her and her son's lottery-ticket cart - is the subject of another article. The mention of the lottery-ticket cart makes me read this one again. The name of the victim is not mentioned, but I realise that this is probably Manoj, Anil's friend.

There are more results spilling onto the next page but I stop there. I sink back into my chair, with a sick feeling in my stomach. It is all rather sensational and incredible, more like a fantastic story than real life. Serial killers only feature in Hollywood films and TV series, not in everyday life in Colombo. And why would anyone want to kill an innocent crippled lottery-ticket seller?

I keep thinking about the little community living in the slum I had visited. The bereaved mother of the dead boy and the fear in her eyes when she spoke about her son. The sick grandmother and the little girl who hadn't taken any notice of us after that first glance. The inquisitive neighbour and her bright-eyed toddler. And the murdered crippled boy who was only a memory...

What a coincidence that the two boys - such good friends - had died violent deaths within a month of each other.

Of course, one was a murder, and the other the result of an accident - two very different types of deaths.

Or were they?

What did the boy's mother say to me? 'The men were very angry and threatened us...'

And the Emergency doctor's words: 'He looked like he had been beaten up...'

Was it possible that the two boys had been involved in something shady? Something that had eventually caught up with them? I remember Aunty Sherine saying, 'Wanathamulla? That place is a hotbed of crime...' My mind starts to work furiously, thinking of drug dealers and underworld gangs. The crippled boy - Anil's friend - had been viciously attacked and murdered.

Perhaps Anil too, had been attacked, before he had met with the accident. That would explain the injuries to his head and face, which the Emergency doctor thought looked like the result of assault. The boy had told the doctor that he had been attacked, but because the driver of the SUV had clearly described the collision, this part of the history had gone unheeded, attributed to ramblings of a confused head-injured patient.

But wouldn't the pathologist have picked that up? Surely the injuries resulting from being assaulted must be distinctive from those resulting from an RTA? I remember the grumpy ill-looking pathologist I had encountered and the strange smell I had caught a whiff of. I am quite sure that the smell was alcohol. If it was, wasn't the post-mortem report questionable? Wasn't it possible that he had attributed all injuries – even those resulting from assault – to the accident? And how could such a senior doctor be allowed to practice while under the influence of alcohol?

My mind is reeling with all these questions bouncing back and forth. I am reading too much into these incidents, I tell myself. It was probably a coincidence, these two boys dying within a month of each other. There is actually nothing to connect their deaths, which are totally dissimilar.

I shut the laptop down, not entirely sure that I have convinced myself.

15

The sleek red BMW that glides up to the front gate as I am leaving for hospital is familiar. The car stops and Aunty Christine's driver Tissa opens the door and jumps out of the driver's seat, leaving the engine running, and greets me with a respectful 'Good morning.'

'Morning, Tissa,' I reply. 'Has Christine Nona sent something?'

'Ah, no, miss,' he says, looking slightly embarrassed. Tissa is a thin, mournful looking man with a drooping moustache. He fidgets for a few seconds and then says, 'I wanted to thank you for visiting Padma...'

'Padma?'

'My sister-in-law. Leela's younger sister.'

'Oh. I didn't know her name was Padma,' I say.

'It was very kind of you and my wife and I truly appreciate it. I know how busy you are, with studies and all.'

'That's quite alright, Tissa,' I reply. 'I'm only sorry I couldn't be of more help… when he was in the hospital.' I pause. 'As you know, by the time I saw him…'

'I understand,' he says, his face clouding over. 'We didn't even know about the accident till the next day. Recently his mother had no idea of his whereabouts.'

He turns, rummages in the front seat and produces a small parcel in a plastic shopping bag. 'This is for you, from my sister-in-law.'

'What's this, Tissa? There's no need to give me anything!'

'It's just some tea…'

'Tea?' I say, surprised.

'Tea leaves. From factory. She works in tea-packing factory, you know. She gets tea leaves at a discount. She wanted to give you this.'

'Please thank her, Tissa.'

'I will. I'll be off now, miss. Have to take the car for a service.' He opens the door and says, 'I can drop miss at the hospital, it's on the way to garage.'

'Alright, thanks.' A moment later I sink into the soft leather cushions in the back seat of the car and it takes off, engine purring smoothly.

'Tissa, I want to ask you something…' I open the bag and peep inside, inhaling the aroma of tea leaves.

'Yes miss?'

'What kind of a boy was he?'

'Anil? He was a good boy, miss.'

'Was he – could he have been involved in anything – illegal?'

He hesitates before answering, his eyes fixed on the road. 'I have been asking myself the same thing. The answer is – I don't know. He was honest but stubborn. He loved his family – would have done anything for that sister of his, even though they didn't have the same father.'

'Ah – I didn't know that. What happened to Anil's father?'

'Anil's father died…she remarried – a useless fellow, a drunkard. He deserted her. We don't even know where he is. She is better off without him.'

'I see.' I notice some papers at the bottom of the bag. 'Tissa, what are these papers?'

'I don't know, she said she found them with his things. She thought you might know what they meant. She said you offered to help.' He brings the car to a gentle halt opposite the main block of the hospital. 'Here we are, miss.'

'Thanks, Tissa.' I hop out quickly, hoping that none of my colleagues spot me leaving the flamboyant red vehicle.

There is something familiar about the figure that limps laboriously ahead of me in the crowded corridor outside the gynaecology ward.

'Morning, Lionel,' I say, overtaking him easily. 'How are you?'

He stops, surprised, and greets me respectfully, a smile spreading across his face. In the bright light of day, not surrounded by dead bodies, he doesn't look sinister at all.

'Good morning, madam. I am fine, thank you. Coming to mortuary again today?'

'No, not today,' I confess. 'I've got ward rounds today.'

'Very good, madam. Anything I can help you with, please let me know.'

'Thanks, I'll remember that. I'll be doing pathology in two months, so I'll definitely see you in the post-mortem room then.' I walk away briskly, and then pause, turning back.

'Oh, by the way...'

'Yes, madam?'

I lower my voice. 'Do you remember a post-mortem done on a young boy with a deformed leg? His name was Manoj. He was stabbed and beaten to death. '

A shadow passes across his face. 'That lottery-ticket seller?'

I nod eagerly. 'Yes that's the one. You remember him?'

'Some cases I can't forget,' he says sombrely. 'I still think about that one. It was about one month ago.'

'Yes that's right.'

'He was one of those beggars that were killed. It was a police case. There were about four or five in Colombo...'

'Yes, I know...'

'Madam, do you want me to find the report?'

'No, not necessary. I'm only telling you because I got to know that that boy was a friend of Anil, the boy who died in the accident.'

He shakes his head. 'That is sad. Both were so young also, no.'

'Yes. They were best friends and they lived in the same *watte.*'

I enter the gynaecology ward, leaving him shaking his head sadly and limping slowly down the corridor. The ward round is just about to begin. I take my place at the periphery of the cluster of students, taking my note book out of my pocket and brushing up the history of my patient.

I whisper to Harsha, 'How did the triple A go?'

'It was super! I got to scrub up and assist!' he whispers back, eyes sparkling. 'What about you? Did you see that boy's family? Sorry I couldn't come with you.'

'Yes, I finally went by myself. I couldn't get hold of Tara either. I have a lot to tell you——' I start telling him about my visit to the slum. 'I'm beginning to think that there's something odd about that death.'

'What do you mean?'

'I think that boy may been assaulted before he was knocked down by the SUV.'

He cocks his head. 'Don't you think you're getting a little too involved in this boy's case? You didn't even know him. And you're not an expert on forensics.'

Stung by his remarks, I reply, 'You'd feel the same, if you had seen his injuries - and listened to his mother's story. They are really poor. You should have seen their home. It's just a tiny little hut, about this big——'

'I'm just saying - it sounds far-fetched. The police would have looked into all this and come up with witnesses. And surely the post-mortem would have shown if there were injuries due to assault? I mean, that's why they do post-mortems - to pick up things like this.'

I snort. 'But I met the pathologist! He was drunk! How can we rely on his findings?'

'Okay, okay, but even if you're right, there's no way of proving it. He's dead and buried now.'

'Cremated,' I correct him. Aunty C had told me it was a cremation.

'Well, dead and cremated, then. So there's definitely no way of proving it.'

'There's another thing – he had a friend, a boy who lived nearby. He was attacked—'

'You two at the back! Are we disturbing your little chat?' Indira's sarcastic words cause the others to snigger.

We mumble our apologies and join the crowd around the first bed as the ward round begins.

When I get back home that evening I upend the bag Tissa had given me onto the kitchen counter. The packet of tea falls out with a soft thud, followed by some papers rolled together and fastened with a rubber band. I empty the contents of the packet into the tea caddy, inhaling the scent of the tea leaves, touched by the gift.

I lay the papers out on the counter and scrutinise them. The largest is a colourful glossy brochure with a photograph of a six-storey building with two wings facing each other in the shape of an 'L' on the first page, and in one corner a picture of a smiling young woman wearing a white coat and a stethoscope around her neck. The caption reads 'Lotus Hospital'.

Lotus again! That name keeps cropping up.

Could the boy have been working in this place? But why keep it a secret? You would hardly expect anything underhand to happen in a hospital, right?

Inside the brochure is a description of the hospital. 'Modern 100-bedded private hospital... State-of-the-art equipment… Qualified specialists…'

A thought strikes me and I check the telephone number printed in the brochure. It ends with four 4s and looks familiar. I remember jotting down the numbers from Anil's call log. I check my notebook and sure enough, the same number is recorded under the name 'Lotus'.

So the Lotus in his phone is not a person, but a place. A hospital. I am intrigued now. Could it be *that* Lotus Hospital?

I pick up the brochure and peep into the living room where Aunty Sherine is busy working, surrounded by her laptop and a sea of papers.

'Aunty, can I ask you a question?'

'Yes… but make it quick. I have a presentation tomorrow and I'm running short of time.'

'Isn't Lotus the name of the hospital where I was born? And where my mother worked?'

She takes off her spectacles and stares at me. 'That's the last question I was expecting!'

'Well, isn't it?'

'Yes, yes. That's why they named you Lotus. Surely you knew that.'

'Yes, but wasn't that an old hospital? This one has the same name but it looks modern.' I show her the brochure.

She takes it, and putting her glasses back on, scrutinises it, reading both sides.

'It's the same institution. They have expanded now. They have put up a new building, in a new location. When you were born it was a small hospital - they called it a nursing home in those days. It was mainly a maternity hospital - a very exclusive one, with anybody who was somebody in Colombo having their babies there. It was a lovely old building, set in a huge garden with lots of trees and flowers. The doctor who started it - he was the one who looked after your mother when she was expecting you.'

'Yes, I know. I've heard the story.'

'She was being groomed to take over from him... but then she fell sick...' There is an awkward silence, and then she clears her throat.

'It's a very big organisation, involved in a number of other areas now as well. Charity work, research, health education, et cetera.'

'Do you know the people who run it now?'

'Yes, they're very well known in Colombo. It's been in the same family - the son runs it now - at least the charitable arm which is the Lotus Foundation. He's a doctor too but has given up practicing medicine and devotes his time to the Foundation. I've had some dealings with them. There's one charity that helps homeless people, another one for amputees. The old man - the one your mother worked for, the one who started it - I think he's still alive but quite poorly. Paralysed, I heard.'

'You know that boy?'

She looks up. 'Which boy?'

'Leela's nephew - the one who met with the accident?'

'What about him?'

'This brochure was found among his things. Tissa gave it to me.'

'So?' She looks puzzled.

'Maybe he had something to do with this place.' I point at the telephone number listed after the address of the hospital. 'And this number was on his phone.'

'You went through his phone?' She raises her eyebrows. 'Why?'

'Umm… just being nosy.' I confess. 'Anyway, it's been returned to the mother.'

She doesn't ask how it was returned, but returns to her work, handing the brochure to me. 'It's just a hospital, Lotus. He could have gone there to visit someone, consult a doctor, apply for a job, there could be any number of explanations.'

'It's a private hospital, Aunty. Look at it - it looks posh. They aren't the kind of people who can afford treatment in a place like this. What do you think his connection with it was?'

'I have no idea, child. Maybe there is no connection.'

'But why would he have the number on his phone?'

She says, exasperated now, 'I don't know. I advise you to forget this and go and do some studying, or something more useful. I need to get back to my work.'

She turns back to her laptop leaving me standing there with the brochure in my hand. I return to the kitchen and sift through the other papers. Among them is a small blue card with a row of letters and numbers on one side, and on the other, a logo printed in black - an illustration of what looks like a cup with an upper jagged edge curling outwards. There is another scrap of paper which appears to have been torn from a notebook, with a telephone number written on it, with a few more numbers scrawled below it.

I think I recognise that number. I punch the numbers on my phone and a few seconds later I hear a recorded message say, 'Welcome to the Colombo Teaching Hospital...'

Yes, I was right – it is the number of the hospital attached to the medical school – that's why the number looked familiar....

The sing-song voice continues '...if you know the extension you require please dial now or hold for the operator...' I enter the numbers scribbled below the phone number. There is a pause, then a click and a different voice – a friendly one – says, 'ENT Department, Nilmini speaking!'

Taken aback, I stammer, 'Er, wrong number, sorry,' and end the call.

I cup my chin on my hands and stare at the three pieces of paper in front of me, none the wiser as to their meaning.

16

The midwives swear that deliveries are more common around the time of the full moon.

It's never been proven scientifically, but throughout history, the effect of the full moon has been blamed for an increase in anything from criminal behaviour to dog bites. The word 'lunatic' is derived from *Luna* – the name of the ancient Roman goddess of the moon, from the belief that insanity and mental instability were influenced by the phases of the moon. After all, the moon does have a gravitational pull on ocean tides, and aren't our bodies too, made up mostly of salty water, like the ocean?

In hospitals, staff recount tales of horrendously busy full moon nights and brace themselves for an onslaught in the emergency units and labour wards every Poya day, the monthly lunar holiday. I have the bright idea of coming in early on Poya day. It's the last week of my rotation and I need to notch up two more deliveries.

Old midwives' tales or not, I am lucky – two women come in together in labour and deliver within half an hour of each other, and I am allowed to deliver both babies, much to the chagrin of Tara, who also has the same idea but comes in just as the second baby's head is crowning. Soon after, yet another woman comes in with a breech presentation (a situation where the baby's bottom comes out first, rather than the head) and we witness a breech delivery conducted by one of the midwives. The baby is premature, and therefore small, and slips out easily, bottom first. If the baby had been bigger, an obstetric disaster could have resulted: obstruction of the emerging head after the rest of the body had been delivered. I had seen illustrations of this dreadful scenario in textbooks: the entire body up to the neck hanging out of the birth passage, the head invisible, unable to negotiate the outlet – a situation that often culminated in the death of the baby.

The midwives – irreverently called 'madwives' behind their backs – are a law unto themselves and firmly believe that they know more about labour and childbirth than any doctor. In some cases they are right – their years of experience greatly outweigh that of a newly qualified doctor. This results in many clashes with the doctors, usually when they fail to keep the doctors informed about all the goings-on in Labour Ward. Today we witness one such screaming match when Indira storms into Labour Ward and yells at the midwife for not calling her in for the breech delivery. The midwife retorts that there was no need to call her since she (the midwife) was more than capable of handling it. They shout at each other like basket-women and we slip past the furious senior registrar as she stands, arms akimbo, in the doorway of the ward, and make our escape to the sound of their raised voices.

As we walk away, Tara says, 'Hey, did you hear what happened to Pathi yesterday?'

'Who?' I ask absently, still thinking of the breech delivery and way the baby had slipped out, buttocks first.

'That pathology professor. Seems he had collapsed and was taken to the MICU unconscious. It was quite a drama.'

She continues, 'And you know what? It seems he collapsed while doing a p.m.' She giggles. 'It's a good thing his patient was dead!'

I stop and stare at her. 'Pathi? Do you mean Professor Pathirana?'

'Yes, he's called Pathi.'

'The pathologist?'

'Ya, that's the one.'

'I met him the other day! Remember, during the gynae list—'

'Yes, you told me about it. Was he okay then?'

'Actually, I did think he looked a bit off...' I remember how he looked, the way he had staggered and almost fallen. 'He was like, pale, and a bit unsteady on his feet. What was wrong with him?'

She shakes her head. 'Uh-uh. I don't know. I only heard that he collapsed.'

I go straight to the hospital's Medical Intensive Care Unit. After obtaining permission to enter from the Sister-in-charge, I slip in unobtrusively and stand by the doorway, scanning the beds.

At first I almost miss him, hardly recognising the cantankerous professor I had met in the mortuary. Lying on the first bed, clad in a hospital gown, he looks thinner and smaller than I remember. The bright blue hospital identity bracelet hangs loosely around his skeletal wrist and he receives a low flow of oxygen through a thin clear tube ending in two short prongs at his nostrils. His eyes are closed and he appears to be sleeping, his breathing slow and regular. The heart monitor connected to leads on his chest beeps softly and reassuringly with a steady rhythmic beat. The tube of a catheter snakes out from under the sheets and empties into a clear bag containing golden-yellow urine. I hardly know the man but I feel a profound sense of relief that he doesn't seem to be in any danger.

A nurse dressed in crisp blue scrubs and a touch of make-up neatly applied to her eyes and lips comes up to me, remarking softly with a smile, 'He's had many doctors and students visiting. He must be very popular. Is he one of your teachers?'

'Er... yes,' I mutter. 'How is he now?'

'Oh, much, much better than when he came in. He was in a coma then, you know.'

'Yes, I heard. Was it...' I hesitate, 'alcohol-related?'

She looks at me oddly. 'No, it wasn't. He doesn't drink at all.'

I stare at her in surprise. 'What was it then?'

What she tells me leaves me dumbfounded. I listen, speechless as she explains what happened.

How could I have been so wrong?

As soon as I leave the MICU, I call Harsha.

'I feel really awful!' I burst out as soon as he answers his phone.

'Why? What happened?'

'I made a big error of judgement,' I confess gloomily. 'You remember I told you about meeting Professor Pathirana, at the mortuary?'

He chuckles. 'The alcoholic?'

'That's just it! I heard he had collapsed while at work and was taken to the MICU unconscious. I thought it must be due to the alcoholism. Or liver problems.'

'Wasn't it?'

'No!' I burst out. 'I went to see him. It was nothing to do with alcohol.'

'Then what?'

'He had been in a diabetic coma!'

He whistles. *'No!'*

'Yes! He's not an alcoholic. Smokes like a chimney, but he's a teetotaller.'

'Oh... so he's a known diabetic?'

'Yes. On insulin. His blood sugar had rocketed for some reason and he had gone into a coma. It was more than five hundred when he had gone into ICU.'

'Wow. Anyway, why are you so upset about it?'

'Well, I totally misjudged him, no? I thought it was alcohol that I smelt on his breath... I jumped to the conclusion that he was drunk.'

'So how do you explain the smell?'

'Don't you get it? That was the smell of ketone bodies!'

'Oh...!' I could hear enlightenment in his voice.

He knows what I am referring to, of course. In diabetic ketoacidosis, a serious complication of diabetes, chemicals called ketones are excreted from the body in large quantities via the urine and the lungs – where they give the breath a characteristic sweet, fruity odour, which, in this case, I had mistaken for alcohol.

'So I was completely wrong about him,' I say.

'Don't feel so bad. How would you recognise the smell if you hadn't come across it before?'

'It's obvious when you think about it. We've been taught all about it! He had all the classic signs. He was thin and wasted, looked ill, and smelt of ketones. Anybody else would have got the diagnosis immediately.'

'I think you're being too hard on yourself.'

'I have this habit of jumping to conclusions...' I say gloomily.

'That's very true, of course!' He chuckles. 'And the most dramatic ones!'

'Poor man. Labelling him an alcoholic...' I shake my head. 'I should have stopped and thought about it. And you know what? You're right. I've been jumping to conclusions about that boy also.'

'Who?'

'The boy from the slum,' I say impatiently. 'The one who was involved in that accident. You said I was reading too much into his death, saying he had been attacked first. And that the injuries due to the attack were missed in the p.m. because Prof Pathirana was under the influence of alcohol at the time. So he definitely wasn't drunk when he did the post-mortem. I was convinced that someone was after that boy and tried to kill him!'

'Prof Pathirana may not have been drunk, but he still could have overlooked something in the p.m. You said he looked ill when you saw him.'

I shake my head firmly. 'No. I've learned a lesson. No more wild imaginings, no more crazy theories. I shall mind my own business from now on.'

He laughs.

'I'm serious! And stop me if you hear me go on about it again.'

Part III

17

It looks like a torture scene from one of those James Bond movies that my father loves to watch, except that here the victim is not struggling to escape from her bonds but lies unconscious on the narrow bed, thanks to the anaesthetic drug that she has just been injected with.

Two electrodes are attached to her forehead, connecting her to a little blue box by long thin wires. The psychiatrist - who actually *does* resemble a Bond villain with his shiny bald head and thick-lensed, eye-distorting round spectacles - presses two soft sponge-like pads attached to handles onto both sides of her forehead. His assistant twiddles with some knobs on the mysterious box, dials up some numbers and then, at a nod from him, depresses a red switch.

As the electricity surges through her brain, her body convulses in response, the facial muscles contracting in a grimace, the teeth clamping down on the piece of soft rubber which had been placed in her mouth to prevent her from biting her tongue. I almost expect the psychiatrist to rub his hands together gleefully and   utter an evil villain laugh, but he merely looks at his wristwatch - timing the seizure - and says, 'Forty-five seconds - that's quite satisfactory.'

The gyn and obs rotation had ended with the traditional 'Ward Party' hosted by us students for the staff of Labour Ward and the gynaecology ward. It was held in the side room of the gynae ward, with a menu consisting of Chinese rolls, *seeni sambol* buns, butter cake, *kavun*, coconut rock and ginger beer – we had contributed one item each. At the party, we presented Indira and Dr Henry Fernando with small gifts (a bottle of perfume for her, a tie for him) as tokens of appreciation.

What follows gyn and obs is a whirlwind of 'short appointments' in which we are assigned to two weeks each in selected medical subspecialities. Two weeks is woefully inadequate to get to know a whole speciality and so the short appointments can be quite bewildering.

We start off with two weeks of psychiatry, perhaps the most bewildering of them all. The Psychiatry Unit is a self-contained unit, located in a large homely cottage in a corner of the hospital, away from the other wards. Pretty flowers and plants grow in the small garden that surrounds it; the only thing that strikes a discordant note is the presence of strong metal bars on every window.

The first thing I learn in the Psych Unit is that it's hard to distinguish the staff from the patients – for more reasons than one. The staff in the unit don't wear the usual white coats or uniforms, but dress in normal clothes so as to make the patients feel less institutionalised. We too, had shed our white coats on the first day and were met at the entrance of the ward by a polite, neatly-dressed young man who greeted us and proceeded to show us around the unit.

It's only when an exasperated-looking woman showed up and started to berate the young man that we realised something was amiss. I assumed that she was a patient intent on causing a disturbance until I heard her scold the young man, saying, 'Ruwan! I have been looking for you everywhere! It's time for you to take your tablets.' It was only then that we realised that the young fellow was a patient and she was a nurse.

On the second day, when the consultant asked us to come in early to witness a session of electro-convulsive therapy – or ECT – I thought he was joking. Until then, I had thought that shock therapy was an obsolete treatment, only seen in horror films about lunatic asylums.

I was amazed to discover that ECT is a very effective means of treating some severe forms of mental illness. It is true that it had received some bad press in the past, but with the availability of drugs that ensure the patient does not feel any discomfort during the process, it is commonly used by psychiatrists the world over.

Our new schedule is quite hectic as we spend long hours in the unit, talking to patients and their carers. I still think about the events surrounding Anil's death, but I am determined not to get involved again. I convinced myself that the two boys' deaths were unrelated. I don't hear anything further from the boy's mother, and I still feel pangs of guilt when I think of the professor I had wrongly labelled an alcoholic.

But the phone call changes all that.

I ignore the call at first, for the number is unfamiliar. But when it rings again I decide to answer, snapping a sharp 'Hello?' into the phone. A male voice, soft and deferential, replies a tentative 'Hullo?'

'Who is this?'

'Er... this is Lionel speaking,' says the voice hesitantly.

Who? I could barely hear the softly-spoken words.

'Lionel. From mortuary?'

Ah... *that* Lionel.

I had almost forgotten the man with the glass eye and the limp who had been so helpful to me that day in the mortuary. The last time I had seen him was when I bumped into him in the corridor – when was it? More than two weeks ago. Surprised and slightly irritated, I wonder how he had got my number. And why is he calling me?

'Sorry to disturb, madam.' The words are barely louder than a whisper. It's like he doesn't want to be overheard at the other end.

'What is it?'

He probably wants some free medical advice. Medical students are constantly consulted by hospital staff who think that advice from a half-baked doctor is better than none.

'When madam is free can come to the mortuary please?'

'Why?' I ask, surprised.

'There's something I want to talk about...'

'You can tell me now.'

'No, not over phone please. Better if madam can come here...'

Irritated now, I hedge. 'Mmmm... I'm really busy... don't know when I'll be able to find the time...'

'I understand,' he says respectfully and politely. 'When madam is free...'

'Alright,' I say reluctantly. 'But I'm not sure when, I finish quite late these days.'

'It's okay, when madam is free,' he repeats irritatingly. 'Thank you.'

I end the call, curiosity gradually replacing annoyance. What could he want to talk to me about? I hope it's nothing to do with the dead boy. I had put that incident behind me.

The next few days flash by in a confusing haze as we learn more about the complex, mysterious world that is psychiatry. It appears to me that the psychiatrists are as perplexed as the rest of us about their discipline. The most senior psychiatrist (the one with the shaven head and coke-bottle glasses), in his initial introductory talk to us, lamented the stigma of mental illness and discrimination that people with mental health problems face. He believed that schizophrenia and depression should be considered illnesses like diabetes or high blood pressure, caused by a biochemical imbalance or a genetic influence. Correcting this imbalance, he said, will cure the disease. The second psychiatrist, a younger man who had long hair and an effeminate manner, when talking to us the following day, pooh-poohed the biochemical imbalance theory and talked about the influence of social factors and environmental trauma on the genesis of mental illness. He said he didn't believe in being a 'drug-pusher' and treating patients only with medications, but was convinced that talking to patients formed a major part of their treatment. Between the two of them, we don't know quite who to believe.

It is no wonder that I completely forget about Lionel's call, and it is only when I see another missed call from his number on my phone a few days later that I remember my promise, and I drop by the mortuary that evening after lectures.

As I descend into the basement, the familiar smell of death and chemicals envelopes me. I find the mortuary assistant in one of the smaller post-mortem rooms, supervising two cleaners who are scrubbing the floor with mops and brushes. Thankfully there are no corpses on the tables. As soon as he sees me he leaves the room and ushers me into the cramped office we had been in before.

'Good evening, madam, and thank you for coming,' he says in his peculiar polite way once we are inside.

'Lionel, why did you call me here?' I ask somewhat sternly.

'Sorry to trouble you, madam. Please sit, and I will tell you.' He crosses to the door and closes it carefully, peering into the corridor before he does so. For one crazy moment I wonder whether he has lured me here for some nefarious purpose. I had not told anyone I was coming here. And why close the door? There's hardly anyone around at this time of the day.

'Please take a seat,' he says. I sit down reluctantly while he remains standing, looking at me with his disturbing squint, which only adds to my unease. I fervently hope he doesn't want to consult me about a hernia or something like that in an embarrassing part of his anatomy.

'And how did you get my number?'

He looks surprised. 'That day – you dialled your number from my phone, no?'

'Ah, yes.' Of course.

'I hope you don't mind me calling.'

'No, that's alright,' I say insincerely. 'But now tell me why.'

'You know that report you checked? The boy who had the accident?'

I nod, relieved that this isn't going to be a medical consultation. So this is about Anil, after all.

'You asked me about that other boy also? His friend?'

I nod again, surprised. 'Manoj? Yes.'

So that's it. He probably wants to show me the other boy's post-mortem report. 'Did you trace his p.m. report?' But why all this secrecy? I already knew that the boy had been murdered – stabbed and beaten to death.

He hesitates and then says in a lowered voice, 'I did, madam. I remembered something about those two post-mortems. I checked the reports again because I wasn't sure, but I was correct. I didn't know who else to tell.'

'What did you remember?'

He glance over his shoulder towards the closed door. 'That boy, the one with the deformed leg—' he pauses.

'Yes?' I say impatiently.

His next words leave me uncomprehending and annoyed. Whatever I was expecting him to say, it wasn't that.

'*One kidney?*'

He nods gravely.

'He had one kidney? Is that it? Seriously, that's what you wanted to tell me?'

Another nod.

'Some people are born like that, Lionel. You didn't know that? You can have a normal life with one kidney.'

I stand up to leave, exasperated now.

'Madam, madam, please sit. You have the other report, no?'

I remain standing, not understanding at first. 'What other report?'

'That other post-mortem report,' he says urgently. 'You read it?'

And then, somewhere in my brain, a neurone fires. And another.

And I remember. Perhaps it was because I had read the words in this very room. A single phrase, just two words, which had not registered when I first skimmed through the pages of that lengthy report. Two words which sprang up from the recesses of my memory now, sharp and clear, as though lit up in flashing neon lights.

18

From the look on my face he must have realised that I had remembered. After a few seconds of silence, I speak first.

'Anil Kumara – the other boy – he had only one kidney too!' I remember clearly now – the words on the second page of the report.

Single kidney.

I remember something else. 'And he had a scar – I saw it.'

He nods gravely.

I touch my left flank automatically. 'On the left side. It could have been a – surgical scar.'

I stare at him. 'Did the other boy have a scar too?'

He nods again.

More neurones fire off while I take this in.

Missing kidneys. Surgical scars.

That could mean only one thing.

'So, they both had their kidneys removed surgically… wonder why…?' my voice trails off.

He looks at me with a grave expression. 'There are people who will pay good money for kidneys.'

I look at him, shocked. 'But that's illegal!'

'Many doctors are doing. They also get a cut. It's a big business.'

'You think they sold their kidneys?' I ask incredulously. 'How can you assume that? It could just be a coincidence.'

'It's a big racket nowadays,' he says.

I say thoughtfully, 'The scar – it looked quite recent. But his mother didn't speak about an operation.'

'Then the family must be not knowing, madam. The other boy – the lottery-ticket seller – he was only seventeen. And this one – twenty years old. I don't think you are allowed to donate until you are twenty-one.'

'Well, I don't know,' I say doubtfully. 'It's possible, I suppose. Kidney donation is very common these days. But even if they did donate their kidneys they could have done it for charitable reasons…' my voice trails off. 'But I'm certain his mother would have mentioned it if she knew.'

'It's a big racket nowadays,' he repeats, shaking his head.

'The kidneys could have been removed for some other reason,' I say. There's a long list of indications for nephrectomy. *Tumours, infections…*

'In both the boys?' He looks sceptical. 'They were young fellows, healthy fellows. Why else?'

'The families will be able to tell us, I'm sure.'

'Madam – I think these boys gave their kidneys for money. And I don't think their families knew about it. I am telling you this because you were concerned about that boy. I didn't know who else to tell.'

'Can you show me Manoj – the other boy's p.m. report?'

'Yes, I have it here. You can make a copy, but don't tell that I gave it, please. And be careful, please.'

As I snap pictures of the report, I ask, 'Why are you telling me to be careful?'

His next words send a chill through me. He says quietly, 'Both are dead now, no.'

I leave the mortuary with Manoj's post-mortem report copied on my phone and my mind in a spin. Surgical scars… and missing kidneys. Was it a coincidence that both boys had had a kidney removed? Or could Lionel be right? They had been best friends. Had they both decided to become kidney donors? And even if they did, could they not have done so for altruistic reasons? If Lionel was right and they had sold their kidneys on the black-market, in Anil's case it *would* explain his absence from home, the sudden purchase of an expensive television set, and the expectation of 'more money' coming in.

I try to recall what I knew about organ donation, particularly kidney donation. As I had told Lionel, kidney donation was becoming increasingly common now. Many hospitals in the country were performing kidney transplants. I know that live kidney donation (a healthy human being donating a kidney to another human) is much more common than cadaveric kidney donation (harvesting a kidney from a brain-dead patient for transplanting). I also know that it is heavily controlled and regulated by law, only altruistic donation being permitted.

I couldn't help remembering Anil's mother's words… 'He was expecting to receive a lot of money...he bought the TV for his little sister...' Receiving money for a kidney is certainly against the law. Could they have been involved in an illegal organ racket? And if they had, how would I know for sure? Maybe their families knew about it. But Anil's mother seemed to be completely unaware of anything of the sort.

When I get home, I head straight for my laptop and open up the search page. I type in the words 'black-market kidney'. Within a few seconds the results appear and I start reading avidly about the world-wide trade in human organs – apparently also known as the 'Red-Market'. I am amazed to read that in the USA a kidney sold on the black-market can fetch more than 100,000 US Dollars, and in Asia about 10,000 to 20,000 US Dollars.

Was there such a market here as well, as Lionel had claimed? Was it possible that the two boys sold their kidneys for hard cash? If they had, what had happened to the money? According to Anil's mother, they were still in need of the money to pay for their new flat. And would the boy really have undertaken such a risky procedure to raise a mere fifty thousand rupees? The sums mentioned in all the articles I read were much larger. Ten thousand dollars was equivalent to more than a million rupees. And where would this shady procedure have taken place?

Was it a coincidence that they were both dead now? Was there any connection between their violent deaths? The questions come whirling into my mind, thick and fast, but I cannot come up with any answers.

Harsha rubs his eyes sleepily as he opens the door of his room, dressed in a T-shirt and a pair of shorts.

'Lotus! What are you doing here?'

'I need to talk to you.'

I had flagged down a passing tuk-tuk and arrived at his boarding house on Maradana Road, where he lived in a small rented room.

He invites me in, yawning, and I sit on the only chair in the room. The room is small and spartan, with only a narrow single bed, a table and chair, a wooden clothes rack and a pedestal fan. A bedraggled blue mosquito-net is suspended over the bed, tied up in an untidy knot. Books are piled on the small table and papers spill over onto the floor. I feel a stab of guilt as I think of my spacious room with the huge desk, roomy antique wardrobe and comfortable bed. The bathroom attached to my bedroom is about the size of this room. Harsha doesn't even possess a laptop; I had seen him use the computers in the college library whenever he needed one. His parents are both teachers in Kandy and they aren't very well off.

'Were you asleep?'

'Yes,' he confesses. 'I started to revise some pharmacology and I nodded off. What's the problem?'

I pour out the conversation I had with the mortuary assistant.

To my surprise, he just rubs his eyes and shrugs. 'So what? There *is* a black-market for kidneys. It's well known.'

I stare at him in amazement. He continues, 'There was this man in my village – he donated one of his kidneys to this businessman whom he worked for. There was no mention of money, of course, but soon afterwards he was seen driving a brand-new three-wheeler. It was obvious to everyone in the village that it was in exchange for the kidney.'

'Really? But it's illegal to accept any kind of compensation—'

He interrupts, 'Maybe. But the man was very poor and I think it's only fair. If somebody had done that for me, risked his life so that I might continue to live, I would happily pay him whatever I could afford.'

'But you'll be breaking the law—'

'Then the law should be changed!' he snaps, uncharacteristically irritably, and then continues, 'Look, even if those boys did get paid for their kidneys, there's nothing you can do about it. I'm sure this kind of thing happens all the time.'

I stare at him, unable to think of a reply to this.

He continues, 'And if their families didn't know about it, now that they are dead, there's no way of finding out where or when it happened.'

I delve into my bag and produce the brochure, waving it in front of him. 'But I think I can!'

He takes the brochure, looking puzzled. 'What's this?

'The boy had this. Don't you think that it's very likely that this was where it was done? Why else would he have this in his possession?'

'It's a brochure for a private hospital.' He looks up, eyebrows raised. 'With your name!'

'Yes, I know,' I say impatiently. 'But don't you think it's possible?'

'It looks like a very respectable hospital. What you're talking about is illegal. It won't be done in a place like this.'

'But why else would he have this?'

'I don't know! Anyway, both boys are dead, so what's the point of speculating?'

'That's just it. Don't you think it's odd that two healthy boys who donated their kidneys end up dead?'

'What are you getting at? You're not suggesting that they both developed some fatal complication? Or that someone bumped them off?' He laughs, and then stops abruptly as he sees my face.

'Oh, come on! You can't be serious. These two deaths have completely different causes. They're totally unrelated.' He folds the brochure and hands it back to me, saying firmly, 'Remember you told me to stop you when your imagination runs away with you? Well, I'm telling you now, stop it! Go home and do some studying. The pharmacology tutorial tomorrow is an important one, the grade will count towards the final exam.'

I start to protest, but a knock on the door interrupts me. He opens the door to find a familiar lanky figure draped against the doorpost. I could see a motorbike parked outside the gate.

'Hi, guys,' Rehan drawls. He is dressed in a T-shirt, shorts and running shoes, and carries his helmet and a spare one in his hands.

'Rehan. What are you doing here?'

'We're going running,' he says, walking in and dumping the helmets on the bed. I know he was helping Harsha to lose weight by running with him several times a week. 'What are you doing here?'

While Harsha disappears to change, I tell Rehan the whole story. He listens with interest, and unlike Harsha, is not sceptical.

'Looks to me like there's only one way you can find out if this really happened,' he says.

'How?'

'It's simple. One of us can just turn up at this place—' he waves the brochure. 'And say we need money and want to donate a kidney. And then see what happens.'

'That's not going to work,' I say. 'Look at us. We're medical students. Part of the establishment. They're certainly not going to believe us.'

'Well, obviously we don't say we are medical students! I could pretend to be a poor person who wants to sell his organs,' he suggests, grinning. 'How would they know?'

'You least of all!' I snort. 'You look rich! Look at those shoes!'

Harsha reappears, dressed for running.

As I prepare to leave, he says, 'Look, forget this incident. There's nothing you can do to change anything.'

Rehan winks at me behind his back. 'Remember what I told you? There's only one way to find out.'

They usher me into the waiting tuk-tuk.

Back at home, I disregard Harsha's advice and push my textbooks and notes aside. Opening my laptop once again, I start browsing through the website of the Lotus Hospital.

The same photograph of the hospital fills the home page. At the top is a row of headings. I click randomly on one of them: 'SPECIALITIES', and a list unfolds. *Cardiology, Cardio-Thoracic Surgery, Dermatology, ENT, General Medicine, General Surgery, Obstetrics and Gynaecology…* the list goes on. Harsha is right. It certainly looks like an established, respectable institution. Every major speciality is represented and the facilities look modern. The rooms are large and furnished like a five-star hotel. On its Facebook page, I found it had received more than 25,000 likes.

I pick up my phone and dial the number of the hospital and a mechanical female voice answers, thanking me for calling the Lotus Group and inviting me to choose from a list of numbered options. As I listen to the disembodied voice I ask myself what I was going to say.

Hello, which extension for illegal organ transplants?

I hang up.

No. I'll have to find another way.

19

I find the barber shop easily enough. Salon Gayan is a small establishment situated on a road leading off the more fashionable stretch of Havelock Road, opposite the Chinese restaurant painted in a startling *rambutan*-red that Dr Rohan Cooray had described. It is sandwiched between a grocery shop called Lucky Stores and a tiny booth offering DVDs for 'only seventy rupees'. Through the glass front I see three clients reclining in barber chairs, in various stages of being groomed. Three more are seated, awaiting their turn. A sign announcing a 'Cure for Boldness' puzzles me until I see the illustration of a bald man below the lettering. A young boy is busily sweeping up cuttings of hair from the floor. Everybody inside is male.

As I step through the doorway the conversation grinds to a halt. All heads swivel towards me, except for one reclining man who has his eyes covered by a mask and some gunk smeared on his face. The cloying aroma of scented hair oils and creams wafts towards me.

'Gayan…?' I say hesitantly, hoping that the eponymous salon owner is present. I remember Dr Rohan Cooray mentioning that the owner of the salon had helped the driver of the SUV to carry the victim after the accident.

All heads turn towards one of the hairdressers – a good-looking, muscular young man with blond streaks in his curly hair and an ear-stud glinting in one ear lobe. He steps forward with a smile. 'Yes, miss, that's me.'

The white T-shirt he wears has a picture of Bob Marley on the front and looks like it has been painted on, outlining his bulging pectoral muscles as clearly as the illustrations in *Cunningham's Manual of Practical Anatomy*. The faded blue denim jeans which are ripped at the knees too, are tight-fitting and he wears fancy black trainers on his feet. He looks more like a Zumba instructor than a hairdresser.

By now the masked man has unmasked himself to gawk at me owlishly, his face covered with a thick yellowish paste except for eyes, nostrils and mouth.

Slightly embarrassed by the undivided attention of everyone inside the salon, I gesture towards the pavement outside, where a small awning provides some shade from the blazing sun. 'May I talk to you for a few minutes?'

He obligingly puts down the hair clipper he is holding, and, excusing himself to his client, steps outside with me, to the obvious disappointment of all the occupants inside.

When I say that I am a medical student who knew the victim of the accident he had witnessed (*tiny white lie*) he is quite willing to talk about it.

'You saw it all happen?'

He nods and says, yes, he had just finished closing up the salon when the accident occurred. The boy wielding the broom has found some sweepings near the doorway which needed immediate attention and is hanging about close to us, unashamedly eavesdropping.

'It was around eight-thirty. I came out of the salon at the same time the boy came running onto the main road. I saw him run straight into the path of the jeep, which was travelling on Havelock Road towards Dickman's Road. It happened so fast! There was a squeal of brakes as the driver tried to stop but the vehicle struck him on the side, *thwack!*' He crashes his right fist dramatically against the open palm of his other hand, causing a chunky silver bracelet to jangle against a copper bangle on his wrist. 'Then he just flew through the air a short distance like this—' his arm moves in an arc, biceps and deltoids tensing. 'And then he landed on the ground and didn't move. He didn't look left or right before he ran across. Didn't look normal, the way he was running. Like a mad fellow.'

'Did he land on his face or hit his head anywhere?'

He shakes his head. 'No, he landed on his back. Didn't hit any other part of his body. I'm sure, because he was just lying there, looking up when we got to him. Blood all over his face and shirt also.'

'What do you mean - you said it didn't look normal, the way he was running?'

'He was kind of staggering and he didn't look right or left like any normal person would have done. Like he was drunk or something?'

'What happened next?'

'Well, the jeep stopped and the gentleman who was driving got out. He was in a terrible state, very excited and upset. Anyway, we — a few others and myself - helped him to put the two fellows into the car and he took them to the hospital.'

'*Two* fellows?'

'Ah yes, two of them. First this boy, then just a few feet behind him was another man also running.'

'Was he also hit?'

'I don't think so. But I can't be sure. He was close behind.'

'Do you think that the first man was being chased by the second?'

He looks thoughtful. 'You know, I thought maybe someone was after them both. They were both running as if a devil was chasing them. But yes, the second fellow could have been chasing the first.' The boy with the broom has abandoned all pretence and has stopped sweeping, listening to the conversation with mouth open.

'And they were both taken to the hospital?'

'Yes - at first the other man didn't want to go, saying he was alright. But when he saw the boy was injured, he agreed to go with him. I think he knew the fellow.'

'You think they were friends?'

'Well, it looked like they knew each other. Although…' He pauses, brow furrowing. 'The second man was different… better dressed, and cleaner. The first fellow was very young, shabbily dressed, in shorts, not shaved, hair was long and untidy. I wouldn't have thought that they were friends. You say you know him, miss? The boy?'

'Yes. Can you describe the second man?'

'He looked about thirty, thirty-five, with muscles like a body-builder. He was wearing black shirt and trousers. Long hair tied up. I've seen him around.'

'You have? Where?'

'Here.' He jabs his thumb towards the salon. 'He has come in here once or twice. I think he lives or works somewhere near. How are they, by the way?'

I realise that he doesn't know. 'Anil – that's the boy – he died.'

'*Aiyo!* What a shame.' He looks shocked. 'And what about the other one?'

'I don't know what happened to him, but he wasn't seriously injured.'

He shakes his head. 'I can't believe that boy died. I'm sorry to hear that. I don't know why he ran onto the road like that.'

'You said – there was blood all over his face?'

'Yes – and shirt also.'

'But – he didn't hit his head or face anywhere?'

'Yes – not that I could see. But there was a lot of blood – definitely.'

'Okay.' I am silent for a few seconds, taking this in. Then I ask him, 'That other man – did he have tattoos?'

He looks surprised and thinks for a few moments before answering. 'Yes, yes, he did.' He stretches his arms out, displaying them. 'All over his arms.'

'Oh. Anyway, thanks for all your trouble, so sorry to take you away from your customers.'

'No trouble, miss.'

'One more thing. Can you tell me which direction they were coming from?' I ask.

'I can tell you exactly where he was coming from.' He takes a few steps forward and points to a small lane about twenty feet away. 'He came running out of that road. He must have come from one of the houses down that road.'

Pleased with the information I had received, I thank him again and leave, flustering the broom boy by smiling sweetly at him in farewell.

I had never noticed this dark, quiet cul-de-sac before, although it opened onto a fairly busy street off Havelock Road, the main road running through this part of the city. Tall trees grew on either side, providing a thick canopy of foliage that allowed only a few chinks of sunlight to filter through, forming a pattern of dancing shapes on the ground. As I enter the road, a leaf flutters down from a branch above. Golden-brown mounds piled up by the side of the neatly-tarred road tell me that the road is swept regularly and kept free of the constantly falling leaves. A board saying 'Private Road' is stuck on the brick wall of the first compound on the right. Above this sign is an older signboard, partially covered by low-hanging branches. On close scrutiny I make out a few letters: 'O' and 'T' also an 'S' followed by '...dens'. The letters that had been painted in-between are faded beyond recognition. The sounds of traffic behind me are muted and seem distant. It's hard to imagine that just around the corner is a busy main road. On either side of the road stretch high walls punctuated at intervals by tall, forbidding gates.

The first set of gates on my left is open and I see a long driveway with several cars parked on it, leading to a large modern house. A sign on the wall informs me that these are the offices of the Horizon Advertising Agency. On the opposite side is a similar house which appears to be a residence. I walk past more high walls and closed gates, through which I glimpse large houses and sprawling lawns. When I reach the end of the road I stop. A massive banyan tree stands next to a wrought iron gate, the entrance to the last compound in that road. Long brown strands snake down from the branches of the banyan tree and dance gently in the breeze - young rootlets that stop abruptly about six feet above the ground, clipped short before they could reach the earth and form new roots to prop up the heavy branches. The gate is closed and locked with a padlock and chain looped around the iron bars. The house beyond - in contrast to the others down the road - looks old. It is a sprawling white three-storeyed mansion with a roof of reddish-brown clay tiles. A broad verandah surrounds the ground floor, and intricate white-painted trellis-work decorates the windows and doors. A long covered corridor lined by wooden pillars connects the house to a second, smaller building behind it.

Around the house is an expanse of green lawn, smooth as a billiard table, bordered by shrubs and flower beds. Trees with thick trunks grow on the perimeter of the compound. Beyond the house, a long shed with a corrugated green roof houses a row of cars.

The sound of a vehicle revving its engine disturbs the quiet and I turn to see a sleek black Audi exiting the adjacent compound through a pair of metal gates which swing open automatically. A uniformed guard salutes from his post inside the gates as the car drives past. Except for the driver of the car, all the occupants are white-skinned. As the gates slowly close, I see an unfamiliar flag fluttering from the upper floor of the large house beyond the gates. A security camera is fixed high on the gatepost; its gleaming black eye seems to be looking straight at me.

I turn around and walk slowly back, wondering what to do next. By now I am certain that Anil had been pursued by someone from one of these houses that night, but there was no way I could possibly find out which. As I pass the only open gate, that of Horizon Advertising at the top of the road, on an impulse, I enter. Rummaging in my bag, I pull out an old envelope and walk up the steps, through the open front door and into the reception.

The young female receptionist is layered with make-up and is busy tapping at the screen of her mobile phone with fingernails that look like red talons. She puts the phone down and inquires, 'Can I help you?'

'Er, yes, I'm looking for Mr Fernando.' I say the first name that comes into my head, waving the envelope in front of me, immediately wishing I had picked a less common name. What if there *is* a Mr Fernando working here?

She looks disdainfully at the crumpled envelope and purses her lips, which are painted the same shade of red as her nails.

'There's no Mr Fernando here,' she says, to my relief. 'What address?' She reaches for the envelope.

'Number four hundred and fifty-one Havelock Road,' I say, jerking my hand back before she could take the envelope from me.

'You're in the wrong road. Havelock Road is that road over there.' She gestures with her hand, then picks up her phone and resumes tapping on it. Her next words send a tingle through me.

'This road is Lotus Gardens.'

Back at home, I pore over the hospital's website once again. This time, I notice a small tab on the home page which says 'Click here for Lotus Foundation'. I position the cursor over it and click. The page changes and I lean back in my chair and stare in disbelief at the photograph that slowly appears, pixel by pixel, and eventually fills the screen.

It is the front view of a large house, painted entirely in white, covered in red clay tiles and surrounded by a broad verandah, with intricate trellis-work above the doors and windows. In the foreground, the imposing mansion is reflected in a circular pond whose surface is scattered with pink and white lotus blooms. I stare at the photograph on the screen, my heartbeat quickening.

It is the same house I had glimpsed through the rootlets of the banyan tree at the end of the lane called Lotus Gardens.

20

A young woman with short wavy hair stands in the doorway, smiling at me pleasantly.

'Can I help you?'

I stammer, 'Yes-I-I have an appointment—'

'Ah, the medical student. Yes, I was told about you. Come in, come in.'

She ushers me into a wide hallway which also seems to function as a reception. The hallway opens onto two passageways on the left and right, and ends at a broad wooden staircase covered with a red carpet. The staircase, which has an ornately carved balustrade, winds upwards and ends in a wide landing. Rays of morning sunlight stream through a large circular stained-glass window on the landing, illuminating the design of a lotus blossom in shades of crimson and pink against a blue background. The woman invites me to sit on a plush red sofa, and I do so, sinking a few inches into its soft depths. I wonder who she is. She doesn't look like a typical receptionist. On closer inspection, she isn't as young as I first thought, judging by the fine little lines at the corners of her eyes, the ever-so-slight double chin, the strands of grey in her hair and the heavy figure which is shapely but not slim and girlish anymore. Forty-ish, I guess; no jewellery, no make-up, unremarkable clothes but beautiful features. The long brown skirt doesn't quite match the blue and white printed blouse, and the black sandals on her feet are low-heeled and plain. I don't claim to be an expert on fashion but I do know that those broad shoulder pads had gone out of style before I was born, and unless they had made a comeback, her clothes were hopelessly outdated. She obviously didn't care too much about her appearance but in spite of the dowdy clothes she looks striking.

As if she read my mind, she says, 'I'm the manager. I'm Soni – that's short for Sonia. What's your name?'

I mumble my name.

'Did you say Lotus?' She laughs in delight and claps her hands together. 'That's quite a coincidence!'

I nod and smile half-heartedly.

She peers at me with a puzzled look on her face. 'Have I met you before, dear? I feel as though I know you from somewhere.'

I shake my head and say politely, 'I don't think so. I've never been here before.'

She smiles, her eyes crinkling at the corners. 'You remind me of someone, I can't quite place who. Anyway, do you mind waiting for a few minutes? Dr Mendis will be ready to see you soon. The receptionist will be in a little later, so I'm holding the fort.'

'No, not at all,' I assure her. 'I'll wait. I hope you didn't have to come in early especially for me.'

'Oh no, it's quite alright!' she says, smiling warmly. 'We're quite used to it. The Director always has an early start.'

She leans against the reception desk and folds her arms, saying chattily, 'So you're studying to be a doctor. You must be quite a clever girl.'

I don't know what to reply to this, so I waggle my head and say instead. 'So you work for the Foundation?'

'Actually I work both for the Foundation and the hospital. Mainly over at the hospital.'

'Are you in the medical field?' I ask politely.

'Yes and no! I would have loved to be a doctor but I'm not clever enough!' She laughs gaily. 'I'm actually a nurse but I work in Admin. Patient Services. My qualifications aren't recognised here. I trained abroad, you see.'

She giggles girlishly. 'So no more emptying bedpans for me! I just push papers around all day.'

Straightening up, she looks at her wrist-watch and says, 'He'll see you very soon. I'm sorry but I'll have to leave you, I'm just popping over to the hospital for a short while. I'll be back soon.'

'I'll be fine,' I assure her. 'Is the hospital close by?'

She looks surprised at the question. 'Yes, of course. Just next door.' So saying, she disappears through the front door. The slam of the closing door echoes through the hallway and I feel quite alone. I wish she could have stayed and chatted to me a little longer.

I sink further into the sofa, hugging my bag to my chest, and look around me. Apart from the sofa and the receptionist's desk, the other items in the vast hallway are a long coffee-table strewn with magazines, a huge potted palm and an antique wooden chest studded with brass knobs placed against one wall. A faint smell of wood polish lingers in the air.

The minutes tick by, and in spite of the manager's reassuringly nice manner, I start to feel nervous about the forthcoming interview. What was I going to say to the man? I pick a magazine from the coffee-table and leaf through it to distract myself, wondering what possessed me to come here.

When I arrived at the offices of the Lotus Foundation earlier this morning, I found myself standing in front of the white mansion whose image I was now familiar with. I had pored over pictures of it on the Foundation's website and other internet sites. There was no doubt that it was the same building that was situated at the bottom of the lane called Lotus Gardens. That particular entrance was either an unused or a little-used side entrance, for this morning I had entered through the imposing front gate on Havelock Road, where the large circular lotus pond that I had seen in the photograph on the website occupied a central spot in the garden in front of the old mansion, dividing the curved driveway into two.

The website also told me that the Lotus Hospital and Foundation were started by a family called Mendis. The internet was full of information and pictures of them. They seem to be well known in Colombo, but although Mendis is a fairly common name I don't recall hearing about this particular family before.

The present director of the foundation too, is a member of the family, according to the information given on the website.

Surprisingly, it had been Aunty Christine who had arranged the appointment with the director of the Lotus Foundation. When I called her to ask her if she knew anything about the organisation, she immediately offered to arrange for me to visit the place.

'I know the family. I can organise it.'

'How do you know them?'

An impatient click of the tongue. 'This is Colombo!' I knew what she meant, of course. In Colombo – essentially a large village masquerading as a city - everyone knows each other (or knows someone who knows someone who knows the person in question) and it was inevitable that someone like Aunty Christine, with her innumerable contacts, would be able to provide me with some information about the Lotus organisation - which is why I had asked her in the first place.

When she said she could arrange a meeting with the director, I had protested. 'But I don't want to meet the director! I just want some information about the place.'

'Nonsense!' she had replied briskly. 'Best thing is to go straight to the top. I know someone who can arrange it.'

As usual, it was pointless arguing with her. She called me back within ten minutes to inform me that the director of the Foundation would be able to see me the next morning at seven.

'*Seven?* That's very early!'

'It seems he's one of these early birds. He gets in at six-thirty every morning. And this way you can see him and go straight to hospital. You won't be missing your work.'

If he is an early bird, I am starting to feel like a worm.

One of the doors leading from the hallway suddenly opens and a deep voice says, 'Miss? This way, please.' A tall figure appears and holds the door open for me.

Startled, I struggle out of the sofa, dropping my bag and the magazine. Grabbing them, I straighten up to face the speaker, Dr Romesh Mendis, owner and director of the Lotus Foundation. I recognise him from the pictures I had found when searching his name on the internet. He ushers me through the door and I find myself in an enormous high-ceilinged room with tall French windows looking out onto a well-kept lawn bordered by flower beds and trees. Tall shelves filled with books line one wall and a vast desk occupies one end of the room. Photographs and paintings dot the wall behind the desk and a sofa and two armchairs are arranged around a small coffee-table in the centre of the room. A long conference table with chairs is placed at the other end of the room.

'Sit,' he says brusquely.

Zero marks for charm.

Not even the hint of a smile on his solemn face, which is fairly handsome except for a slightly too-large nose.

Maybe he's just not a morning person.

After I seat myself on one side of the massive desk, he drops into the black leather chair opposite me and gazes at me impassively. Despite the early hour, he is clean-shaven and dressed quite formally and neatly in a crisp white shirt, beige trousers and a glossy red tie. His salt-and-pepper hair is cut short and his thick eyebrows too are speckled with grey.

I stare back, refusing to be intimidated.

'So how can I help you, Miss…er…?'

'De Silva.'

'Miss de Silva. What can I help you with?'

What do I say?

'Er… I would like some information about the Foundation.'

'And why do you want to know this? Are you writing an article about us?'

'Yes, I'm planning to.' It isn't a complete lie since I'd been asked to contribute an article to the College magazine.

'Which newspaper do you work for?'

'I don't. Work for a newspaper I mean. I'm a medical student and I'm writing an article for the College magazine.'

His expression softens. 'Medical student? I see.' I delve into my bag and fish out a notebook, open it and sit there, pen poised, hoping he wouldn't notice that it was my pathology notebook.

Just then the phone on his desk rings, and, excusing himself to me, he answers it, speaking in a lowered voice.

My gaze travels onto the wall behind him and wanders idly over the pictures hanging there. A younger version of himself clad in a graduate's cloak, smiling proudly and clutching a rolled-up degree certificate. Another one of him in cricketing whites, holding up a huge silver cup, surrounded by jubilant team-mates. A long photograph that looks familiar - a crowd of people lined up in three rows in front of a building which looks like the Anatomy Block. And a large painting of an older version of himself, a portrait of a man looking regal in a red cloak, who gazes sternly down at me. The face looks familiar - maybe I had seen pictures of him too on the internet. He looks like an ancestor, probably the father or maybe the grandfather, judging by the similarity in features and the identical too-large nose - obviously a familial trait. Much like my nose, which I had always thought was too large for my face. There is another picture that looks out of place among the others, a faded, sepia-toned photograph depicting bare-chested men loading barrels onto a bullock cart supervised by a man in a white suit and hat.

He puts the phone down and says abruptly, 'You look familiar. Do I know your parents?'

Taken aback, I gape silently at him for a few seconds before stammering, 'No... no. I don't think so.'

He frowns. 'Are they doctors?'

I don't know why I lie.

'No,' I say, poker-faced. Why is he being so nosy? Or is he just following the customary Sri Lankan style of social preliminaries? *Which is to find out whose son/daughter you are, what your mother's maiden name is and which school your father attended, all in the first two minutes of conversation.*

He waits expectantly but I stay silent.

'Right,' he says abruptly. 'Let's get on with this. I suppose you want to know about the beginnings of the Foundation, and some of the work we do?'

'Yes, please,' I say, glad that he has dropped the subject of my parents.

'It all started with my great-great-grandfather,' he says rather pompously. The cushions of his chair makes a soft hissing sound as he settles back and links his fingers together. 'Hugo. Hugo Mendis. You may have heard the name?' He looks at me inquiringly.

I shake my head.

'No?' He seems surprised. 'Okay, to continue – he was born in a small village down South, son of a humble carpenter.' The lines sound well rehearsed and almost biblical. I could see that he has told this story many times before.

He continues, 'He amassed a small fortune from plumbago. They used to call him "the Plumbago King".'

The Plumbago King? Seriously?

I picture old Hugo sitting on top of a pile of plumbago, wearing a jewel-studded crown, holding a sceptre in one hand and a huge bag of money (his small fortune) in the other.

'That's interesting.' I say politely. 'Plumbago?'

'Yes. Do you know what that is?'

'Er… not really,' I confess.

'It's graphite.' He looks at me severely as if reprimanding me for my lack of knowledge.

'Oh…'

'Well, initially he dealt with coffee, and cinnamon, but it was plumbago that really made his fortune. At that time Sri Lanka

- then Ceylon - was one of the main suppliers of plumbago to the British Empire.'

Pointing to the faded photograph I had noticed earlier, he continues, 'That photograph shows barrels of graphite being transported from the mines.'

I gaze at the photograph again, feigning interest. Does he really think anyone would be interested in how his great- (or was it great-great-?) grandfather made his pots of money?

For want of anything better to do, I scribble 'plumbago king' in my Path notebook.

'Tea—'

'Tea as well?' I say, starting to write it down.

'No - would you like some tea?'

'Oh, no thanks,' I say. 'Please continue.' I wonder what he would have done if I had said yes. The place seems deserted and it seems like the staff don't believe in turning up for work before the boss does. Then I notice the empty cup and saucer on the desk, with dregs of tea in the cup.

'He became something of a philanthropist, contributing to various charitable causes.'

I nod, trying to look interested, wondering whether he had prepared the cup of tea himself.

'He had fourteen children.'

Fourteen?' The pen drops from my hand and rolls under the desk. I dive below the desk to look for it. While I scrabble around, I glimpse perfectly-creased trouser legs and polished, expensive-looking brown leather shoes. His socks are a dark blue with a black stripe and don't match the shoes.

'That's a lot,' I say, emerging from under the desk, pen in hand.

'Not unusual in those days. There were eight daughters and six sons. The second, a son, was my great-grandfather. His son, Leo, was my grandfather. It was he who built this place.'

'It's a beautiful building.' This time I am sincere. 'So is the garden.'

'Of course, this was used as a residence at the time. This room was actually the living room.' He appears pleased by my comment. 'My father then converted it into a nursing home.'

'A nursing home? So this was the original Lotus Nursing Home?' I ask, deeply interested now, a thrill of excitement running through my body. *So this is the place where I was born!*

'Yes, it was.' He looks surprised. 'You know about it?'

Flustered, I say, 'I've heard of it. It used to be quite well known, I'm told.'

'Yes, yes. Very well known. Well, to get back to my grandfather. He too, was a philanthropist like his grandfather before him, and spent a lot of money helping poor people, building hospitals and the like.'

'With your great-grandfather's - I mean great-great-grandfather's money.'

He stares at me. 'Yes. Then, we come to my father, Dr Edwin Mendis. He studied medicine and specialised in obstetrics. When he returned from his training in England he started a hospital exclusively for women. He wanted to provide a peaceful and safe environment for mothers to deliver in. Thinking this place would be ideal, he decided to turn this into a nursing home. He built a house on Rosmead Place and moved the household there. Then he modified this place to be used as a hospital. The labour ward and operation theatre were in a separate building which he added on, and connected to this block with a corridor. You can still see the old lift that was used to transport patients between floors.'

'But then the hospital moved?'

'Yes. In this day and age, the idea of a stand-alone institution specialising only in one discipline, is - in my opinion - primitive. We need the backup of a multi-disciplinary team. What about ICUs, what about blood banks, what about mothers and babies who need referrals to other specialities? It was time to integrate. There had to be a new hospital - one which offered everything.' He is waving his arms now animatedly.

'And what about you, Dr Mendis?' I ask. 'What is your role?'

'I trained as a medical doctor too. But my aim is to carry on with the work my grandfather started. So I started the Foundation. I've been involved in it for the past fifteen years or so. When the new hospital was built next door, I made this building the headquarters of the Foundation.'

I scribble down *Foundation'* but the pen has stopped writing after its fall. He sees this and hands me a pen from a pen-holder on his desk. I take it and pretend to write in my notebook. He talks about the different types of work the Foundation does. 'There's basically two areas. The part that my grandfather was interested in. Homeless people, the disabled, things like that. And the medical side. Research, health education, et cetera.'

'And your father? He's still involved in the hospital?' I ask, trying to draw the conversation back towards the subject of the hospital.

'My father is almost eighty now. Unfortunately he suffered a series of strokes some years ago. As a result, he can hardly move, and is unable to speak.'

'Oh,' I say awkwardly. 'I'm sorry to hear that.'

'Yes, well, it's hard to see him like that...' his voice trails off. He seems to have forgotten me momentarily. 'He used to be such a live wire. He was, at one time, one of the most sought-after doctors in the city. His brain is still active, of course. The strokes affected only his motor functions. It's almost like a "locked-in" situation. There is a slight improvement from day to day but...' he sighs deeply.

I want to ask him more about the hospital but the moment seems to have passed. He is silent, probably thinking about his father. He clears his throat, reaches into a folder on his desk and hands me a sheaf of papers. 'Here is some literature about the work we do. I hope you have enough information for your article.'

I stuff the papers into my bag and thank him.

'Do you think I could visit the hospital too?'

'Yes, anytime. Take this.'

He hands me a small blue laminated card. 'This is what our volunteers carry. It gives you access to the hospital at any time. If you show this at the reception they'll let you have a look around.'

The phone rings again and he says, 'Excuse me, I think we'll have to end it there.'

'Yes, thanks a lot. I'll be off now.' I pick up my bag and leave the room as he answers the phone, swivelling his chair around so that he faces the garden. Outside, I look at the blue card he handed me. The words 'Friends of Lotus' are printed on it in black letters. I turn it over. On this side is a logo, a picture of what looks like a shallow cup, viewed from the side, with a jagged upper edge. It is the same design that was printed on the blue card that was among Anil's belongings, and now, I recognise it for what it is. A stylised lotus flower in bloom, viewed in profile, petals outspread and pointing upwards.

21

I gaze at the plump arm before me in despair. There's no hint of anything that even remotely resembles a vein, no inviting blue line under that thick layer of subcutaneous fat that I can aim my needle at. In desperation I tighten the tourniquet that encircles the upper arm and its owner utters a yelp of pain as the tight band pinches her skin. She is an obese, big-breasted housewife and is seated on a chair with her arm outstretched on the armrest.

'Sorry,' I mutter, using my forefinger and thumb to flick the centre of the antecubital fossa, the space in the crook of the elbow which normally houses a network of veins.

I'll never make a good phlebotomist. Where the hell are her veins?

A quick wipe with an alcohol swab and I decide to go for it, plunging the needle through the skin and aiming for a faint blue thread that has appeared in response to my frantic tapping. She yelps again but I ignore her this time.

Oh shit. An ominous blue bulge appears under the skin, signifying that the needle has passed right through the walls of the vein, leaking darkly-coloured venous blood into the tissues.

Cursing inwardly, I say cheerfully, 'Oh, sorry, I'm going to try that again,' and I withdraw the needle, applying a cotton wool swab and asking her to keep her arm flexed. I think wistfully of the man in whose vein I had successfully inserted an intravenous cannula a few days ago in the Emergency Unit – a young construction worker whose veins had bulged like pipes under his taut, tanned skin.

I utter a silent prayer before trying again, this time on the opposite arm, ignoring her grumblings. This time the venepuncture gods look kindly on me and I see the faint backflow of blood appearing in the hub of the needle, telling me that I am indeed within the vein. I hold my breath, concentrating on keeping the needle absolutely still until the required ten cc of blood fills the syringe.

Both the patient and I draw simultaneous sighs of relief as I release the tourniquet, withdraw the needle and slap a small square of sticky tape on the tiny puncture wound, asking her to keep her arm flexed for five minutes. She heaves herself out of the chair and lumbers off, grumbling loudly to herself *(about my skills, no doubt – or lack thereof)*.

I have never been very good at drawing blood, unlike Tara, my phlebotomy partner who is rostered with me to come in early this morning and collect blood samples from the patients for lab tests. She invariably enters even the most difficult veins with the unerring instincts of a vampire.

The first patient I attempted this morning had ended up looking like a pincushion, with no less than four squares of sticky tape on her arms covering my failed attempts. The patient – a sweet old woman – had been uncomplaining, which somehow made me feel even worse.

As I stick labels on the little glass tubes containing the blood samples, Tara passes me and whispers, 'Not bad! You got in on the first shot. She looks like a tough one.'

I whisper back, 'No I didn't. I had to prick her twice. She was not amused.'

She sticks a label on a vial of blood that she has collected, holding it up against the light and admiring the deep red liquid in the little glass tube.

'Some of us are planning to meet up tonight and go out for dinner,' she says, placing the tube carefully on the counter. 'Like to join us?'

'Ah, where are you going?'

She shrugs her shoulders. 'Haven't decided yet. Maybe that posh *koththu* joint on Flower Road.'

'I'd love to come, but...' I pause.

'What? What's your excuse this time?'

I say reluctantly, 'There's this meeting I want to attend.'

'Meeting? What meeting?'

I fish the invitation out of my bag. 'Look.' I had discovered the card among the sheaf of papers that Dr Romesh Mendis had thrust at me before I left his office. It is an invitation to a symposium hosted by the Lotus Foundation to be held that evening - one of a series of monthly meetings held to discuss various medical topics.

She pulls a face. 'But this looks boring! "Medical Symposium!" Why do you want to go for this?'

'I'm actually curious about this organisation.' I point at the logo and the words at the top of the card.

She reads the words and says, 'Why? Because it's got your name?'

'No, no. Remember that boy from Wanathamulla? Who died after that RTA?'

'Yes, but what's this got to do with him?'

'I think there's a connection between him and this organisation.' It sounds lame even as I say it.

'You're still hung up on that boy's death?' She shakes her head and gives me her trade-mark eye roll. 'Anyway, what time does it start? You could join us later.'

'It starts at five-thirty. I thought I'll go there straight after our last lecture this afternoon. Do you want to come too?'

She looks at me in mock horror. 'No thanks!'

Scrutinizing the invitation, her eyes widen. 'This is at the Lake Hotel!'

'Yes, I know.'

'You can't turn up there looking like this!' She points to my clothes.

'Why not?' I protest.

'It's a five-star hotel. Everyone will be dressed up.'

'But it's just a meeting—'

She interrupts me. 'No, I have a plan. Come home with me after lectures and I'll lend you something to wear.'

'No, that won't be necess—'

'No, you must. Otherwise you'll look out of place. Trust me. And after that, you're joining us for dinner.'

I open my mouth to object and then shut it. From experience I know it's no use protesting.

'That's settled, then.'

A tuxedoed waiter ushers me into a large hall dominated by a glittering crystal chandelier the size of a small car. Several people are seated on a podium and a presentation is in progress. The speaker, a short balding man with a goatee beard, is just visible above the profusion of purple and mauve orchids which deck the lectern. One side of the room consists entirely of huge panes of glass overlooking the calm waters of the Beira Lake. Twinkling lights from the buildings lining the far shore reflected in the darkening water look like fairy lights. Another waiter materialises next to me bearing a tray containing a variety of drinks. There's white wine, red wine and whisky but I settle for what appears to be a fruit drink (a liquid coloured a vivid orange with little bits of chopped fruit floating in it) and take a seat in the last row, attempting to pull my dress down over my knees as I do so. Tara is about three inches shorter than me and the black lace dress she lent me ended a good six inches above my knees.

The speaker is holding forth about some form of kidney disease which is affecting farmers in the dry zone of the country. I have never heard of this condition before and I listen with interest. On two large screens on either side of the podium, slide after slide flashes up, showing the numbers of patients inflicted with this incurable disease. According to his estimates *(somewhat exaggerated, surely?)*, a staggering quarter of a million people would die of this condition in the next three decades unless something was done now. It seems that nobody knew what caused this, although he seemed to hold the view that the cause was related to environmental pollutants in the water that these unfortunate people were forced to drink: from wells and streams in the dry zone. More impossibly crowded slides follow showing the results of analysis of water samples in the afflicted areas.

Fifteen minutes later he is still waxing on and my attention is waning. I sneak surreptitious glances around the room and spy a few familiar faces from the hospital, but I seem to be the only medical student present. There is a wheelchair at the front of the room occupied by a white-haired old man – I wonder who that is. I mentally thank Tara for forcing me to change my clothes; everyone is very smartly dressed, the women in glittering sarees or dresses and the men in suits and ties. Someone from the row in front of me turns around and gives me a broad smile and a wink; it is Renuka, the pathology registrar, looking glamorous in a red saree and her hair done up in a top knot. Finally, the slide show comes to an end and a smattering of applause follows the speaker's final dramatic statement that the government *must* provide pipe-borne water to these people or *everyone would die*.

The moderator, who I recognise as being a prominent physician, thanks him and introduces the next speaker. At the mention of his name I sit up in my seat and take notice.

'...the director of the Lotus Foundation, which sponsors these monthly discussions. Dr Romesh Mendis!'

Louder applause this time.

He takes his place behind the lectern and smiles at the audience. I study him closely. Today he is wearing a dark blue blazer over a white open-necked shirt and grey trousers, and the smile lights up his face, making him appear young and relaxed. He greets the audience and then launches into his talk.

'I'd like to thank all of you for attending this month's symposium, which focuses on kidney disease, an area which the Foundation is actively involved in. This meeting also commemorates World Kidney Day which falls this month. For those of you who don't know this, World Kidney Day is observed annually on the second Thursday in March. Last month's meeting was on cardiovascular disease and it was very well attended too.

Some of you may be unfamiliar with our work, so let me present a summary of the work we do.'

Most of what he says next I have already heard from him or read on the website but it sounds different listening to him here. He is certainly a very good public speaker, speaking simply and clearly and I can sense that the audience is mesmerized.

'...the purpose of *this* particular symposium is to increase awareness of kidney diseases, as well as prevention and some of the treatment methods, with an emphasis on transplantation. As you know, we actively encourage living organ donation and are currently campaigning for more organized cadaveric donation in this country, including the "opt out" system on driving licences. If this system is eventually implemented, consent is presumed, and any person who is certified brain-dead after a road traffic accident will be considered a potential organ donor unless they have previously chosen to opt out. We also provide counsellors to families of brain-dead patients who are potential cadaveric donors ...'

He pauses and takes a deep breath before he continues, as if what he has to say next is not going to be easy.

'In an ideal world, everyone would donate altruistically to others who need a kidney. But as you all know, the amount of organs available for transplantation falls dismally short of the requirement. Even in our country, where the number of altruistic live donors is much higher than in most other countries, many patients languish, doomed to a lifetime of dependence on dialysis machines because of this imbalance.'

He pauses again, and then says quietly, 'Every day, patients die waiting for the kidney that never comes.' Everyone is silent.

'My family has personal experience of the pain that these patients suffer. My mother suffered from chronic kidney failure and was one of the first recipients of a transplanted kidney in this country. She lived for many years after her transplant. Ever since then, my father, who is here with us today, has worked tirelessly to help renal failure patients.'

The old man in the wheelchair must be his father.

He continues, 'In her memory, the Foundation has performed several kidney transplants free of charge for deserving patients.'

He waits for the applause that follows this statement to die down.

'In my view, there is only one way in which we can meet the demand for kidneys.'

Another pause. The audience is quiet, their attention fully engaged. A click of the remote control and the slide changes. A single word is written on it, large white letters on a dark blue background.

COMPENSATION

Murmurs of surprise ripple around the room. I hear people near me muttering loudly.

'What does he mean by compensation?'

'Money?'

'Surely not! Paying money to organ donors?'

'Madness!'

'Everyone knows that's illegal.'

'The man is either insane or stupid.'

He holds up his hand, smiling serenely. I am inclined to agree with the last sentiment.

'Wait! I know what you are about to say. But there's more.' He clicks once more and another word appears below the first.

REGULATION

'I'll explain what I mean by these two words.' He takes a few steps forward, descending from the podium and moving closer to the audience.

'All over the world, there is a growing realisation that compensation of living organ donors has many benefits.'

The slide changes, this one showing a research study published in an American journal. He jabs his finger towards the screen.

'This study shows that paying donors for kidneys actually saves money!'

I don't particularly like the man, but I feel sorry for him. The audience is not going to let him get away with this crazy talk.

'How is that possible, you may ask?' It certainly looks as if many of the audience were asking this, judging by expressions on their faces - perplexity, confusion, and in some, anger.

'This is because, in the United States, the wait for a kidney can be as much as two to three years, and the cost of undergoing dialysis during that period is much more expensive than say, paying ten thousand dollars for a kidney.'

Several hands immediately shoot up in the air as people start to shout questions and comments at him. I catch only a few of them.

'You can't put a price tag on human organs!'

'What about poor people? They will be exploited to provide organs for the rich!'

He continues calmly as if he hadn't heard them. 'In addition, the rate of organ donation will inevitably rise, and more organs will be made available.'

A man stands up and says, 'What you're proposing is against the law! And unethical, to boot.' I recognise him. He is a dermatologist and has nothing to do with kidney transplantation.

Another man stands up and says, 'Hear, hear. I agree. I am a lawyer and I can tell you that according to section 7 of the Transplantation of Human Tissue Act of 1987—'

He turns to the man and interrupts him. 'So, let's legalise it! And regulate it so that no one gets an unfair advantage over another. The rich and poor both will have an equal opportunity to receive a kidney.' He turns to the dermatologist. 'You're talking about ethics: tell me, is it unethical to reward someone for risking his life and his health for another person?'

The dermatologist looks confused and there are more rumblings from the restless audience. I recall Harsha voicing almost the same words in his room the other day.

'Policemen, firemen, soldiers – these people risk their lives every day to carry out their jobs. Surely we don't expect them to do this for free? They receive payment for what they do. And as long as payment remains illegal, the black-market in kidneys will thrive, driving the prices up even further, and vulnerable groups will continue to be exploited. We know this is happening.'

The slide changes, and this time it shows a photograph of a woman carrying a baby standing in front of a ramshackle hut, with mountain peaks in the background. 'This woman lives in the Nepalese village of Hokse where almost every healthy young adult has sold one of their kidneys. Brokers from India convince these poor people to donate their kidneys in return for paltry sums of money. Most of the money earned goes, of course into the brokers' own pockets.'

There is silence as everyone gazes at the slide. He continues, 'Before this can happen in our country, let's turn the black-market into a *white* market. I believe this will achieve two things: increase the supply of kidneys, and protect the vulnerable poor from exploitation.'

Someone shouts from the middle of the audience, 'And how do you propose to do this?'

He says quietly, 'What I propose is to have a register of recipients and a register of donors and then match them accordingly. Recipients and donors do not approach each other directly. Pay the donor directly from a central fund with money that would otherwise be spent on dialysis. Eliminate the brokers, the black-market and the exploitation of poor people.'

'It would never work!' someone shouts from the back. 'Tell me one country where this happens.'

He looks up, searches the audience and answers simply. 'It has worked for the last twenty-five years or so in Iran. It is probably the only country where there is a waiting list for donating rather than receiving a kidney.'

That silences everyone for a few moments. The moderator, who looks shaken, seizes his chance and stands up, thanking the speaker for his interesting ideas.

'We'll have time for more questions at the end of the whole session,' he says. 'There'll be a short break now before we go on to the next talk.'

I feel rather shaken myself. It's the first time I have heard of the concept of legalising payment for human organs. I can't help thinking of what Lionel had told me. Surely it can't be a coincidence that I had just heard the director of the organisation that I suspected of being involved in the kidney racket propose that payment for organ donation be made legal? Was it possible that he already practiced what he preached in his own backyard?

A few people get up and follow him out of the room, presumably to quiz him further. I decide I have heard enough, and sidle out of the room, handing my half-empty glass to a waiter.

Outside the room, I see a cluster of people surrounding him, talking animatedly. Snatches of conversation reach me as I pass.

'You're crazy to even suggest such a thing!'
'It's absolutely brilliant, the best idea I've heard in years...'
'It'll never get past Parliament—'

He is busy fending off their questions, and doesn't notice me as I slip past and head for the lift. As I wait for the lift to arrive, I hear a squeaking sound and turn to see the wheelchair bearing the white-haired old man approaching the lift, pushed by a man dressed in a white shirt and trousers. They are accompanied by a woman dressed in a shimmering blue silk saree with a silver border, silver necklace and earrings and carrying a silver clutch. She has a thin narrow face with sharp attractive features, finely-shaped eyebrows, with her hair piled on top of her head in an elegant knot. As we stand there, I feel the woman's eyes boring into me. I gaze steadily ahead, ignoring them, but after a few moments I start to feel uncomfortable. I smooth my dress down and wonder why she is staring at me. Is the dress too short? I should never have worn it. Is there something wrong with my hair? Or is it the lipstick that Tara had smeared on my lips before I left her place? I did tell her it was too pink.

Fortunately the lift arrives quickly, heralded by a 'ping', and I step aside politely, allowing their group to enter the lift first. The process of manoeuvring the wheelchair into the elevator causes some distraction and I manage to sneak a surreptitious glance at the two of them. Yes, the white-haired old man has definitely got to be the director's father - the face is craggy and wrinkled but the resemblance is striking. And hadn't he told me that the old man was paralysed after a series of strokes? That would explain the wheelchair. I wonder who the woman is. From the proprietary way that she fusses around the wheelchair man she could be his wife, but she looks a lot younger than him. And far too young to be the mother of the director, who looks at least fifty. And in his talk didn't he mention that his mother was dead? Could she possibly be a daughter? Although there is no family resemblance here at all. Maybe she's another relative or a second wife?

Just then a woman dressed in a red *salwar kameez* bedecked with gold sequins rushes into the lift before the doors slide close and she and the woman in blue greet each other effusively, pecking each other on the cheek as they do so.

The woman is heavily made up, and her lipstick and high-heeled sandals match the colour of her outfit. She calls the woman Saro. 'It's lovely to see you both,' she gushes. 'And doctor is looking so well today.' This to the man in the wheelchair who responds only with a perfunctory grunt, staring straight ahead.

They chat till the doors of the lift slide open again on the ground floor. I notice that that the woman called Saro still shoots glances at me while talking to the other woman.

As they head towards the exit the woman turns and looks at me again curiously, her finely shaped eyebrows almost meeting in a thoughtful frown.

22

There are about half-a-dozen photographs in heavy frames still leaning against the wall in the spare room beside the old almirah, where I had left them the last time I had been there. I soon find the one I am looking for. Even through the thick layer of dust that coats the glass I recognise the distinctive architecture of the Anatomy Block which forms the backdrop of the photograph. After I wipe the glass clean with some damp wads of toilet tissue, I sit back and scrutinise the photograph.

There is no doubt about it. It is a copy of the same photograph I had seen hanging behind Dr Romesh Mendis' desk in his office at the Lotus Foundation. I spot my parents immediately, seated next to each other in the front row. So he must have been a medical student at the same time as them. After careful inspection, I think I recognise a younger, slimmer, longer-haired version of him standing in the third row.

I pull down the box files once more and rummage through the one filled with photographs. Below pictures of myself taken in infancy and childhood I find some photographs of my parents taken while in medical school. Pictures – the colours faded now – taken on trips and parties, some in the bus, some at the beach. A group photograph taken inside Peradeniya Gardens. A cluster of laughing girls at the foot of a cascading waterfall, fully clothed and splashing each other with handfuls of water. Another one showed a group of boys dancing on a beach, one of them with a guitar slung around his neck. I pick up the photograph of the girls and try to spot my mother. There she is, a few inches shorter than the others, knee deep in water, her sodden clothes clinging to her body. My eyes are drawn to another figure standing at the edge of the group smiling and looking on – a tall, fair-skinned girl with a striking, beautiful face. After studying the photograph a little longer I realise who she reminds me of. She looks a lot like the woman I had met at the Lotus Foundation – what was her name? Sonia. But the girl in the photograph is slim and has long hair cascading onto her shoulders. Could it be the same woman, or was this just a chance resemblance? She had told me she was a nurse, not a doctor. I stare at it for a few moments more before leaving it aside and picking up the next photograph. Maybe it was a relative – a sister, perhaps, who had studied medicine at the same time as my parents?

I shuffle through the next few photographs trying to spot Dr Romesh Mendis. Most of them show either or both of my parents, but in one group photograph, taken atop Sigiriya, I recognise him, standing at the back of the group, a few inches taller than the rest, with windblown hair and a grin on his face.

I select a few of the photographs and replace the rest in the box. Trotting downstairs, I find my aunt in the kitchen inspecting the contents of the refrigerator with a dubious eye.

'Aunty Sherine, have you seen this photograph before?' I show her the photograph of the girls standing under the waterfall.

She casts a cursory glance at it and replies, 'From where did you get that? It looks old.'

I explain to her where I had found it and point out the tall, slim girl with the long cascading hair. 'Do you recognise this girl?'

'I've defrosted the fridge. It needs a thorough cleaning,' she says. 'It looks quite filthy. What do you say?'

'Yes, yes, go ahead.' I ask her again, 'Do you know who this girl is? You must have met most of their friends, no?'

She squints at the picture and says, 'I can't see the face clearly without my glasses. But you're wrong, dear. I was still in school then and they had so many friends I couldn't keep track of all of them. I remember just a few names. This face doesn't look familiar. Why don't you ask your father? Anyway, why are you so curious about her? Who is she?'

'She looks like someone I met recently,' I say. 'I'll email a copy to him and ask him if he remembers.'

Back in the spare room, I start to replace the boxes and my eye falls on the box containing my mother's medical files which is also lying on the floor. I hesitate, and then open the box and start to leaf through the pages of her file again slowly, remembering with mild amusement the last time I flicked through it, panic-stricken and paranoid after that lecture on breast cancer. I open the file again, this time more calmly than the last, and browse through the pages leisurely.

Fifteen minutes later, I join Aunty Sherine downstairs where we have dinner together after cleaning out the refrigerator. When I come up to my room it's quite late, but I spend some time searching for more information about the Lotus Foundation on the internet before I finally go to bed after midnight.

When I next open my eyes I look up in surprise. A glittering chandelier is suspended above my bed. *How did that get there?*

The door opens and a tall man in surgical scrubs and a cap and mask enters the room. He crosses to a corner of the room, opens a box, lifts out an object, and turns slowly to face me. His features are blurred but as he approaches me they sharpen and I recognise the face of Dr Romesh Mendis.

What is he doing here?

Then I recognise the object in his hands – it is a kidney, red and glistening and dripping blood. I look down and see a large gaping cut in my abdomen. In panic, I try to rise but my limbs refuse to obey me. There is a flash of lightning followed by a deafening clash of thunder as he leans over me. I hear a voice shrieking, and I turn my head. A woman stands next to the bed, her clothes damp and plastered to her body. Her hair is wet and tangled and her eyes are wild but I recognise her – it is my mother. She looks at him and screams, 'No! No! You can't put that in her!'

I stare helplessly as he looms over me, ignoring her. She continues to scream, 'No! It's the wrong kidney! It's the wrong blood group!'

I sit bolt upright in bed with my heart pounding in my chest. I look up - there is no chandelier. The room is dark and there is no one else with me. With profound relief, I realise that it had just been a dream. But the thunder and lightning are real - there is a storm raging outside and the rain is pelting down, beating against the windowpane like a constant drum roll.

My heart gradually resumes its normal rhythm but those words keep echoing in my ears. '...*it's the wrong blood group... wrong blood group... blood group!*'

A flash of lightning lights up the room and I have a 'light-bulb' moment - literally. The clash of thunder that follows is so loud it rattles the window panes.

Now, I understand why I had that niggling feeling after I first leafed through the pages of my mother's file. Wide awake now, I sweep the sheets aside and jump out of bed. Once again, I tip-toe to the spare room and open that box. But I know, even before I open the grey folder, what I would see there, on the first page.

Flashback to my first year, Physiology Lab. The young demonstrator telling us that today's practical would be on blood group testing. Laughter and jokes as we take samples of blood from each other and then perform the tests for grouping blood.

A drop of anti-A, a drop of anti-B, look under the microscope for evidence of clumping.

The demonstrator checking our results and telling me, 'You have the rarest blood group. Group AB constitutes just 4 percent of the population.'

She walks to the whiteboard and scrawls the letters denoting the blood groups. A. B. AB. O. Then she draws some sweeping lines connecting the letters. 'This is how blood groups are inherited.' She uses me as an example. 'Let's say the child is AB. One allele from each parent. An A from one parent, a B from the other. These are the possible combinations.' More squiggly lines and letters scribbled on the whiteboard. She looks at me and says, 'So your parents have to be either A, B or AB. It's that simple.'

It's that simple. I'm AB. My parents have to be A, B or AB.

So how come the little box on the first page of my mother's file next to the words 'Blood Group' were filled out with the words 'O positive'?

23

The text message from Harsha simply said 'Come to Wd 32'. I am used to this. He and some of the other students constantly comb the wards looking for interesting and unusual cases.

Unable to make sense of the information I had discovered last night, I had fallen into a restless sleep and woken up late, wondering if it had all been a bad dream. I had no time to ponder on the matter because I had to rush to the Psych Unit. Fortunately, both consultants were away at a conference and nobody was keeping track of us today. Most of the other students had already left the unit. I hung around for an hour talking to some of the patients and then decided to join Harsha in Ward 32, grateful for the distraction.

Ward 32 is familiar territory. It is where we had followed our very first general surgical rotation, in our third year. I find Harsha chatting to Dr Shani Pieris, the surgeon in charge of the ward.

Dr Pieris is a renowned gastro-intestinal surgeon and authority on bowel cancers. Slim and dark with her long hair tied up in a knot, she is dressed, as usual, in a crisp cotton saree and her trade-mark high heels. I always wonder how she manages to stay neat and crease-free clad in six yards of starched cotton all day long. The few times that I had been required to don that wretched garment I had battled to keep it together around me, and the saree usually became a sorry, crumpled mess within an hour of putting it on.

This morning, she looks elegant in a pale blue number with a dark blue border, the pleats neatly pinned across her left shoulder. I sneak a peek at her footwear; today she wears strappy blue wedge-heels, at least four inches high. I had often spotted her svelte track-suited figure jogging around Independence Square, her portly lawyer husband huffing and puffing a few metres behind. We all adore her but I suspect that Harsha has a terrific crush on her.

She greets me warmly. 'It's so nice to see my old students coming back to this ward. My present lot aren't as interested as your group was. Those rascals just disappear once the ward round is over.'

Harsha beams with pleasure at her statement.

'I'm off to theatre now. Feel free to stay and see some patients. There's a thyrotoxic patient in Bed Two, we're prepping him for surgery next week. And you can examine the abdomen in Bed Six.'

As soon as she leaves, Harsha asks, 'What happened? Why were you late?'

I answer evasively. 'Overslept.'

'Come, I want to show you something.'

He leads me to the corridor outside where a bed is reserved for the 'dirty' cases; i.e., patients with badly infected wounds. The occupant is not in bed, but is seated on a chair by the bed enjoying his meal - thickly-sliced bread piled on a white enamel plate like doorsteps, surrounded by a yellowish puddle that could have been dishwater or dhal curry. A mug of steaming plain tea on his bedside locker completes his meal. He chomps away contentedly, dipping chunks of bread into the yellow gravy and shoving them into his mouth, his edentulous jaws moving rhythmically from side to side. He takes no notice of us as we stand there, watching him in fascination. It is the first time I have seen someone actually enjoying hospital food.

He looks like an Old Testament prophet, with a straggly grey beard and tangled white hair reaching to his shoulders. The leathery skin on his face is grimy and criss-crossed by deep furrows.

'He's a vagrant,' Harsha says in an undertone. 'He gets himself admitted to hospital every now and then because he's got this foot ulcer.' I see it now, covered with a white dressing, on the upper part of his left foot. 'I think he just comes in whenever he wants a square meal and a bed for the night. The wound is really chronic - it's been there for months. I've seen him before, a few months back.'

'Why did you want me to see him?' I ask, puzzled.

'Let's wait till he finishes his food and I'll show you.'

In a few minutes the old man places his plate aside, empty and wiped clean. Harsha bends down and says a few words to him. The old vagrant merely nods and picks up the chipped mug containing his tea. Harsha pulls out a pair of gloves from his pocket, slips them on and squats down, saying, 'Look.' He picks up the flimsy gauze covering the wound, uncovering it with a flourish.

At first I just see a large open sore on the upper surface of his foot. I wonder why Harsha insisted on showing me this repulsive wound. Leg ulcers are extremely common and I had seen dozens of patients with chronic wounds like this.

'What's so special—' I start to say, and stop, blinking. Am I seeing things? The floor of the ulcer seems to be moving, shifting. I step closer and gasp in shock. The old man is quite unperturbed by our interest in his wound, and continues to slurp his tea with obvious enjoyment.

No, I am not seeing things. Occupying the floor of the ulcer is a mass of writhing, wriggling, plump maggots. Dozens of them, looking like animated grains of rice, happily feeding on the rotting detritus in the depths of the wound.

Harsha, gratified by my reaction, covers the wound carefully, thanks the old man and apologises to him for disturbing his meal. As he does so, he bumps into the bedside locker and knocks a small bundle onto the floor. We both bend down to gather the contents of the package - probably all the old vagrant's worldly belongings – which had been crammed together into a plastic shopping bag.

'This wound is disgusting!' I hiss as I gather some of the scraps of paper that had fallen out of the bag. 'Shouldn't the maggots be removed?'

'Yes, he's booked for a wound toilet tonight. Actually, the maggots are doing him a favour,' he whispers back. 'They're pretty good at cleaning up the dead tissue in wounds. Did you know that maggots are used as a treatment? For necrotic wounds?'

'Eeuw. You're joking, right?'

'No!' he insists. 'I'm serious. I've been reading about it. Studies have shown that they are as effective, if not more effective, than surgical debridement.'

I am still not sure if he is joking or serious. I can't imagine anyone consenting to have those fat, squirming little creatures deliberately placed on any part of their bodies.

He holds out a crumpled plastic bag, and we start to replace the objects that had fallen out. First, a pair of spectacles with round metal frames (unbroken, luckily), and an identity card so tattered and faded the writing is illegible, the face on the card just an amorphous greyish blob. Next, some scraps of paper with writing on them, and a few pieces of card, one of which is his hospital registration card, signifying that he is, indeed, a frequent flyer.

I pick up a small blue card and stare at it. It looks familiar. That sea-blue colour, a row of numbers and letters on one side and the now-familiar logo on the other. It is almost identical to the card I had discovered in the bag given to me by Anil's mother.

'What's that?' asks Harsha.

'This card – I've seen one like it before.' I tell Harsha about the card I had been given by the dead boy's mother. 'I wonder where he got this from...'

'Let's ask him.'

The old man tells us that the card was given to him by some people who run a free clinic.

'What kind of clinic?' I ask him.

A walk-in clinic especially for street people, he informs us. Held every Monday. Anyone could walk in straight off the street and get free treatment, he says.

'Free medical treatment? Really?'

Yes, he confirms, free treatment, but only if you are registered.

'Registered?'

'Yes.' He points to the card. 'They give you this once you register. They do blood tests and all.'

'You need to register?'

He shrugs. 'Yes. They have a computer. All our details in there.'

'So – anyone can be registered in the clinic?'

'Yes. As long as you give them a phone number. A contact number.'

He tells us he usually gets his wound dressed there every week or two, and has been frequenting the clinic for the last few years.

'Years?'

'Yes, yes. Very long time. But this——'

He points to the blue card once again. 'This they gave only recently. Last year. New system.'

He continues, 'Once you have the blue card it's very easy. Any Monday you can go there and get treatment.'

'And it's free?'

'Yes,' he nods. 'All free.'

He tells us where the clinic is located – in an old house in Kitulwatte, next to the Colombo cemetery.

So that was what that blue card was. I wonder why Anil had one in his possession. He didn't seem like a person who was in need of regular medical treatment.

24

At night, the slum is transformed. Darkness conceals the filth and the squalor, and the tiny dwellings, shabby and dilapidated by day, appear quaint and toy-like under the diffuse light of the street lamps. All the denizens of Wanathamulla seem to be out and about, infusing the place with a carnival-like atmosphere. Loud music blaring from a small shop competes with the '*taka-taka-taka*' of metal against metal emanating from a *koththu-roti* maker in an eatery opposite. A row of blinking coloured lights is strung across the entrance of a small shop selling SIM cards and mobile phones.

It takes me a few minutes to find my bearings on foot and get to Ambawatte Lane. This time the neighbour's door is closed and my knock is answered immediately by the boy's mother who greets me with a welcoming smile after an initial look of surprise. There is another person with her, a young girl dressed in a black T-shirt and skinny blue denim jeans sitting on the settee. Seeing me, the girl jumps up and disappears through the flimsy curtain into the room beyond. I wonder who she is.

I sit on the settee once again and thank Padma for the packet of tea leaves. She sits on one of the green plastic chairs, smiles sadly and says. 'It was nothing, miss. You were very kind, coming to see us and returning the phone.'

'Where's the little girl? Your daughter?' I ask, looking around. The television is switched off, but the photograph of the boy still occupies its place on the cabinet. The garland of jasmine flowers has been replaced by some *araliya* flowers floating in a small glass dish. Dim light from a naked light bulb suspended from the ceiling illuminates the dingy room.

'Champa? She's gone to temple with her grandmother.' Leaning forward, she asks, 'Miss, did those papers mean anything to you? The ones I put in the bag?'

'That's what I wanted to talk to you about,' I say, glad of the opening she has given me. 'Tell me, did your son have an operation recently?'

A sudden crash, the sound of breaking glass, comes from behind the curtain, making us jump. She starts up, but sits down again when a female voice calls out, 'It's alright, Padma Akka. I dropped a glass. Sorry! I'll clear it up.'

She settles in her chair and looks at me, bemused. 'Did you say an operation?'

'Yes - a surgical operation.'

She shakes her head. 'No, not recently. He had an operation for appendicitis when he was twelve, and a tooth extraction also, long before that. Why, miss? Why are you asking this?'

'What about his friend? Manoj? Did he have any surgery recently?'

'Manoj?' She appears perplexed by my question. 'I don't know. I don't think so. When he was small he had some operations on his leg. Why, miss?' she asks again.

'Just an idea I had, after going through those papers.'

'Well, Anil certainly didn't have. I'm not sure about Manoj. But you can ask his sister.'

'His sister?'

'Yes, that's his sister in there.' She gestures towards the curtains. 'They live close by. She visits me all the time.' Raising her voice, she calls out, 'Menaka! Come in here, will you.'

Only silence meets this request. She calls out again, louder. 'Menaka!'

The girl appears in the doorway, moving the curtain aside.

'This is Manoj's older sister,' Padma says. '*Nangi*, this is that girl I told you about—'

The girl mutters an acknowledgement, looking sullenly at the floor, her hair falling across her face. She is slim, with shoulder-length hair cut in layers framing an attractive heart-shaped face.

'She was asking if Manoj had any operation recently...'

The girl shakes her head firmly, still looking down, hands clasped together with fingers interlocked. She says, 'No, no operation.' Her fingernails and toenails are painted with blue nail-polish.

She's lying, I'm sure of it. I can tell from the way she froze when the question was asked, and the way she avoided my eye when answering.

'Are you sure?' I ask.

'Yes,' she says loudly and clearly, tossing her hair back, and then, 'Padma Akka, I have to go. I'll see you later. Sorry about the glass.'

She opens the rickety front door and disappears through it. It slams shut with a bang.

I jump up and say, 'I have to go too.'

She gets up, saying, 'Last time I couldn't even give you a cup of tea. Now also you are going without having anything?'

'No, no,' I say hurriedly. 'Thank you, but no.'

'A soft drink even? Fanta?'

I thank her again, refusing the soft drink, and leave quickly, looking up and down the narrow lane as I leave the shack.

I catch up with the girl about twenty yards away. She is walking rapidly, heading towards the canal.

'Menaka! Wait!'

She turns around and sees me, and continues to walk away. I grab her by the wrist and pull her to a halt.

'Stop it! I'm in a hurry. I have to go somewhere.' She tries to twist her arm away but my grip is vice-like. I am sure she has information about her brother and his best friend, and I am desperate to find out what it is.

'You know about the operation, no? He must have told you.'

'There's nothing to tell.' She looks around uneasily.

'I promise I won't tell anyone that you told me.'

'I can't talk to you here.'

'Why not?'

A dark shadow flits past, and she jumps nervously, but it is only a woman clad in a black abaya. The woman turns back and looks at us curiously, her face a pale blur in the darkness. I drop Menaka's arm and she rubs it with her other hand.

'It's dangerous. Somebody might see.'

'Who?'

'The last time you got away lightly.'

'What do you mean?'

'The last time you came to see Padma Akka. They slashed the tyre of the three-wheeler.'

'What? No, that was just a flat tyre.'

'No. That was them.'

'Them? Who's them, Menaka?'

Her eyes darken. 'I can't talk here,' she says again. 'Meet me at the salon at the Borella junction. It's behind the bus stop, next to the cycle shop.'

'When?'

'Tomorrow evening?'

'What time?'

'Six.'

'I'll be there.'

She turns away and disappears into the darkness.

25

The salon is called Salon Bright, and looks anything but. It's housed in a dingy block directly behind the main bus stand in Borella. I'm at the bus stop at five fifty-five, keeping an eye out for her. Several buses stop and leave, leaving only me and a mangy black mongrel sleeping inside the bus shelter. At six-fifteen I am convinced that she's not going to show up. Had she asked me to meet her outside the salon, or inside? I'm tempted to ask for her at the salon but I can't muster the courage to knock on that door. At six-twenty the door to the salon opens and, to my relief, she peers out, sees me and beckons.

It turns out that she works in the salon. Like the other girls who work there, she is dressed in a uniform - a white top similar to the scrub tops we wear in the operating theatre, and a pair of blue trousers. With make-up on and her hair set and falling in layers around her face, she looks smart and sophisticated, quite unlike the fearful girl I had met the previous evening.

She ushers me into a room with a high couch rather like the examination beds which are found in the hospital. There is a tall stool crammed with bottles and jars and some kind of apparatus on wheels standing next to it - a glass cylinder half-filled with water, with assorted tubes and nozzles protruding from it. I am not sure what it is - a gadget to deliver some kind of beauty therapy, no doubt. The room is small and sparsely furnished but everything looks clean and there is a strong floral fragrance in the air.

She says, 'Please sit.'

I look around, and finding nowhere else to sit, hoist myself onto one end of the couch, legs dangling, and wait expectantly.

To break the ice, I ask, 'How long have you been working here?'

'Almost one year,' she says, pushing her hair behind her ears. Red highlights in her hair gleam when it catches the light. 'I'm following a course in beauty therapy and hairdressing.'

'That's nice. Do you like the job?'

'I love it,' she says, her face lighting up. 'It's my dream to own my own salon one day.'

'Tell me about Manoj.'

Her face changes instantly. She pulls out a low stool from under the couch. Crouching down on the stool, she begins, hugging her knees. 'He was my *malli* – five years younger than me.'

She pauses and I prompt her. 'Did he have polio?'

'No, not polio. He was born with a deformity in his leg. He had lots of operations when he was very young – at the Children's Hospital – but they couldn't correct it completely. He could walk, of course. But with a limp.'

She hesitates and continues. 'Manoj didn't do well in school. His mind couldn't cope with anything very complicated. So he ended up selling lottery-tickets. We bought this cart for him – like a tricycle. He used to sell tickets all over Borella, Baseline Road, Maradana Road, and he got to know all the beggars and street people in the area.'

'The beggars?'

'Yes. You know most of the beggars who beg around Borella live around here. They aren't really homeless. Some of them live in our watte. To most of them begging is a job, like any other. They set out every morning and come back to their homes at night, like going to work in an office. There's this woman I know – she pays her neighbour five hundred rupees and takes her baby for the day.'

'What!'

'Yes.' She nods. 'I heard that they give the baby something so that it doesn't cry. A drug to make it sleep, or arrack - something like that. They can earn one thousand, two thousand rupees per day. It's very organised.'

'What happened with your brother?'

'Anyway, through them, he got to know about this clinic which provides free treatment for homeless people.'

This must be the same clinic that the vagrant told us about.

She continues, 'One of them told him that they had been approached by someone there and asked about kidney donation.'

I feel a shiver of anticipation at her words, which she uttered in a matter-of-fact manner.

So it's really true - what I had suspected all along.

'For money?'

'Yes - but they did not say that. They said that they would receive compensation - a reward. They were sworn to silence - they said it would not be given if they told anyone.'

'And that's how he got the idea?'

'Yes,' she says sadly, nodding.

'But why did he do it? Was he in need of money?'

She says resignedly, 'We are always in need. He did it for us. My mother and me. We needed money for the new flat - we have to give up our house—'

I nod. 'Yes, Padma told me about the new flats. What about your father? Doesn't he help?'

She exclaims scornfully, 'Him? All he can do is drink!'

'Oh—'

'We don't depend on him at all,' she says dismissively. 'I had to borrow money to pay for the course I'm following. So we were in debt. And Manoj knew I wanted to start my own salon.'

'He told you he was going to do this?'

'Yes - but only after it was all arranged. He told Anil and me. Before he went into hospital for the operation.' Her eyes fill with tears and her voice breaks. 'I blame myself. I should never have let him. My poor malli. I should have been the one. I would rather have him alive than all the money in the world.'

She tears a few sheets of tissue from a box on the stool and blows her nose loudly before continuing. 'Anyway, Manoj pretended to be a beggar and went to the clinic. That was a few months ago – in November. They registered him, did a check-up and some blood tests. He attended the clinic a few more times. Nothing much happened. By then he thought it was probably a lie – the story about the kidney thing. He stopped going there, and then one day, they called him. That was about two months ago – I think it was sometime in January. They wanted to do further tests. Then that they told him that there was someone who matched his blood group and asked him about the operation.'

'Did they say who this person was?'

'No.' She shakes her head. 'But later he found out – it was someone from a Middle East country.'

'Are you sure?'

'He saw them – dressed in those long robes. And that headdress. And speaking in their language – Arabic.'

'So he must have been away from home a few days? For the operation?'

'Yes. Four days. He told my mother he was going to stay with a friend. Anil told me they agreed to pay Manoj two lakhs. But they paid him only fifty thousand and said the rest would come later. Anil was very angry and said that he – Manoj should demand his money. He said that they were cheating Manoj – taking advantage of him because he was not very sharp. He said that he should be paid much more. At least nine or ten lakhs.'

'But what happened to Manoj?'

'He had the operation. Everything went well and he was sent home after four days.'

'Where? Where was the operation done?' I ask eagerly.

She looks up, surprised, her black eyeliner smudged by tears. 'Why, at that hospital. Lotus Hospital.' Once again, she spoke in a matter-of-fact way but my skin tingles with goosebumps when I hear the words. *So it really is true.*

'He said the hospital was wonderful. He had a big room on the fifth floor, like a hotel room. There was a TV and a fridge also in the room. And the food! He could order anything he wanted.'

I prompt her again. 'What happened after the operation?'

'They didn't pay all the money they promised. He went back to the place several times and asked for the rest of the money. They promised to pay the balance in instalments. Then Anil also went to the free clinic and was registered with them. He was angry about the way they treated Manoj, but he was determined that he wouldn't allow himself to be cheated. But Manoj – he became frustrated, and finally threatened to go to the police...' her voice trails off.

'Did he?'

'No, of course not. We warned him and told him he must not. No, he just wanted to scare them and get his money.'

'But do you think his death had anything to do with that? Wasn't it one of those beggar killings?'

'That's what the police said,' she says scornfully. 'But he wasn't a beggar. Everyone in this area knew that. I know it had nothing to do with those other killings.'

'So you think they wanted to stop him from going to the police?'

'I think so. But I don't have any proof.'

'But why did Anil do it?'

'He really needed the money. He said he would be careful.'

'Nine or ten lakhs? A million rupees? That's a lot of money. What did he need it for?'

'For his sister, of course.'

'His sister?' I ask, surprised.

'Yes, Champa. He was hoping that she could be cured.'

'Cured? Cured of what?'

'Didn't you know? Champa is deaf.'

'No,' I say slowly, shaking my head. 'No, I didn't.'

She continues, 'About two years ago she fell ill – she was in hospital for about a month. Brain fever. It left her deaf.'

'But – cure her? How?'

'I'm not sure. There is some treatment and it's very expensive. Some kind of hearing aid that has to be inserted near the brain.'

More flashbacks. The cheerful voice answering the phone, 'ENT department, how may I help you?' The fragment of newspaper with the article about the deaf and dumb charity.

'His mother knows nothing about this,' she says, watching me anxiously. 'Please don't tell her.'

'I won't,' I promise.

There is a knock on the door and somebody shouts, 'Menaka! Full leg waxing and eyebrows!'

'Coming!' she calls, jumping up from the stool and wiping her eyes quickly with a tissue.

'Menaka, wait!' I say. 'There's one more thing I have to ask you.'

'What is it?' she asks hurriedly. 'I have a client waiting.'

'You said "they" were watching. Who is "they"?'

'There's a man – he works for the hospital. He has a cousin who lives in our area. They visited Padma and threatened her once. The cousin – he's a real thug. He's been in prison also. He spies on all the neighbours and feeds information to the other fellow.'

'Have you seen the other man? Do you know his name?'

'I don't know his name. But I have seen him. He comes on a motorbike. He's tall and strong, with long hair and tattoos all over his arms.'

'Treatment for deafness?'

Nilmini, the secretary in the Ear, Nose and Throat Department turns out to be a plump girl with a personality as cheerful as her telephone manner.

'Yes. An artificial device.'

'Hearing aid?'

'No, something more complicated than that - something that is implanted or inserted near the brain?'

'Do you mean a cochlear implant?'

'Ah…yes. I think it could be that.'

I tell her Anil's name and ask if he had ever called to inquire about a cochlear implant.

She says, shaking her head, 'No, I don't recall the name. We get a lot of inquiries.'

'His sister's name is Champa - she's deaf. She's about six or seven years old.'

She exclaims, 'Yes, now I remember her! She came with her brother - that's the boy you mean? I remember that. I was wondering why the parents didn't come with her.'

It turns out that the little girl is on a list of patients awaiting the procedure for implanting the device.

'Isn't the treatment here free?'

'The operation is free but the implant is not. It's impossible to provide the implants free of charge because they cost so much.'

'How much?'

'One million rupees,' she says.

'What!' I almost drop my bag in shock.

'Yes. It's very expensive. And that's the cheapest kind. There are more expensive implants.'

'One *million*! For a hearing aid?'

'It's not a hearing aid. It's much more complicated than that. A hearing aid just makes sounds louder. A cochlear implant sends signals directly to the auditory nerve. Look.' She points to a poster on the wall. 'This is the internal part of the device, which has to be surgically implanted. It's a major operation which takes about two to three hours. Then a few weeks later the external part is fitted behind the ear. That part looks a little like a hearing aid. After that the patient has to be trained how to interpret the sounds he hears through the device. It's a long process.'

'But how do people afford it?'

'Well, usually they start a fund and collect donations. Sometime they get help from an organisation – or from the government – the President has a fund for such things. It sometimes takes years for people to collect the money. In a year or two the government hopes to provide the implants free of charge.'

'Had Anil started a fund?'

'I think he said he would apply to the President's fund for part of it. But he said he would be able to get the balance.' She opens a CR book and flips through the pages. 'Here it is. Here's her name. I remember now, he actually said he would have the money soon and scheduled the operation for May.'

When I leave the ENT Department a few minutes later, I finally understand why Anil risked his life and became a black-market kidney donor. How else could he obtain the astronomical sum of money to pay for the cochlear implant that would restore his sister's hearing?

Part IV

26

The moustachioed doorman at the entrance of the Lotus Hospital is dressed in a pristine white uniform decorated with buttons and braids, complete with white shoes, gloves and peaked cap, and could easily have been mistaken for the captain of a ship. At the sight of the blue 'Friends of Lotus' card, he waves me in with a broad smile. Once I pass through the busy reception, I find myself standing in a bright atrium enclosed by a clear dome through which I can see the sky. A water feature consisting of a pond with miniature waterfalls cascading down several levels occupies the centre of the atrium.

As the manager Sonia had told me, the hospital was built on a block of land right next to the Foundation. I spot a large board which appears to be a map of the hospital. It tells me that all the clinics are on the ground floor and the wards on the first, second, third and fourth floors. I peep into one of the waiting rooms outside a clinic. Comfortable-looking cushioned chairs are laid out in rows, and one corner is occupied by a water-dispenser and a coffee- and tea-making machine. I follow a group of people into a lift and let myself be transported upward. Soft music plays inside the lift. Some people get off at the third floor and I follow them. Outside the lift a sign with an arrow pointing to the left says Cardiology and a similar one pointing to the right says Urology. I head for the stairs and start climbing up to the next floor.

A familiar figure comes down the stairway carrying a large cardboard box.

'Dias!' I exclaim. 'What are you doing here?'

It is the burly attendant from the Trauma unit.

He stops, looking flustered. 'Madam!'

'Do you work here?'

He puts the box down and scratches his scalp, looking embarrassed.

'Yes, madam. Sometimes I do a shift when I am off duty. Just to earn a little extra. They pay well.'

So he moonlights here. I knew that some of the government hospital staff supplemented their modest incomes by working in private hospitals when they were off-duty.

'Madam is here to see a patient?'

'I'm just looking around. Dias, what's on the fifth floor?'

'Fifth floor? Some patient rooms. VIP rooms. For big shots.'

'Do they have foreign patients here?'

'Sometimes.'

'Are there any right now?'

'In fifth floor? I'm not sure madam. Today I didn't go there. Last week, there were some people - foreigners. Chinese, I think.' He pulls at the outer corners of his eyes, making them appear slit-like.

'How about the sixth floor?'

'Offices. And lecture hall.'

'Dias, did you know that boy who died in the Trauma ICU had been a patient here?'

'No! But he looked like a very poor boy.'

'Yes, he was. He lived in the Wanathamulla slum. So you didn't ever see him here?'

He shakes his head. 'No, madam.'

'Will I be able to get on to that floor?'

'The fifth floor? There's a security guard there always—'

'Can you take me there?'

He looks uneasy. 'I don't know madam. We can't go there without a reason. I have to take this box to the pharmacy now. They are waiting for it.'

'Let's go now, Dias. Won't take long—'

He suddenly jumps to attention, picks up the box and vanishes down the stairs, almost dropping it in his hurry. Almost immediately I see the reason for his sudden disappearance. Descending the stairs towards me is the lanky figure of Dr Romesh Mendis. He is deep in conversation with another man.

He sees me and halts, a look of surprise on his face.

'It's you again.'

I nod in acknowledgement and an awkward silence follows. His companion breaks away, saying, 'Sir, I'll attend to that matter now.'

He barely acknowledges the man's words, merely jerking his head in response. He addresses his next words to me.

'You're very interested in this place, aren't you? More research for your article?'

I say boldly, 'Actually, there was somebody who had been a patient here…'

'Oh? And who was that?' He takes his phone out of his pocket and glances at the screen.

'A boy called Anil.'

Still looking at the phone, he inquires, 'And how is he doing?' His tone is polite and uninterested. 'I hope he had a pleasant experience here.'

'He's dead,' I say flatly.

He jerks his head up and looks at me. 'Dead? What happened?'

That's got his attention.

'Oh, he didn't die when he was here,' I say. 'He died a few weeks later.'

He looks relieved. 'Ah. Well, I'm sorry to hear that, but I don't think you can blame the hospital for what happened a few weeks later.'

'He had an operation here.' I couldn't believe I was saying this out loud.

'Oh? Were there complications?'

You could say that.

I carry on recklessly. 'He donated his kidney.'

'Oh. Yes, we do perform a limited number of transplants. But what happened to your friend? I'll try to look into it.'

'He wasn't a friend.'

'No? I thought you said—' He looks confused.

'He was promised money—'

'Money?'

'For the kidney.'

He says incredulously, 'Money for the kidney? That's impossible.'

I go on, '...and the kidney went to a foreigner.'

His expression becomes serious, almost stern. 'Right. I think that's enough of this nonsense now. Either you are some kind of troublemaker or you are completely mad. You're talking about something that's completely illegal!'

'How can you deny it? I know you do that kind of thing here. I was at your talk.'

'Talk?' He looks bewildered. 'What talk?'

'The meeting at The Lake. The one about kidney disease.'

'Oh... in that case you should understand that this is exactly what I am trying to prevent! Why would this hospital be involved in something that I am passionately against - the exploitation of kidney donors? What I'm trying to establish is a registry...' his voice trails off. 'Oh, what's the use? You don't understand what I'm talking about! Nobody does...' There is no mistaking the despair in his voice and I am silent, regretting my outburst. He seems to be talking more to himself than to me now.

He looks up at me suddenly. 'And you think I am doing this for money?' He laughs bitterly. 'Just look around you. You think I want to make more money?'

I don't know what to say to this.

Why did I start this conversation?

He says angrily, 'I think you should leave now and not come back here again. Come with me, please.'

He escorts me to the lift and punches the 'Down' button vigorously. We stand in stony silence until the lift arrives. When the doors open, he steps in, holds the door open and I follow meekly.

At the next floor the lift stops, the doors slide apart and the woman called Sonia steps in. He acknowledges her with a stiff nod but to my surprise she doesn't respond to him but smiles brightly at me instead. She seems to sense the awkward atmosphere for she does not say anything, and for the next few seconds as the lift descends we stand in silence like statues.

In the crowded atrium she waves to me and disappears down a corridor. He marches to the entrance with me, and as I walk down the driveway, I turn around and see him talking to the doorman, pointing at me as he does so.

At the gates of the hospital, I stop, looking for a tuk-tuk. A small car draws up alongside and its driver pokes her head out of the window, calling out, 'Hello again, dear! Can I drop you somewhere?' It is Sonia, driving a small green Maruti which has a large dent on the front bumper.

'No thank you, I was just looking for a tuk,' I say, surprised.

'Come, I'll drop you at the junction, you can catch one there.'

She insists and I agree. She lifts up a giant black handbag which occupies the passenger seat, and I hop in, fastening my seat belt. The inside of the car, like the outside, looks rather well-worn, and is cluttered with bags and papers. She dumps the bag on my lap and, shooting a sidelong glance at me, inquires, 'So, were you visiting a patient?'

'No,' I say, shaking my head and picking up an empty plastic bottle that is rolling around on the floorboards near my feet. 'Just collecting some more information for my article.'

'Oh.' She takes the bottle and tosses it onto the back seat. 'Well, if I can help in any way let me know. Is there anything in particular?'

'Well, there is something else.' I hesitate, and then continue. 'There was a boy who was a patient here – he underwent an operation. I wonder whether I can find out anything about it.'

'I'm sure you can. Who was the patient?'

'His name was Anil Kumara and he was a kidney donor—'

I stop in mid-sentence and gasp as she slams on the brakes, narrowly missing a tuk-tuk that had slowed down in front of us. The bag on my lap shoots forward and I clutch it before it drops off onto the floor.

'Sorry,' she apologises. 'These three-wheel drivers! I still haven't got used to them.'

It looks to me as it was her fault but I don't say anything. My heart is still racing.

'Tell me dear, you were saying...'

I wait for my thudding heart to settle into its normal rhythm before continuing. 'This boy underwent an operation to donate his kidney here. But a few weeks later he was killed in an accident. That's how I came across him, at the Colombo Teaching Hospital.'

'Really, that's so sad. But what did you want to find out?'

I say eagerly, 'Is it possible to trace his file? Find out if he really did undergo the operation here?'

'Yes, I can certainly look into it. When did you say it happened - three weeks ago?'

'Yes, roughly. I don't know the exact date—'

'Never mind, I'll try to find out. Write down his name and your number on this piece of paper.'

'Great - thanks a lot.' I scribble on a scrap of paper which appears to be a receipt for a parking fee and place it in the glove compartment which has lost its door.

'Okay, I'll see what I can do.'

She pulls over to the side of the road. 'Here you are then.'

'Thank you.'

I wave at her from the pavement as the car pulls away.

What a stroke of luck it was running into her again. She could be my eyes and ears inside the hospital.

27

'Got a few minutes?'

I look up from my desk to see Aunty Sherine poking her head through my bedroom door.

'Yes,' I say, surprised. She rarely invades the privacy of my room.

She enters and sits on the end of the bed and starts to flick through the pages of *Muir's Pathology* which happens to be lying on the bed. She grimaces at an illustration and puts the book down.

'I'm a bit concerned about you, child,' she begins.

'What? Why?' My tone is defensive and I continue reading.

'You seemed to be preoccupied with what happened to that boy.'

I don't reply.

'Actually, preoccupied is putting it mildly. It's seems to be more like an obsession.'

'Well, no one else is concerned about it,' I say.

'Of course they are. He has a family to worry about that. Let them deal with it. Lawyers will see that they are compensated.'

I turn to face her. 'His family? He's only got his mother, grandmother and little sister. Three helpless females! And now they live in terror because of what happened to him. And I don't think they can afford lawyers.'

She stares at me. 'How do you know? You haven't been to see them, have you?'

I stare back mutely.

'*Lotus.* You mean you actually went into that *mudukku?*'

'Yes, I did,' I say defiantly. 'What's wrong with that? You said you've been there many times.'

'That's different. I belong to an organisation. I have people to support me. You went there alone? That's not a place for a young girl to go wandering about on her own. It's full of thugs and rowdies. To say nothing of the drug-dealers and criminals...'

'I wasn't alone,' I say. 'I went with Sunil.'

'Who?'

'That tuk-tuk guy. The one who always parks at the top of our road.' I avoid mentioning the second time I went there, by myself, at night.

'That long-haired johnny?'

'Yes.'

She gazes at me in disbelief and clicks her tongue in that way that aunties do.

'I don't know what to say to you, Lotus. I really don't think it's safe for you to go there. Don't you have better things to do with your time?'

'Actually, it seemed alright to me. There were plenty of people about and it looked very safe.'

She shakes her head slowly. 'And what do you mean, they live in terror?'

'Aunty Sherine, something bad happened to that boy. I'm sure of it. I was just trying to find out more about him.'

'Lotus, bad things happen to people. That's life! It's not your responsibility to sort it all out. You should concentrate on your studies. This medical course is not a joke.'

I stay silent. She gazes at me for a few moments and then says, 'I'd like you to talk to someone—'

'Who?'

'My friend Menik. You know her, she's been here a few times.'

I remember Menik, a tall, anorexic-looking lady with long, wavy henna-streaked hair, flowing clothes, chunky necklaces and bilateral nose-studs.

'Isn't she a psychologist or something?'

She nods.

'Oh no! You can't be serious!' I stare at her in horror.

'It'll just be a little chat. You don't even have to go anywhere. I'll ask her to come here—'

'You think I need *counselling*?'

'I think it would do you good to talk to someone. About any issues you might have...'

'I talk to you, don't I?'

'It would be good to talk to an outsider, someone neutral.'

'Well, I don't want to!' I say stubbornly. 'And what are these issues I'm supposed to have?'

She is silent.

'Well?'

'You're always by yourself.'

'No, I'm not. I have you,' I protest.

'Of course you have me. But I'm not your parent, no? And I'm not even home most of the time. What about friends, people your age? When your father left you here he was hoping that you would have a normal life. But you don't mix with others, you don't have many friends.'

'Of course I have friends!'

'So where are they? How come I never see them? When your parents were in Medical College it was one party after another - picnics, night-clubbing, dances, there were friends in and out of the house. But you don't do any of those things... you even stopped attending the annual dance, what do they call it?'

'Mednight.'

She is right about that. After that first one, I had no wish to attend another for as long as I lived. I shudder as I recall that night. Amongst other things that happened, the seniors had forced on the juniors drinks that were heavily spiked with arrack and most of them had ended up quite intoxicated. There was copious vomiting all over the dance hall, with some students passing out and having to be revived with glucose drips. Call me fastidious, but having to pick my way through a sea of vomitus trying to resuscitate comatose colleagues is not my idea of a good time.

'I told you about that,' I said. 'Don't you remember the first time I went?'

'Yes, but now you're a senior,' she says reasonably. 'That time you were a first-year and the seniors were just having fun at your expense.'

'Well, I really don't like that sort of thing,' I say stubbornly.

She shakes her head. 'You need to spend more time with other people.'

'I do!' I protest.

'No – you're always hanging around here, inside the house. And now you're fixated on what happened to this boy. Why? You should spend the time on your studies.'

She gets up from the bed and says, 'Anyway, the next time you want to do something like that, tell me. I'll come with you.'

After she leaves I walk across to the window, and gazing out, wonder if she is right. Am I really a loner, an anti-social misfit as she seems to believe? It's true that I had never invited any of my fellow-students to this house, although I'd been to many of their homes.

And then, the thoughts that I had been blocking out these last few days come tumbling back into my mind, like a raging torrent through a dam that has just given way.

What was the reason for the discrepancy in the blood groups? Could it just be a clerical error?

I had recently read an article bemoaning the high incidence of human errors in medical practice and one of the examples quoted was the recording of blood groups. The author of the article claimed that the commonest cause of reactions following blood transfusion was wrongly labelled blood being transfused. So surely it was possible that someone had carelessly entered the wrong blood group in my mother's case file?

But if it wasn't, the only conclusion that I can draw is a mind-boggling one that I can't believe I am even considering so calmly.

That I couldn't possibly be the biological child of the woman I had known as my mother!

If I wasn't, it could explain some things. The blood groups, for starters. And the fact that I look totally dissimilar to both my parents. She had been petite and dark and pretty, and he is short and plump. I, on the other hand, am thin and tall, taller than either of them. And she certainly had had fertility problems. Had she, in the end, given up hope of having a child herself and decided to adopt? And resolved never to reveal that to the child? And woven a web of lies about the child's birth in order to maintain this deceit?

But why?

There is no shame in adoption. Had my mother been unable to face the truth that her reproductive system had failed her utterly and totally, and had been unable to fulfil her intense maternal urge?

And what about my father? Is that the reason that he had left me here after she died? Because I was not his flesh and blood?

I could ask him, of course.

But how? I'm not due to see him for a few weeks and it's not exactly the kind of question one can pop casually during a Skype call.

Hi, how's the weather there? By the way, am I adopted?

28

'Madam, excuse please.'

As I emerge from the pathology block after a lecture, I hardly hear the quiet, respectful voice the first time and the words are repeated, a little louder, by a short, dapper man with a pencil-thin moustache dressed in a white shirt and black trousers standing patiently outside the entrance. Shelton, the peon who works in the Dean's office, is a familiar figure around the college. He has the slim build and youthful look of a schoolboy but I know that he has been working in the college for at least twenty years, and is married with teenage children.

'What is it, Shelton?'

He says, 'Dean Sir wants to speak to you, madam.' Shelton always addresses us students as 'madam' or 'sir'.

Alarm bells jangle in my mind. Why would 'Dean Sir' want to see me? As far as I knew he wasn't even aware of my existence.

'Are you sure he wanted *me*?'

'Yes I'm sure, madam,' he says, producing a small slip of paper with my name written on it. 'Please come with me to office.'

He trots off and I follow him slowly, trudging across the grassy courtyard in the centre of the campus, feeling like a schoolgirl being summoned to see the principal. Being asked to meet the dean was unheard of. Most students went through medical school without speaking to the dean even once.

The dean's office is on the first floor, right next to the library. Shelton asks me to sit on a chair outside the door and he disappears inside, saying, 'I'll tell Shanthi Miss that you are here.'

I receive curious looks from students who are passing to and from the library, and I gaze stonily ahead, ignoring them. In a few minutes, Shanthi, the dean's secretary, a pleasant middle-aged lady wearing a green saree emerges and greets me politely. I realize that I am biting my fingernail and hastily put my hand down.

'Come, dear. Dean will see you now.' The sympathetic look she gives me before she ushers me into the office makes me even more nervous. She leaves immediately, leaving me alone with the man himself, Dean of the Colombo Medical School. I stand there for a few seconds before he looks up from a large desk crowded with papers and books and says, 'Ah, come in and sit down, please, I won't be a minute.' He continues what he was doing – scribbling his signature on some letters.

Professor Ashley Ranasinghe is a benevolent-looking man in his late fifties, as bald as a basketball except for a few wisps of silvery-grey hair around the sides and back of his head. The large brown-framed spectacles perched on the end of his nose are attached to a black cord around his neck and he wears a loose white short-sleeved cotton shirt with a Nehru collar. The top button is undone, and a ballpoint pen peeps from the front pocket. Although I can't see the rest of his attire, I know he would be clad in khaki trousers and well-worn brown slip-on leather shoes without socks on his feet – his unvarying daily attire. His wardrobe is probably full of identical white cotton shirts and khaki trousers, I think to myself irrelevantly. I am struck, not for the first time, by the contrast between the way the academic and clinical teachers dress. The hospital specialists are, for the most part, nattily and fashionably turned out, whereas the academic staff seem unconcerned with style, sometimes appearing downright scruffy. It is hard to believe that I am in the presence of the world's foremost expert on *Plasmodium vivax*. I know he is the author of a book and scores of research papers on this species of the Malaria parasite, and his expertise is sought by the WHO and other similar organisations. It is largely due to his contributions that Sri Lanka has been declared a malaria-free country. The last (and only other) time I faced him across a desk had been at my parasitology oral examination, the *viva voce*. He had asked me a question about tapeworm infestation. I had been somewhat excited and had mixed up the life cycles of the beef tapeworm and the pork tapeworm. He had gently made me realise my error and I managed to extricate myself and we had carried on with the viva smoothly thereafter.

I sit gingerly on the heavy chair opposite him and drag it forward slightly, producing a loud scraping noise. He looks up sharply, frowns, and continues his task. Bits of rattan from the woven chair seat scratch the back of my knees and I try not to fidget. The smell of dusty papers, books and leather surrounds us. The walls are crowded with framed photographs of past deans who frown down at me disapprovingly, and an ancient ceiling fan rotates furiously overhead, making a sound like a small cyclone and threatening to blow away the papers on his desk. Behind him, two tall bookshelves crammed with leather-bound volumes stand like sentinels on either side of the large window which overlooks the grassy square outside. Laughter and snatches of conversation drift up from outside where students pass on the path below. I wonder why his office isn't air-conditioned, like most of the others. I had only been there a few minutes and was already beginning to sweat. Or maybe that wasn't because of the heat.

He finally stops scribbling and looks up, laying his pen down and picking up a green folder. To my dismay I spy my name and initials stamped in large letters on the folder. Why did he have my file in front of him?

'Your academic record has been fairly good up to now, Miss, er… Miss de Silva,' he says, leafing through the folder.

So why am I here?

'But I have called you here to talk about something else.' He places the folder on the desk and inspects me through his spectacles. One of its earpieces is broken and it looks like it has been taped together with a piece of Sellotape. His next statement is completely unexpected.

'You've paid a visit to the Lotus Foundation recently?'

I am speechless with surprise. He looks inquiringly at me and I nod, still unable to speak. How could he know about my visit?

He says in a matter-of-fact way, 'Look, what you do outside this college is generally not my business, but you can't go about making a nuisance of yourself. The director of the Foundation brought this to my attention. This won't do, this won't do at all. I can't have my students harassing doctors like this.'

I answer as calmly as I can despite the outrage I feel. 'I did go there, sir, but all I did was meet him and discuss the work of the Foundation. I didn't harass him at all.'

'He claims that you accused him of unethical practices.'

If the cap fits. 'Umm... not exactly, sir. He must have misunderstood me.'

'Dr Mendis is a very eminent member of our profession, as was his father before him. Not only that, he is a generous benefactor of this medical school, being an alumnus himself. Did you know that all the computers in your library were gifted by him?'

I shake my head and try to look suitably impressed. 'No, sir, I didn't know.'

'I don't want you giving him trouble or causing this institution any embarrassment. Is that clear?'

'Yes, sir.' Meekly.

'That's all.' He pulls out another pile of papers and starts leafing through them.

With that dismissal, I stand up to leave. When I reach the door he looks up and says, 'If you have any issues about unethical practice, you need to take it up with the Medical Council. Is that understood?'

'Yes, sir.'

I leave his office and head straight to the library next door, just needing a place to sit and think. I find a free chair in the corner near the Anatomy section and throw myself into it, fuming.

How dare he?

I am not angry with Dean Ranasinghe, of course. It is Dr Romesh Mendis I am furious with. The pompous director of the Lotus Foundation. I can't believe that he had actually called the dean and spoken to him about my visits.

Why would he do that unless he had something to hide?

29

'I have to do something about this!'

I had just cornered Harsha, Rehan and Tara in the canteen and told them about my meeting with the dean.

'But what can you do?' asks Tara.

'We need to prove that this organisation - this man - is secretly obtaining kidney donors by offering money and not only that - they are cheating these poor people and obtaining their silence by threats and violence. I heard him give a talk about it - he was actually proposing legalising payment for human organs!'

'Seriously?'

'Yes! At that symposium I went to.'

'But how can you prove it?'

'We have to think of some way.'

'You said it yourself,' points out Rehan. 'We can't turn up there and ask questions. You said you've been to that place and they kicked you out.'

'That's the hospital. I think we should have a look at that free clinic also. We might be able to find out something.'

'I'll come with you,' offers Tara.

'Okay, great. Let's do that this afternoon. It's Monday - they should be open today.'

'We need someone who can pretend to be a kidney donor,' suggests Rehan.

Harsha shakes his head. 'But not one of us.'

'Someone who can register in that clinic?' asks Rehan.

'No, that would take too long. Manoj, the crippled boy –
he was only contacted about two months after he registered. We
can't wait that long. We must find another way.'

After a few seconds silence, I exclaim, 'I know just the
person and I'm sure he'll help.'

'You want me to make phone call? No problem, miss.'
Sunil grins at me obligingly, his brilliant white teeth gleaming
bright against his dark skin. He had picked Tara and me up
outside College after lectures.

'It's not just the phone call. They may contact you and ask
you to come there. Are you willing to do that?'

'Yes, sure. But what is this call about?'

I begin, 'Remember that family I visited in
Wanathamulla...?'

It takes me about ten minutes to clue Sunil in and explain
what was required of him.

I ask him again anxiously, 'Are you sure you're okay with
this, Sunil?'

'Yes, miss, sure. No problem.'

I hesitate and then say, 'I think that something happened
to those boys because they got involved in this business. I don't
want anything like that to happen to you.'

'I can take care of myself, miss. Don't worry. I'm happy to
help.'

'It could be dangerous, Sunil. You remember that flat tyre
you had? That could have been done by these people.'

'Ah… I knew something had been done to the tyre that
day. But don't worry, miss,' he says again. 'I'll be careful. I know
karate also.'

'Alright, Sunil. Just make the call. Let's see what happens.'

'Now let's go to that Kitulwatte place,' urges Tara. 'I'm
pretty curious about it.'

'Look, there's the cemetery. It must be close,' exclaims
Tara.

We pass the Kanatte roundabout and turn into Kitulwatte Road. Not knowing the exact address of the free clinic, we drive around for a few minutes before we spot the signboard with the familiar lotus logo. The clinic is situated in an old house with a porch surrounded by a large garden. The garden is overgrown and looks neglected. A white BMW is parked under the porch. Sunil stops outside the gate and switches the engine off.

'Look! Somebody's coming out.' Tara says.

A man dressed in a blue shirt and striped sarong slowly descends the short flight of steps leading up to the front door. He has only one leg and uses a pair of crutches. He hobbles slowly down the driveway and out of the gate. He doesn't look up as he passes us - he is busy negotiating the ruts in the road with the crutches. I catch a glimpse of his face - he is unshaven and his skin is greasy and worn.

'Must be one of the patients who attend the clinic.' I whisper after he passes us.

'Come on,' says Tara. 'Let's go in.'

Tara and I make our way down the driveway.

'Nice car,' she whispers, looking at the vehicle parked under the porch. 'Look! It's brand new. The seats have still got the polythene covers on.'

We climb up the steps and enter what must have been the living room of the old house, which seems to function as a waiting room. It is a far cry from its luxurious counterpart in the Lotus Hospital. There are three wooden benches, a ceiling fan, and not much else. Three people are seated on the benches. As we stand there hesitating a man dressed in a white shirt and trousers appears, and shouts 'Next!' A thin woman wearing a faded skirt and blouse with a bandaged foot wrapped in a plastic shopping bag rises from a bench and shuffles slowly into the room beyond.

The man looks inquiringly at us.

'We'd like to speak to the doctor, please,' I say politely.

The man - presumably a nursing assistant or attendant - disappears inside the room and a few moments later, a man wearing a white coat appears in the doorway. He looks about forty, with longish hair and a raffish look.

'I'm Dr Herath. Can I help you?'

'Hi, we're medical students.' I flash my blue card at him. 'We have permission to look around the clinic. I hope that's alright.'

He looks surprised. 'Medical students? Yes, certainly. Come on in.'

The room inside is quite different to the waiting room. As we enter, the cool blast of an air-conditioner hits us welcomingly. There is a large desk with a computer, a small sofa, a refrigerator and a television set, and brightly-coloured curtains made out of a striped handloom fabric. A partition divides the room into two.

'Nothing very exciting goes on here, you know. I'm just about to see this diabetic woman with an infected wound on her toe. You can watch, if you like.'

The woman with the bandaged foot is lying on an examination couch behind the partition. The attendant deftly unwraps the soiled bandage and exposes the bare leg, revealing a suppurating wound on the big toe.

We watch as Dr Herath deals with the woman efficiently, cleaning and dressing the wound, wrapping her leg up again and checking her blood sugar, asking her to come back in a week's time. He gives her a pack of tablets which she stuffs into her blouse and then limps off after wrapping her foot carefully in the plastic shopping bag and thanking him gratefully.

He washes and dries his hands and crosses to the refrigerator. 'Drink?'

We refuse and he opens the fridge, taking out a can of Coke. I catch a glimpse of the contents of the fridge before the door swings shut. In addition to more soft-drinks there are some cans of beer.

'Take a seat,' he says, sinking into the chair at the desk and loosening the knot of his tie. We seat ourselves on the sofa. Popping open the can, he takes a deep swig, sighing with satisfaction after the first swallow.

'We don't get many medical students who are interested in this sort of thing,' he says, eyeing us curiously, his gaze lingering over Tara, who had recently added blue highlights to her hair and was looking particularly striking. 'This is the first time anyone has visited.'

'Oh, we're interested, very interested,' Tara assures him, rather too eagerly, I think.

'How did you hear about this place?' he asks.

There is a silence. Tara looks at me. 'Er… a patient at the hospital told me about it,' I say quickly. 'An old vagrant, a homeless man with a leg ulcer.'

He nods. 'Ah, yes. Most of our patients are that type. But you said – you had permission to look around?'

'Yes, we spoke to someone at the Foundation,' I say.

'Who did you speak to?' He seems to be asking a lot of questions.

'Er… I don't remember their name, sorry.'

'Was it a man or a woman?'

'Er… a man, I think.' I wish he would stop interrogating us. I didn't want to mention Dr Romesh Mendis' name. What if he called him up to check on us?

'And you can't remember his name?'

I shake my head and ask, 'So how exactly does this clinic run?'

He seems dissatisfied with my answers but moves on to explain the running of the clinic.

'It's free. All patients are given a basic check-up when they first come in. We keep records—' he gestures towards the computer. 'So we know their history. There's a small procedure room where we can even perform minor operations under local anaesthesia. For example – I suspect that woman's toe will have to come off if it's not getting better by next week.'

He swivels the screen of the computer around so that we could see.

'Look – I type in 'Sumana' followed by this ID number…' he says as he types the digits on the keyboard. 'That's that last patient's ID.'

He presses 'ENTER' and the screen changes, displaying a page detailing the woman's medical history and the results of some blood tests.

'There you are! It's very easy once they are in the system.'

'That's very impressive,' I murmur. 'These poor people are very lucky to have a service like this.'

'Yes, it's pretty good,' he says complacently.

'So this is a weekly clinic, isn't it? Where do you work the other days?'

'I'm attached to the Lotus hospital.' Tara and I can't help exchanging glances. 'I work in the Surgical Department. You know – assisting in surgeries and looking after post-op patients.'

'And what if any of these patients needs hospitalisation? Would they be taken to the Lotus Hospital?'

He bursts out laughing. 'No way! They wouldn't be able to afford it. That's a private hospital. Very, very pricey!' He takes another swig from the can. 'No, they would be referred to a government hospital.'

'So, no patients from this clinic would have been a patient there then?'

'No.' He frowns and asks, 'Why do you ask that?'

'No reason,' I say innocently.

I waggle my head at Tara, signalling that we should leave, and thank him for his time.

'No worries,' he says.

He tosses the empty can into a bin and rises to accompany us to the door.

'Oh, we can see ourselves out.'

'I'm just going outside anyway for a fag.'

He watches us as we walk down the driveway. I turn around and see him lighting a cigarette.

A loud roar makes us both jump and Tara grabs me, pulling me out of the way of a huge black motor-cycle which turns into the gate and zooms up the driveway. There is a crunch of wheels on gravel as the bike comes to a stop under the porch.

We clamber into the tuk-tuk and I glance back as the rider dismounts and takes off his helmet with well-muscled arms. He's dressed completely in black. Long wavy hair tumbles out of the helmet onto his broad shoulders. At a distance, his arms look dark and hairy.

'Oh my gosh! That must be him!' It is not hair; they are tattoos - intricate designs that crawl up his arms and disappear under the sleeves of his black t-shirt.

'Who?'

'The tattooed man! I'm sure of it!'

'Miss, I have seen him too. At least, I've seen the bike. That day in Wanathamulla. It was parked outside one of those houses.'

'How do you know it's the same bike?'

'It's a special one, miss. Look at that design.' He's right. On the side of the bike is painted a design in bright colours, tongues of flame in red, orange and yellow.

The two men greet each other and then turn and look at the tuk-tuk.

'I don't like the look of that guy,' says Tara nervously. 'Shall we go?'

'No, wait.' I fumble in my bag and pull out my notebook. 'I have an idea.'

I rifle through the pages till I come to the page where I had scrawled the numbers I had copied from Anil's phone.

'This number - it was the last one in his call list. It was the only one which wasn't saved under any name. I called it before but the phone was switched off.'

'So?' asks Tara, puzzled.

I am already punching the digits on the keypad of my phone. I hold the phone to my ear and then, after a few seconds, I hear it ring at the other end.

The other two have realised what I am doing. The three of us turn around as one and peep out of the tuk-tuk at the two men who are still standing by the front door of the old house. The rider of the motor-bike looks down, reaches into the hip pocket of his jeans and pulls his mobile phone out.

I end the call before it can be answered and say urgently, 'Let's get out of here, Sunil. *Now!*'

30

The next day, Sunil rings up with disappointing news. He says that he called the number I gave him and inquired about the possibility of being a kidney donor. He said that he had been told that there was a 'reward' given to such donors. The person he spoke to had told him that although he could donate his kidney there was no question of a reward.

'So they didn't ask you anything else?'

'No, miss. He just hung up. But he took my number.'

'Maybe they'll call you back. Let's wait and see.'

So much for my grand plan.

I check my phone hopefully for calls or messages from Sonia, but there are none. I wonder whether she had forgotten her promise to me, or whether she couldn't find any record of Anil being a patient at the Lotus Hospital.

My father, on the other hand, replies my email about the old photograph immediately, but doesn't offer very much new information.

Dear Lotus

That photograph brings back memories. Where did you find it?

To answer your question – I recognise the girl. She was not a medical student, but a friend of one of the other students who joined us on some of our trips and picnics. We often invited our friends along too. I think her name was Sonali (I could be wrong) but I can't remember her surname or whose friend she was. It's been thirty years and my memory is not what it used to be!

I hope you are doing well in your studies. I'll be in Colombo for 5 days in June. Let me know if there is anything you need.

love
Thaththa

I wonder whether the girl in the photograph was related to the woman I had met. The resemblance was uncanny. But without knowing her surname or any more information about her it was impossible to know. I resolve to ask Sonia the next time I happen to meet her. I wish I had asked for her phone number the last time we met.

'Miss, they called back.' Sunil's words on the other end of the phone are uttered in a hoarse whisper and send a thrill of excitement through me. I know immediately what he means, of course. And who 'they' are.

'Sunil, that's great. What did they say?'

'This man – he asked if I was still interested in donating. I said yes, then he asked me to come for some tests.'

'Oh... what else?'

'I asked about payment.'

'And?'

'He said something could be arranged.'

I catch my breath. 'Really? Money?'

'Yes. But I was to tell no one. And miss?'

'Yes?'

'I recorded it.'

'What?'

'On my phone. I recorded the call. I got a new phone and it can record—'

'Fantastic! We have proof, then. I need to hear it. Where are you now?'

'I'm there.'

'What? Where?'

'In that house. In Kitulwatte.'

'What are you doing there? I didn't ask you to go back there.'

'They asked me to come here.'

'You should have told me!'

'I tried to call, miss. Phone was switched off.'

'Oh… yes. I must have been on the ward round. Anyway, what are you doing there now?'

'I'm in toilet, miss.'

'Toilet?' *Is he mad?*

'I'm calling from toilet. I can't speak loud. They asked me for urine sample.'

'Sunil, just get out of there now. You don't need to do any tests or give any urine sample. We have the proof.'

'They have already taken the blood. It's okay, miss. If I stay here I can find out more.'

'No. Get out of there. That man, the one with the tattoos – he may recognise you. You need to get out of there before he sees you. How did you go there? In your tuk?'

'Yes, of course.'

'And where is it?'

'I parked outside gate, miss, like earlier—'

I click my tongue impatiently. 'Sunil! They might recognise the tuk! Just leave! Now!'

'Alright, miss.' Then, 'I have to just finish giving this sample…'

'Now, Sunil. And call me as soon as you are outside.'

Aunty Sherine listens in silence to the whole story. She shakes her head in disbelief. 'So you were right all along…'

'..and so, I need to tell someone, someone who will be able to look into all this.' I finish.

She stands up. 'Yes, I think I know who to speak to.'

She makes a call and her friend Superintendent Boteju turns up at home soon after and she makes me tell him the whole story again. Things move quite swiftly after that. Sunil is also interviewed and I am told that the police feel that they have sufficient grounds to launch an investigation into the Lotus Hospital and the free clinic.

Two weeks later, it is all over the news.

The headline in the Sunday paper reads 'PRIVATE HOSPITAL INVOLVED IN ORGAN TRAFFICKING!'

It goes on to say that the director of the Lotus Foundation, as well as some doctors working in the Lotus Hospital were being questioned about the alleged sale of kidneys to foreigners, in response to a complaint made by a concerned member of the public.

The article is accompanied by a photograph of the hospital. I stare at the picture, finding it hard to believe that the string of events which had started with Aunty Christine's text messages to me one Friday morning had led to this. Would all this have come to light if I hadn't got caught up in the boy's death? What if I hadn't read her text message till much later? What if I hadn't called her back? What if I hadn't arrived in the Trauma ICU at the very moment I did? What if I hadn't looked in the drawer and picked up that mobile phone?

What if?

What if…?

31

The Dermatology Unit looks clean and inviting with a profusion of potted bougainvillea in pink and magenta blooming outside the entrance. As we step onto the broad verandah outside the ward, I notice a peculiar odour - not the usual chemical smell of antiseptic or the sickly smell of infected wounds, but a sour unpleasant odour which reminds me of stale unwashed clothes.

After the hectic pace of gyn and obs, and the complex intensity of psychiatry, I tell myself that two weeks of looking at a few assorted skin rashes will be plain sailing - but the very first patient I see is a startling and disturbing sight. As we troop into the unit I see a middle-aged man propped up on the first bed, lying with his eyes closed, only a thin sheet covering the lower half of his body. There's hardly any skin visible on the poor man at all: every square inch is covered in blisters of all sizes. Some of them have burst, leaving pink, raw areas which look really painful. I wonder what skin disease he has been struck down with. Whatever it is, it looks serious.

The musty odour is stronger inside. Halfway down the ward I realise what it is. It's the smell of diseased, shedding skin. Most of the patients are sitting in bed, surrounded by fragments of their desquamating skin - myriads of tiny flakes which are scattered all over their sheets, their clothes, and the floor. I always thought skin rashes were just a bit of a nuisance but some of these patients are quite ill. The dermatology registrar, a pretty female with a lisp and a stunningly clear complexion herself informs us that some skin diseases can be fatal. She rattles off some jaw-breaking names; I only manage to catch one – something called SSSS, in which I think that one of the S's stood for skin.

It seems that the consultant in charge of the unit is on vacation so the young registrar shows us around the unit and talks to us about the importance of skin diseases in the whole scheme of things. She lets us leave early and I am glad to get away from the smell which is starting to make me feel nauseous. I feel really sorry for the patients who are inflicted with these awful diseases that threaten their lives and transform their whole appearance.

I am never going to complain about my acne again.

That afternoon, I decide to do something rash myself.

Catching a tuk-tuk right outside College, I ask the driver to drop me off a short distance from the Lotus Hospital. Avoiding the busy main entrance with the fancily-dressed doorman, I sneak around the side of the building where I spy a sign which reads 'Staff entrance'. The security guard in the booth outside the small door is busily occupied with the task of exploring his nasal cavity using his forefinger with the diligence of an ENT specialist, and doesn't even look up as I scurry past.

The Medical Records Department is located deep in the bowels of the hospital – the furthest corner of the basement. Most of this floor is occupied by the Radiology and Imaging Department – this where the X-ray machine, CT scanner and MRI machine are kept.

I follow the sign that says Medical Records, which leads me to a long deserted corridor with a green door at the end of it. Receiving no answer to my knock, I turn the knob and push the door open hesitantly. The heavy door swings open, creaking loudly, and I slip through into a large, windowless, dimly lit room. Rows of tall shelves reaching up to the ceiling and crammed with boxes and files stand in rows, casting long shadows on the floor. There is no one in sight and a ghostly silence hangs over the place.

The doors swings back slowly, hinges still creaking, and shuts with a loud slam, making me jump. I venture down one of the narrow aisles separating the shelves, my footsteps echoing eerily.

Where is everyone?

'Can I help you?'

I gasp and swirl around, startled, to see a stooped, bow-legged figure standing behind me, its face completely in shadow.

Where did he come from?

My heart thudding against my ribs, I stammer, 'Uh... I need to look at some records...'

The figure moves slowly out of the shadow with a peculiar side-to-side waddle and I see a wizened gnome-like man with a shock of curly white hair and large spectacles with thick black rims, his face creased with dozens of fine lines.

He squints at me from under bushy white eyebrows. 'What records?'

He works here? But he looks ancient!

'I need to look at some Labour Ward records.'

He takes a step closer and peers up at me curiously. He is at least a foot shorter than me and has bow-legs so pronounced, a small dog could have trotted between his legs with ease.

'And you are..?'

I produce the blue 'Friends of Lotus' card. 'Medical student.'

'Ah.' He takes the card and scrutinises it, then hands it back to me, shaking his head. His eyes are bright and cat-like, a light grey in colour. 'Very sorry. That's not enough. I need written request with director's signature if you want to retrieve a patient file.' He hobbles across to a desk in a corner of the room and settles himself behind it.

'No, I don't want to retrieve a patient file,' I assure him, following him to the desk and trying to think which of the seven dwarfs he resembled the most. 'I just want to look at some old records. A Labour Ward register.'

'Hmm,' he goes, crossing his arms on his chest. 'Need head of department's signature for that.'

It looks like this is going to be more difficult than I had anticipated. 'Look, I've got special permission from the director to look around. This is important to me. It's…' I hesitate. 'It's a personal matter.'

'Personal?'

'Yes,' I say, my mind working rapidly. 'You see, there's this boy.'

'Boy?'

'Yes.' I try to add the right amount of desperation to my voice. 'We plan to get married. But - his parents insist on matching our horoscopes. My family don't believe in that kind of thing, so I don't even have a horoscope. But if I can just find out the time of my birth - I know that's always documented in the delivery record…'

'You were born here?' He regards me with new interest.

'Yes. In the old hospital.'

'Old hospital?' He shakes his head. 'Those records not here.'

'Oh…' Disappointment floods through me. 'Then where?'

'In storage.' He gestures toward the back of the room. 'Locked up. I'll have to search for them. That is long time ago. More than twenty years, miss.'

'Look, could you please do this for me? I can wait.'

He purses his lips, and then says, 'Write down your date of birth,' pushing a piece of paper forward. I eagerly write on the paper and hand it back to him.

He studies the scrap of paper. 'No guarantee. Some records have perished. And some eaten up.'

'Eaten up?'

'Rats!' he says succinctly.

'Oh…but you will check?'

'Come back tomorrow.'

'Tomorrow? Oh, thank you so much, Mr—'

'Just Jansz.'

'Mr Just Jansz?'

'No, just *Jansz*. Everyone calls me Jansz.'

'Oh. Thank you, Mr – I mean…Jansz.'
He stands up and ushers me to the door.
'What time shall I come?'
'You can come any time. I'm always here.'
The door swings shut in my face.

32

The next morning, we assemble outside the Skin Clinic and meet the dermatology consultant Dr Alwis, who has turned up after an obviously relaxing holiday. He is in a jovial mood and greets us cordially. We spend two hours in the clinic looking at all manner of skin rashes. It wouldn't be so bad if they were only on the hands and face and maybe the feet, but being forced to inspect bumps, blisters and eruptions in what people call their 'private parts' is not my idea of a fun morning.

Ugh. Sometimes, private parts are best kept private.

I am impatient to return to the Lotus Hospital, so when the rest head back to College for a Community Medicine lecture, I part from them. Com Med is not my favourite subject anyway, and this series of lectures on Epidemiology is delivered by the most boring lecturer on the planet, who is said to have once fallen asleep during one of his own lectures. At last week's lecture, he had half the batch nodding before you could say 'Typhoid Mary'.

Once again, I sneak in through the staff entrance and find Jansz in his underground lair, seated at his desk, perusing the sports page of the Daily News which is spread in front of him. As soon as he sees me, he quickly closes the paper, hops off his chair and leads me to a long table on which lies a large book with a thick blue cover and a dark brown spine.

'You're lucky, miss,' he says. 'I found the register. It was here, with all the other recent ones. I think someone else must have taken it out of storage.' He wipes the cover with a dust-cloth, and then pulls out a chair with a flourish. 'Sit.'

I sit as bidden and gaze at the book, conscious of the beating of my heart, which seems to be galloping away at a rate of about one hundred and fifty beats per minute. He switches on a desk lamp and a yellowish light bathes the desktop. There are brown patches on the blue cover where the covering has disintegrated, but other than that, it seems to be in fairly good condition.

I open the book. Age has turned the pages a creamy yellow and their edges a dark brown. The first page is blank except for some words written in block letters in black ink, now faded to a light brown: LABOUR WARD REGISTER. MAY-JUNE. The year is written below. The year I was born.

I turn to the next page. The pages are divided by vertical lines into columns, each with a different heading. *'Name of patient'*, *'Mode of delivery'*, *'Time of delivery'*, *'Sex of baby'*, *'Weight of baby'*, and a final column with the heading *'Complications'*.

With fingers that are trembling now, I turn the pages slowly and carefully.

Am I doing the right thing here? What if it is all a lie? What if there is no record of my birth in this book?

I stop at the page for the third of May and then resolutely, turn to the next page. I have to know. I have to find out.

The fourth of May. My birthday.

I try to ignore the fluttering in my chest and concentrate on the writing on the page. There are six entries for that day. Three normal deliveries, one forceps delivery, and two Caesarean sections. Holding my breath, I scan the list of names.

Her name leaps out at me from the bottom of the page and my breath escapes in a long sigh of relief. There it is, my mother's name, the fifth on the list, hand-written in a neat, flowing script. Her full name, followed by the words *'Emergency LSCS'* in the next column. The fourth column contains the words *'female'*, and the fifth *'2.2 kg'*. In the last column is written *'Eclampsia, PPH'*. I knew that, of course. She had developed high blood pressure and had a seizure shortly before I was born, and had then gone on to have a post-partum haemorrhage. She had battled and survived two of the three most deadly complications of pregnancy.

So there it is - in black and white. Faded black ink, on creamy discoloured white, but still clear enough. The record of my birth to the woman I knew as my mother. So she had definitely given birth to me in the old nursing home, just as had been told to me. It wasn't a lie.

But how could I explain the blood groups?

It had to be a mistake, it just had to be.

The blood group recorded in my mother's medical file had to be a clerical error. There was no other explanation.

I couldn't argue with the evidence on the page before me. Once again, I had stressed myself out for no reason at all.

I snap a picture of the page with my phone, making sure I replace my phone in my bag this time.

'I hope the time is good for you, miss.'

Startled, I look up, to find bright eyes gazing shrewdly at me behind the large owlish spectacles. 'What?'

'Your time of birth, miss. I hope the horoscopes will match.'

'Ah-ha!' I laugh weakly. I had completely forgotten the bogus excuse I had fabricated yesterday. Patting my bag, I say, 'Yes, yes, I hope so too. I have it right here. Thank you so much.'

He nods, closes the book carefully and says chattily, 'You know, I was working there when you were born, miss. In the old hospital.'

'Really?' I look at him, surprised. 'You've been working for the hospital for that long?'

He cackles. 'I started long before you were born! Almost fifty years now!'

I eye him with awe. Unless he had started work in his teens, that would make him at least seventy now. Surely that was way past the retirement age?

'So, what was it like then? The old hospital,' I ask curiously. 'I heard it was very popular back then.'

'Nursing home,' he corrects me. 'It was a nursing home back then. Yes, it was very well known. All the famous people in Colombo came to deliver their babies there. Film stars, cricketers' wives, politicians' wives. Beautiful place, too. Airy rooms, large garden, full of shady trees. Old Sir was a very well-known doctor then.'

'Old Sir?' I query.

'Yes. Dr Eddie. Young Sir's father.'

'And you always worked here, in Medical Records?'

'No, no. When I was younger I was very active, worked in office. When I started to get arthritis they transferred me here.' He winces and pats his knees. 'This new place has too many floors. Have to go up and down all the time! Not like the old place. And I don't like lifts, you know. Boxes hanging by wires! I don't trust them. And what if there's a power cut?' He shakes his head sagely.

He folds his arms across his chest and continues, 'Too much standing, walking up and down the stairs when working in the office. My doctor said, better to change job. And my veins also were getting very coarse.'

'I beg your pardon?' I ask, puzzled.

He bends down, and to my astonishment, pulls up his trouser leg and twists a bony leg around to display a network of twisting, knobbly blue cords on the inside of his leg. The skin looks pale and unhealthy and is stippled with tiny blue spider-like marks.

'Oh...' I say. 'You mean varicose veins?'

'Yes, that's what I said,' he says impatiently, rolling down the trouser leg carefully. 'Doctor said, mine are very coarse. And I have a bit of gastric also.'

I interrupt him, anxious to change the subject before he can relate any more of his medical history or expose any other part of his anatomy to me. Not for the first time, I wonder what it is that leads people to disclose their entire medical history whenever there's a doctor or a medical student within a five-foot radius. It doesn't seem to happen to any other profession. I can't count the number of social occasions that have been ruined by the presence of some hypochondriac wanting to discuss with me that twinge in their back (or leg, or chest, or stomach) or their most recent cholesterol (or LDL, or HDL, or sugar) level. 'My mother - she worked in the old hospital - I mean nursing home.'

'Your mother? What's her name?'

I tell him her name. 'She was a doctor. Remember her?'

He frowns in concentration. 'Yes, yes I do. You're her daughter?'

'Yes. What do you remember about her?' I hasten to add, 'I was quite young when she passed away, you see. I don't remember her very well.'

'She died? I didn't know that.' He pauses, brow furrowing. 'Come to think of it, I do remember now - she left suddenly. I heard she became ill...'

'Yes,' I say. 'She had cancer.'

'I'm sorry to hear that. She was a nice lady. Always had something nice to say to me. "How are you, Jansz? How are your knees today, Jansz?" I had a bit of the arthritis then too, you know. Not as bad as now, of course. Oh, she was a nice lady, very nice.'

His brow furrows. 'Actually, I remember when she delivered. She had some complication, was quite serious after childbirth.'

'Yes,' I say eagerly. 'That's right. She did have some complications. Do you remember anything more?'

'No,' he says. 'But everyone in the nursing home was talking about it at the time. She was well known to all the staff, you see. I remember everyone in the office being very concerned about her. We were very happy when we heard that she recovered. And the baby was also alright.'

He looks at me sharply. 'So that baby was you. Can't imagine...'

He continues, 'And now you are going to be a doctor also.' He shakes his head and says again, 'Can't imagine. Makes me feel very old.'

'Is there anyone else like you who also worked here at that time? I would love to talk to anyone who knew my mother.'

'Yes, there are a few. Very few. Matron Yvonne. She's a nice lady.'

'How old is she?'

'Quite old, older than me!' he replies promptly, grinning. 'When I joined the nursing home as a young fellow she was already working there. She ran the whole place.'

'So she would have known my mother?'

'Definitely.'

'Where is she now?'

'She retired – about ten, fifteen years ago. I heard she lives with her daughter now.'

'Do you know where she lives?'

He shakes his head. 'No. She used to live in the Bambalapitiya Flats before she moved in with her daughter. She used to call me regularly to find out how I was doing. But I haven't heard from her for a few years. I heard she was ill. She must be about eighty, eighty-five now…'

'Is there anyone else?'

'There's Miss Saroja of course.' He cackles. 'But of course she doesn't work here anymore.'

'Saroja? Who is she? And why doesn't she work here anymore?'

He chuckles roguishly. 'She doesn't have to work, no? Not after she married the boss.'

'She married the director? Dr Romesh?'

'No, not him, the old boss. His father. Dr Eddie.'

Confused, I say, 'But – I thought his wife was dead.'

'Yes, his first wife died. Dr Romesh's mother. The director married again when he was quite old – must have been in his fifties or maybe even sixty. She was a young nurse then. She was definitely working here when your mother was here.'

'Oh…I think I've seen her.' The woman in the blue saree at The Lake, accompanying the old man in the wheelchair into the lift. The woman in the red *salwar* rushing into the lift had exclaimed, 'Saro, it's lovely to see you.'

'So does she have children?'

He shakes his head. 'No children. Shortly after they married he had a bad stroke. He recovered partly but could never walk. Or talk. That's what happens if you marry an old man,' he says philosophically, and hastens to add, 'He's lucky, of course, to have her. She takes very good care of him. Dr Romesh also has no children. Very unlucky. Married a very rich girl from England, but no children. Now divorced.'

I digest this information when he says suddenly, 'Oh, I forgot. There's Miss Sonia.'

'I've met her. She used to work here then, too?'

'Yes, but only for a short time when she was much younger. Actually, I don't remember her very well. Looked quite different those days. She has been abroad for a long time – about twenty years.'

I think about the three people he mentioned who may have known my mother. The step-mother of the director who was now being investigated by the police? *No, thank you.* I'll steer clear of that family for the time being. The manager who seemed nice and helpful? But she had only worked here for a short time and had spent most of her time abroad, so it was unlikely that she would have anything to tell me about my mother. And an eighty-year-old woman, in poor health? I sigh. It looks like I'll have to settle for the old matron. It would be nice to talk to someone who had known my mother. I had so few memories of her.

'Can you tell me how I could get in touch with the Matron – Yvonne?'

'Yes, I think I have her number somewhere.' He waddles off into a little room behind the desk and reappears in a few minutes, thumbing through the pages of a tattered notebook.

'Ah, here it is…' He reads out a telephone number. 'And here's another one I have jotted down. A cell number. You can try that also.'

33

The first number seems to be inactive. I get the standard recorded message saying that it is not in use. I try the second one, and, after a few rings, a woman's voice answers, 'Hello?' In the background I hear indistinct voices and a telephone ringing.

The voice sounds like it belongs to a younger woman, not an eighty-year-old. 'I would like to speak to Yvonne, please. Matron Yvonne?'

I hear a sharp intake of breath followed by a few moments of silence and then, 'Who is this? Who's speaking?'

I give her my name and she says 'Lotus? That's your name?'

'Yes, Can I speak to Yvonne? Is this her daughter?'

'Yes, I'm her daughter. Why do you want to speak to her?'

'Er… I want to talk to her about my mother. I think she knew her.'

This time the silence is so long that I check the phone to see if we are still connected.

'I'm sorry, you can't speak to her.'

'Why not? Is she ill?'

A long sigh, and then, 'My mother passed away two years ago.'

'Oh!' I can't hide the disappointment in my voice. 'I'm sorry to hear that. How did she – what happened?'

'She had cancer. Liver cancer.' She asks again, 'Why did you want to speak to her?'

'I think she knew my mother. They used to work at the same hospital. My mother is dead too. She died fifteen years ago.'

'Your mother? What was her name?'

I tell her. Another long silence follows.

'Hello?'

She clears her throat. 'I don't know if I should be telling you this...'

'What?'

'I think there is something you should know...'

'What? Is it something about my mother?'

To my frustration, she says she can't talk anymore because she is at work, at an office on Duplication Road. I offer to meet her after work and she agrees to meet at a pastry shop close to her office at five-thirty that same evening.

'Ranil called,' Aunty Sherine calls out from the kitchen when she hears me entering the house. 'A message for you. He wants you to call him back. I've written his phone number down for you.'

'Ranil? Who's Ranil?'

'SP Boteju. He called to update you on the case.'

'Oh, him. What did he say?' I join her in the kitchen and pour myself a glass of water.

'The director – that is your Dr Mendis – has been cleared! They think he was not involved at all.'

I can't believe it. 'Really? He had nothing to do with it?' And I had been convinced he was behind it all.

'They are questioning some other doctors who they think are definitely involved – a surgeon and three others.' She pauses and says, 'And that's the other thing.'

'What?'

'He wants to meet you.'

'Who? The policeman? I thought he wanted me to call him.'

'No. The doctor. Dr Mendis.'

'What?' I splutter, almost choking on the water I am sipping.

'Yes. He contacted me.'

'But why?' I'm still gasping and she comes round to me and thumps me on the back vigorously. 'Whoa! That's enough! And I don't want to meet him! It'll be totally weird!'

'It doesn't have to be. I mean, he's been cleared. I told you.'

'And how did he get hold of you?'

'I'm sure it would have been easy to track us down. He knew your parents back then. He said he'll send a vehicle to pick you up once you fix a time. And I don't know why. To explain things, maybe?'

'Explain what? And are we sure he's in the clear?'

She nods. 'Yes, they're quite sure, after their investigations and the statements of the other doctors involved. They of course claim that the mastermind was a woman working there, that she was behind it all.'

'A woman doctor?'

'No, not a doctor. She was one of the administrators. A manager or something.'

A sudden chill came over me. 'What's her name?'

'Sonia, he said. Sonia something.'

'What! It can't be!'

'Why, do you know her?'

'Yes! Well, I met her there. I can't believe it. She's a really nice woman.'

'Well give him a call if you want the details.'

'Yes, yes, I will.'

'How well did you know this woman?' she asks curiously.

'Not very well. I spoke to her a couple of times.'

'Oh, and not only that. It turns out that that's not her real name.'

'Oh, really? Then what is it?'

'Her real name is Sonali—'

The glass in my hand falls to the ground with a crash. I run out of the room, my mind in a spin.

'Lotus! What on earth…Lotus! Pick up the——'

'Wait! I'll be back!' In my room, I rummage on my desk till I find what I am looking for.

I run back and show her the photograph.

'Look,' I say breathlessly. 'That's Sonali.'

She peers at the photograph, holding it away from her. 'Hang on, it's not clear, let me get my glasses…'

Putting on her spectacles, she says, 'Isn't this that photograph you showed me the other day? Isn't that your mother? How could that woman be in this photo?'

'Because Sonali was this girl who was friends with someone in their group. I asked Thaththa about her. He said she was a friend of someone in their batch. She was invited to some of the outings.'

She takes off her glasses and stares at me. 'That's an unbelievable coincidence. So she must have known them. Does she know who you are?'

'I don't think so. She never asked about my parents. Oh wait – once she said I reminded her of someone she knew. But that's all.'

I stare at the photograph again. 'Have they arrested her?'

'No. She has disappeared.'

'What?'

'Yes. They only want to question her, but she seems to have gone abroad. She left some time ago, before all this came up. They're trying to locate her. And you say you actually met this woman. What a drama!' She shakes her head and hands me a dustpan and brush. 'Here, clear this mess up. Oh, and he also said that it was your idea that gave them a breakthrough in the case. Now they have evidence that the boy was attacked.'

'My idea?'

'Yes. Something about a security camera?'

'Ah, yes.'

'Anyway do call him. He'll give you the details.'

I'm at the pastry shop by ten past five, and, entering the place, I take a seat facing the door. It is actually a coffee shop, one of those trendy overpriced outlets that are now springing up all over Colombo. I ask for an iced-coffee but the boy behind the counter, who has an alarming amount of acne eruptions on his face, says they 'don't do' iced-coffee. Instead, he suggests what seems like the next best thing, something called an iced-coffee frappe. In a few minutes I am served a monstrous glass filled with a milky brown liquid topped by a few inches of foam, whipped cream and some shavings of rich dark chocolate. I take a cautious sip and look around me impatiently. A group of noisy teenagers occupy a table nearby, laughing and chattering.

When she opens the door and walks in, I know immediately this has to be Yvonne's daughter. She looks around, and spotting me, beams and walks across.

She is a plump, jolly, middle-aged woman dressed completely in blue – a smart navy blue trouser suit with blue ear-studs and a matching necklace made of large blue and gold beads. She carries a blue handbag and another larger shopping bag.

'You must be Lotus,' she says breathlessly, dumping her bags on a chair and wiping her sweaty brow with a handkerchief – blue, of course. 'It's so hot outside! Nice and cool in here.'

Her name is Charmaine and she works as a secretary in an audit firm nearby. I ask her what she would like to drink and she opts for a nice cup of tea. The pimply boy, not surprisingly, says they 'don't do' tea – nice or otherwise – so she settles for a mug of hot chocolate instead.

I wait for her to settle down, and then ask her, 'What can you tell me about my mother?'

'Aney darling! I got the shock of my life when I got your call! Asking to speak to Yvonne like that!'

'I'm sorry about that,' I say. 'I had no idea that she had passed away.'

'I know, I know, dear, that's quite alright. It's just that it gave me such a shock, and her death anniversary coming up next week also—'

I prompt her gently. 'You were going to tell me something…'

'Yes, you're right.' She settles back in her chair and begins. 'I have heard my mother speak of your mother. She loved to talk about the old days when she worked in the nursing home. She was a senior matron there, you know.'

'I know,' I say. 'Jansz at the hospital told me about her. He's the one who gave me your number.'

'Jansz?' She looks puzzled.

'An old Burgher gentleman who works in the Medical Records Department.' I describe the dwarf-like man.

'Ah, yes.' Her face clears. 'Uncle Trevor. Yes, they were friends. I haven't seen or heard from him for years. He still works there?'

'Yes. He told me she more or less ran the place back then.'

'Yes, that's right. She worked there for years and years, joined when Dr Eddie Mendis started the place. He was such a famous doctor! The father of the Dr Mendis who is in charge now. Do you know them?'

I nod. 'I have met Dr Romesh Mendis. And I've seen the old man… in a wheelchair?'

'Yes, that's him. Poor man. He can't do anything for himself now. But back then!' She waggles her head vigorously. 'My mother practically worshipped him.'

She sips her hot chocolate and continues. 'She was quite a character too! She worked till she was about seventy. The stories she used to tell about the nursing home! The difficult cases, the bad patients. That famous triplets case – do you remember?' Before I can reply, she exclaims, 'No, of course you don't! You probably weren't even born when that happened.'

She puts the mug down and her face becomes sombre as she continues, 'About three years ago she was diagnosed with liver cancer. I got the shock of my life when she told me. She had an operation, but the cancer had spread. After the operation, she moved in with me.

'The last few months before she died, she was very unhappy. She told me there was some matter she had to settle but refused to tell me what it was. When I kept asking her what she meant she said she was too ashamed to tell me. She kept saying that her illness must be punishment for what she had done.'

She shakes her head. 'I couldn't imagine what she was talking about. She had been such a good matron, and everyone spoke so well of her. I thought maybe it was some old hospital scandal, but I couldn't remember anything like that.'

'Do you think it had something to do with my mother?'

'Yes, I'm sure.'

'Why do you think that?'

'Wait, I'll explain… she made a lot of phone calls, trying to contact someone. Some international calls too. She got very frustrated because it seemed like she couldn't get hold of whoever it was.'

'And you have no idea who that was?'

'No. But it was a woman.'

'A woman?'

'Yes. This woman came to see her – but that wasn't the person she was trying to find.'

I lean forward eagerly. 'A woman came to see her? Do you know who it was?'

She nods. 'Yes.'

'Who?' I ask breathlessly.

'She was someone she used to work with. She came in a big white car – a Benz – with a driver.'

'Do you know her name?'

'I heard my mother call her Saroja.'

'Saroja?' She must be talking about the old man's wife. I describe the woman in the blue saree I had seen at The Lake.

'Yes, that's what she looked like. Thin and dark, but quite nice-looking. She was wearing trousers and a kurta top.'

'She's Dr Edwin Mendis' second wife. Didn't you know that?'

'Is she?' Her eyebrows arch in surprise. 'No, I never knew that. I know he remarried but I never met the second wife before. But then, I was abroad for many years. I came back when Mummy fell sick.'

'So what makes you think she was not the person your mother was desperate to find? And why did you say it had something to do with my mother?'

'I think she asked this lady - Mrs Mendis, you say - to find this person for her. I served the lady a drink, then my mother said that they had something confidential to discuss and asked me to leave the room. She stayed for about an hour. But when she was leaving, I came to show her out and my mother said to her—'

'Yes?' I prompt.

'She said, "You'll do your best to find her, won't you?" And that lady replied, "It won't be easy."'

She takes a sip of her drink. 'Then, my mother said, something like, "I owe it to her. Now that Lakshmi is no more."'

'She mentioned my mother's name!' I exclaim.

'Yes. I'm quite certain about that. Then Saroja said, "What about the child?"'

'The child?' I whisper.

'And my mother said, "First do this." '

'What happened then?'

'Well, my mother was expected to live a few months more but a few days later she developed a complication and was rushed to hospital. A blood clot in the lungs.'

She shakes her head. 'She died the next day. I only saw that lady once more - at Mummy's funeral. She didn't talk about anything that had happened between them.'

'So that's all?' I can't hide my bitter disappointment. 'You don't know anything else?'

'No, that's all I can tell you, dear.'

'Didn't you try to find out? Ask Mrs Mendis, maybe?'

She shakes her head. 'No, I didn't. I had enough on my plate already, what with the funeral and all. And settling her other affairs.' She shrugs her shoulders. 'And anyway, it didn't have anything to do with me, no? Or she would have told me. I think Mrs Mendis would have done what she asked her to and it was probably settled.'

I am silent, thinking about the information she has given me and almost miss what she says next.

'…she must have otherwise the other woman wouldn't have come, no?'

I look up at her, startled. 'What did you say?'

'I said, Mrs Mendis must have contacted the person otherwise she wouldn't have come.'

'Who?'

'That woman. I never found out her name.'

'Wait.' I speak slowly. 'Do you mean that this person – whom your mother was trying to locate to settle some past debt or something like that – actually came to see her?'

'Well, *somebody* came. I don't know if she was the one. She turned up a few months after Mummy's death. Asked for my mother. Didn't say much.'

'What did she look like?'

'Aney darling, it was almost two years ago and she was only there for a few minutes. She was wearing these huge sunglasses, they covered half her face. But she was a nice-looking lady, fair and tall, and spoke very well.'

'What did she say?'

'I told you – she didn't say much.'

'Did she seem upset by the news of your mother's death?'

'Yes, she did, actually. She had no idea. But as I said, she didn't say much and left quickly.'

'Is there anything else you can tell me? Anything at all that you remember about that woman? Or the meeting with Mrs Mendis? Are you sure you didn't hear any more of their conversation?'

'You mean – did I eavesdrop?' She looks offended. 'No, I never. Anyway, the door was closed.' She leans forward. 'But I remember one thing.'

'What?'

'When that lady - Mrs Mendis - was leaving after talking to my mother, she looked—' she pauses, searching for words and I wait with bated breath.

She concludes the sentence using what appears to be one of her favourite phrases.

'She looked like she had just got the shock of her life!'

It feels surreal to be sitting in this room again, being offered a plate piled with Lemon Puff biscuits by Dr Romesh Mendis. I pick one and grip it nervously. Talk about an awkward situation. Because of my actions, this man had been questioned by the police, his institution and staff investigated and been given the worst publicity ever.

We are seated at the coffee table in his office at the Lotus Foundation where Aunty Sherine had dropped me off ten minutes earlier. I had been reluctantly persuaded by her to accept his invitation to meet, but I declined her offer to accompany me inside. This time the actual receptionist showed me into his office, where he rose up from behind the desk to greet me. I may have been imagining it, but his clothes seemed to hang loosely on his tall frame - it looks like he has lost a bit of weight since I last saw him.

'Look - I know we didn't get off on the right foot—' he begins.

Understatement of the year!

I nibble on the biscuit. He shifts around on the sofa restlessly. 'I knew your parents, you know.'

So he's done his homework. I hope he's forgotten that he already asked me about them, and I lied to him.

'I know,' I mumble, mouth full of Lemon Puff crumbs. I point to the long photograph behind his desk. 'We have the same photo.'

'Ah…' he nods. 'It's been a long time, but I remember them well.'

He asks after my father, and then, after an awkward pause he clears his throat and continues. 'You do understand that I had nothing to do with this business? There'll be an official statement to the media to say that the Foundation was not involved, but I wanted to tell you in person.'

'But the clinic was part of the Foundation,' I point out, wondering whether I should believe him.

'Yes, yes, you're quite right.' At that moment he looks quite bewildered and lost and I feel a pang of guilt. 'If I am guilty of anything, it's that I was too trusting. I left the running of the clinic and hospital entirely in the hands of others because I was so immersed in this place. I should have kept a closer eye on things.'

You certainly should have, mate.

He doesn't wait for a response, so I pour myself a cup of tea while he rambles on for a few minutes more on the same theme.

He gives a hollow laugh. 'I suppose I should thank you. If you hadn't come poking your nose here, all this might never have come to light.'

Poking my nose? That's a bit strong…

Then abruptly, 'Are you on your way to classes?'

'Sorry…what?'

'I mean - my driver can drop you—'

'Oh, there's no need. I'm going home anyway—'

He insists and I agree. I finish my tea and he accompanies me to the front door and even opens the door of the waiting car for me.

'Thank you.'

'Don't mention it. And thank you for coming.'

As the car turns on the curved driveway I glance back. He is standing on the front steps, staring after the vehicle. Seeing me look back, he lifts one hand up hesitantly. I realise he is trying to wave. I lift a hand in response as the car accelerates and turns out of the gates onto Havelock Road.

34

'So it was your idea to check the security cameras from that Embassy?'

'Actually it was the residence of the Ambassador, not the Embassy,' I correct Harsha. 'It's right next to the back gate of the Foundation. Yes, I noticed the security cameras the day that I went there.'

'That's brilliant!' Tara exclaims.

'Awesome!' from Rehan.

'Well, it hadn't been that easy, apparently. The Ambassador's security people were reluctant to release the recordings. Finally the Ambassador agreed after somebody high up in the foreign ministry spoke to him. Fortunately they had kept the old recordings - they keep them for three months before erasing them. It was dark and the pictures weren't very clear but they could identify the tattooed man. He's been arrested.'

We are huddled in a corner of the crowded canteen and I am relating to Harsha, Tara and Rehan the telephone conversation I had with SP Boteju the previous evening.

'And what did it show?'

'I haven't seen the recording myself but apparently, it was more or less what I imagined. It shows the boy and the man arguing outside the gate. The man then punches Anil in the face - he tries to run away but the man grabs him and basically beats him up. He kicks his chest and bangs his head against the gate.

The boy manages to get up, kicks the man who stumbles, pulls a knife. He manages to wriggle away but gets nicked – there was a stab wound on the body. He runs towards the road with the man chasing him. That's all that's seen in the recordings – there were two cameras placed at different angles. But we know that when he gets to the main road he dashes across. He must have been desperate to get away – he was running for his life. I don't think he looked to the right or the left...' I pause. 'We know what happened next.'

There is a silence.

'They don't think that the attack was planned,' I continue. 'It's not a very private place – it just happened to be deserted at that time. I think they met just to talk but it went badly. I think he must have just wanted to frighten or threaten the boy. Or maybe Anil accused him of harming his friend. I don't know...'

Harsha says, 'So, it's good news for the man who knocked him down, no? The driver of the jeep. Since the boy died of head injuries which were the result of the assault, he's not responsible for the death.'

'Yes, I suppose you're right.'

'And what about the kidney racket?' asks Tara.

'Look, this hasn't hit the press yet – the police are still investigating. So keep it quiet, okay? They're questioning four doctors and a few other workers from the hospital. The director of the Foundation has been cleared. They've interviewed the staff, and it seems pretty clear that foreigners were being sold kidneys from local donors – something totally against the law. And it was being done completely under the radar – without any official or legal approval.'

'So who was behind it?' asks Harsha.

'They're still investigating. There was a woman who worked there, a manager.' I pause, and then continue. 'I met her once or twice. She has disappeared, probably gone abroad.'

'You met her? What was she like?'

'Quite nice, actually. I can't believe that she was involved. Apparently this was happening before, on a small scale, but in the last two years – ever since she joined the hospital – the numbers had increased. She had been a nurse in the UK, Australia, Singapore, the Middle East. She had contacts in all these countries. The doctors who are being investigated claim that it was she who channelled the foreign patients here. But the police can't find any evidence that she was involved so I'm not so sure. It's just that they can't find her now.'

I pause to take a sip from my cup of tea. The other three listen with rapt attention.

'The homeless charity was being used as a source of kidney donors. They run the free clinic for street people. The clinic is completely above board – it's been running for years. Somewhere along the line, someone has had the idea of exploiting these poor people for this purpose. When their routine medical checks were done, the people attending the clinic were blood-grouped and tested, and whenever a possible client turned up, they were approached, depending on their blood group and how healthy they were. One of the doctors who they think is involved was the doctor in charge of the free clinic. Tara – you remember? We met him.'

Tara nods vigorously. 'I didn't like the look of him.'

'Yes, he seemed quite suspicious of us.'

Harsha says, 'And the director had no idea?'

I shake my head. 'None at all. I thought he was involved at first, but now I believe that he had nothing to do with it.' I pause and continue, 'And he seems to be a bit of a dreamer, really. Rather than a schemer, if you know what I mean.'

Rehan pipes in. 'And the beggar killings? What's the connection?'

'That's still an unsolved mystery. There's apparently no connection. But there's going to be another investigation – to see if the previous beggar killings are connected. If they find that those victims too, were kidney donors – well…'

'You mean – they could have killed other donors too?'

I shrug. 'Don't know. It's a theory. The police think that the lottery-ticket seller might have been killed because he threatened to report the kidney racket to the police. He hadn't been paid what he was promised. The other victims were basically homeless people and beggars. They were easily intimidated. And they were paid – something. Enough to keep them happy. And they paid them in small instalments, delaying further payments. These poor street people had no idea of the market value of their kidneys. Who knows whether they were even told what was going on. As long as these people stuck to that sector of the population they were safe. But these two boys were a bit more savvy. Manoj pretended to be a beggar, his sister told me. As he was crippled they believed him. Once he had undergone the operation and had received some payment, his friend was spurred to do the same thing. He needed money to pay for a cochlear implant for his sister – she had become deaf after an attack of encephalitis. If the tattooed man was responsible for the attack on Manoj, well, it was just coincidence that his murder was considered to be one of those other beggar killings by the police. And convenient.'

'Do they know how many were done?' asks Rehan.

'They're still investigating, but they estimate at least fifty.'

'Wow!' exclaims Tara. 'That many?'

Rehan claps me on the back. 'So it's all wrapped up, then! The mysterious case of the boy from the slum!'

I echo, 'Yes, all wrapped up.'

35

It is about five-thirty that evening when I ring the bell of the big house on Rosmead Place. It is an imposing three-storey building with tall pillars and a flight of black marble steps leading up to the front door. A gardener trimming a hedge with a pair of shears opens the huge gate for me and a manservant opens the carved wooden front door. I ask to see the lady of the house. He asks me to wait, and a few minutes later the woman called Saroja appears, dressed in an orange-and-black batik kaftan which sweeps the floor. Her hair, which had been elaborately coiffed the last time I saw her, is tied back loosely and the only jewellery she wears is a thin gold chain around her neck. She doesn't appear surprised to see me. After the initial flash of recognition I think I see a look of relief on her face.

'I knew you would walk through these doors one day,' she says simply and enigmatically.

I blurt out, 'I want to talk to you about my mother. You knew her, didn't you?'

She nods and says, 'Come in.' I step into a hallway whose gleaming black marble floor reflects several brass oil lamps of varying heights, all polished to a dull gleam. An old-fashioned hat-stand made from a rich dark wood occupies one side of the hallway. I see my face reflected in the long oval mirror framed in the centre of the hat-stand, a look of grim determination on it. The servant shuts the door behind me and melts away. Saroja leads the way into a large sitting room. The room is darkened and I can just make out the shapes of a long couch and some armchairs arranged around a low table on a dark coloured carpet. She crosses the room to the window and pulls on a tasselled cord which draws the heavy velvet curtains back, letting rays of evening sunlight flood the room.

It is only then that I see the white-haired figure slumped in the wheelchair by the window, next to a small round table crammed with ornaments. The old man blinks at the bright light and utters a guttural sound. She gestures towards a chair and turns the wheelchair around so that he faces the room. His right arm grasps the armrest of the wheelchair but the left hangs down to rest in his lap, clawed and useless. Unsure how to greet him, I nod stiffly in his direction and take a seat on an upright chair, which is heavily carved and upholstered in a dark-red velvety fabric which matches the curtains. He continues to make unintelligible sounds, peering at me through bleary eyes which are rimmed by sagging eyelids. It is hard to believe that this gibbering, crumbling man was once a giant in his field, sought after by the cream of Colombo society for his medical expertise.

Crossing the room, Saroja closes the door softly and takes a seat on the couch, which is also ornately carved and upholstered in the same velvety fabric. An absurd number of red, amber and yellow silk cushions embellished with little hexagonal mirrors are scattered on the couch behind her. A large rectangular framed painting depicting a chunky brown nude woman with an egg-shaped face, heavy-lidded eyes, a long pointy nose, and bizarre geometric shapes in the background dominates the wall behind her. I recognise it as a work by a famous local artist whose name eludes me.

'I know I was born in the Lotus Nursing Home,' I begin. 'But can you tell me about her? Did you know her?'

'Yes, I did,' she says. 'I was working as a nurse in the Nursing Home when she first came there.'

She looks at the man in the wheelchair. 'Your mother – Lakshmi – was one of his favourite protégés. She was clever and hard-working. She first came to see him because she had difficulty in conceiving, after several years of marriage.'

'I know all that!' I interrupt her. 'I want to know what the old matron told you. The one you went to see.'

She looks shocked. 'Yvonne? You know about that?'

'Yes. I spoke to her daughter – Charmaine.'

'Ah, yes.' She nods, rises from her chair, and picking up a napkin lying on the old man's lap, wipes a trickle of saliva from his chin. He has stopped trying to speak, but continues to stare at me with eyes that are now bright and alert. 'Maybe now is the time…'

She returns to her seat and continues, 'Lakshmi was like a daughter to him. He would have done anything for her. He tried very hard to help her and everyone was happy when she finally conceived.

'Everything was going well – until the third trimester. Her blood pressure started to rise and she developed pre-eclampsia. Her husband had left for England at the beginning of the pregnancy but was planning to arrive in time for the birth of the baby.'

She pauses, and I say, 'What happened then?'

She hesitates, looking at the old man, and then says, 'What I am going to tell you next is what Yvonne told me.'

I lean forward eagerly.

'I haven't told a soul this before now.' There is a stirring from the figure in the wheelchair. 'There was another woman who worked in the nursing home. She found herself pregnant, and she came to Matron for help. She was not married, of course. She was an orphan and had been brought up in a convent. She didn't have any family to speak of. They agreed that the best thing for her would be to give her baby up for adoption after delivery as she was quite young and apparently, there was no question of marriage. She flatly refused to name the father at that time.'

I start to feel uneasy.

'In the meantime your mother's condition was getting worse. She threw a seizure and had a haemorrhage in her womb – a placental abruption. She was rushed into theatre for an emergency Caesarean. She went on to have a severe post-partum haemorrhage.' She looks strangely at me. 'Sadly, the baby was stillborn.'

'No it wasn't!' I correct her. 'You're wrong. That baby was me.'

She looks at me with that same expression and continues. 'It was a girl. Your mother was unconscious, of course. She was well sedated even before the Caesarean because of the fit and she was kept in a coma for twenty-four hours afterwards. She never saw the baby.'

She's wrong, of course.

She has to be.

The baby wasn't stillborn; it survived. It was small and weak, and had to be kept in an incubator, but it survived. That's what my mother told me. I had pictured that scene in my mind a hundred times – the mother lying unconscious, the little baby small and weak, fighting to live…

She broke into my agitated thoughts. 'The other woman's water broke prematurely around the same time that your mother developed these complications. Labour had to be induced and she ended up having an emergency section too. That baby was small but healthy.'

Why is she telling me this? I don't want to hear this. I want to know about my mother.

There is a grunting sound and I turn to see the old man struggling in his wheelchair, his mouth working frantically, but no words emerge.

'She had wanted to give the baby away… it was arranged for the baby to be given for adoption. But when she went into labour she changed her mind. He thought it was better for her this way… she was only twenty and didn't have any family to support her…' her voice trails off and I realise she is not talking about my mother.

What is she trying to tell me?

I stare at the old man, my heart filled with dread. He gazes back, his eyes blinking and his lips moving jerkily. *What is going through his mind?*

'Do you mean...she gave the baby up? And my mother adopted that baby?' I say, fearfully. 'No! It can't be. She wouldn't have kept that from me. And I checked the birth record! It said that she gave birth to a live baby.'

'Matron Yvonne saw to it that the records were in order,' she says.

What does she mean by that?

'No! My mother wouldn't have lied to me. She told me about how small I was... because of her illness.'

'You were small – because you were premature. She didn't lie to you... she just didn't know.'

'She didn't know? What do you mean?'

'Don't you see? They both didn't know.'

'Who? My parents?'

'Your parents? Yes. But I'm talking about the two women. The two mothers.'

'You mean... the other woman...'

'She never wanted to keep the baby... it was going to be adopted anyway. Your mother had wanted nothing else but to have a baby... in his mind there was only one solution.'

I try to speak but the words don't come out. One by one, the pieces of the puzzle are falling into place but the picture that is being formed in my mind is too fantastic, too horrible to contemplate.

36

'He didn't – he didn't swap the babies?'

I almost choke on my words, waiting for a contradiction or a denial from her.

But instead she nods, and when she speaks next, her voice sounds strained. 'They were both sedated after their operations. Your mother didn't wake up till the next day. He told the other woman that her baby had died. She was very upset at first, but gradually realised that this was the best solution for her.'

'And – my mother?'

'Got what she always wanted – a beautiful baby girl. She was so happy, that was his reward.'

I try to stand up but I feel the room whirling around me, spinning out of control. I sit down again, holding on to the arms of the chair, avoiding looking at the figure in the wheelchair.

'And you – you did nothing? Said nothing?'

'I didn't know,' she says, her face clouding. 'I was only a junior nurse at the time. I didn't even work in Labour Ward. I didn't know any of these things till I visited Yvonne just before she died. She sent for me when she knew she was dying. There were only two people on earth who knew. She – and him.' She looks at him. 'He swore her to secrecy but she was torn by guilt. When she found out she had terminal cancer, she decided she had to tell someone before she died. He – never told anybody. After his stroke he couldn't. Even if he wanted to.'

She looks across the room, and for the first time, addresses the old man directly. 'I don't know what possessed you to do such a thing.' Her voice breaks. He stares back unblinkingly. 'It must have been a moment of madness... '

I wait till the room stops spinning and say carefully, 'So what happened to her? The other... my... the other woman?'

She says slowly, 'Yvonne told me that he - my husband - gave her money so that she could make a fresh start. She went abroad and disappeared from their lives.'

She pauses and continues, 'I didn't see her again till one day - about two years ago, when she turned up at the hospital and asked to meet me.'

'She came back?' I exclaim.

'Yes, she came back. She asked if she could get a job. She had changed her appearance and looked completely different. She had married - and divorced - when she was away and had changed her name too. I didn't recognise her at first.'

'But how did you know? That it was her? Whom Yvonne talked about?' I ask breathlessly.

'Yvonne told me. To make sure, I looked up the records - and looked up which other woman delivered around the same time as your mother and had had a stillbirth. The record was changed, you see.'

'I looked up the labour ward register too. But I never looked at the other names.'

'I recognised the name. When she came back it was difficult to refuse her a job. You see, she had studied nursing abroad, worked in many hospitals and had quite a lot of experience.'

I feel my heart turning to lead, heavy inside my chest, sinking down into my abdomen, pulling me down with it. *It can't be...*

She says slowly, 'I didn't know what to do. I didn't know what Matron would have wanted me to do. There was no one I could talk to about it.'

I scrabble in my bag, pull out my phone and start looking for the photograph I had taken of the Labour Ward register. But even before I find the picture, and zoom in on the list of names on the page, I know.

'Sonia?' I whisper.

She nods sombrely. 'Yes, Sonia. She used to work as a receptionist in the old nursing home. Back then, she was called—'

'Sonali!' I interrupt her. There it was, *Sonali*… right above my mother's name. I had not paid attention to any of the other names on that page, five other women who had delivered their babies on the same day. 'Yes, I know.'

'Yvonne had tried to get in touch with her too – at first. She had worked in so many hospitals in different countries. When she had no success in finding her – it was then that she told me.'

'So she never knew.'

'No.'

'Didn't Matron Yvonne ask you tell her?'

'No, she didn't. I know she wanted to – at first. But it seemed impossible to trace her, so she thought she would never come back. I tried too, but I had no idea where to even start. She turned up a few months after Yvonne died. I don't know if that was a coincidence, or if one of the messages actually reached her.'

'She must have received a message,' I say slowly. 'Yvonne's daughter told me someone – a woman came looking for her. That must have been her.'

I look at her. I am still reeling from the shock of her news but there is more I have to find out. 'But the father – do you know who it was?'

She stares at me with a strange expression on her face.

'The affair was a secret – they knew his parents wouldn't approve...'

'Did she tell you who it was?'

She doesn't answer immediately. 'His parents knew he was involved with someone but they didn't know who. They were anxious for him to marry someone else - someone from abroad, the daughter of a rich friend. So they sent him away.'

'And he didn't do anything?' I say bitterly.

'He never knew about the pregnancy.'

'She never told him?'

'She never told him. He was whisked away and by the time she knew she was pregnant, he was engaged to someone else. She knew they would never be able to marry.'

'So - he still doesn't know?'

'No,' she whispers. 'I haven't told a soul till today. It's been a living hell for me. I know Yvonne wanted her to know, but I couldn't bring myself to tell her. And how could I tell him? I don't know what he would have done. I was in a quandary when I found out. I had to think about you also. And your family.'

'Did she tell them? About the father? At the time?'

'She told them - later. After she was told the baby died. But that was too late. If only she had spoken earlier. Everything would be different. But by then the baby - you, had been given to Lakshmi. There was nothing he could do. It would have broken her heart if she had been told the truth and the baby had been taken away from her. It nearly killed him, finding out that he had given his grandchild away...'

'Grandchild?' I swear I felt my heart stop beating for a moment.

'Yes. My dear child. This - this is your grandfather.'

I felt as I'd been punched, a second blow while I was still reeling from the first.

'It was his son... it was Romesh.'

I stand up and face the old man. He looks up at me, his eyes welling with tears.

I cry, 'You monster! How could you do such a thing?'

'Lotus, sit down - it was a terrible thing to do but don't you see, he only did it because he loved your mother so much—'

Hot tears prick the insides of my eyelids as I rush to the door, wanting only to flee this room. I fumble at the door handle when I hear a strangled cry followed by a crash. I turn, my vision blurred by tears, and see him trying to rise from the wheelchair, the shattered remnants of a crystal vase lying on the floor next to the table.

I reach him just before he lurches forward. I hear Saroja cry out. He falls against me and I stagger backwards, losing my balance and landing clumsily on the soft carpet with his weight on me.

He lies there gazing at me, his body across my lap, face contorted. His body is frail and surprisingly light and he smells of talcum powder and Eau-de-Cologne mixed with the faint ammoniacal smell of urine. I can clearly see the arcus senilis in both his eyes - a thick grey ring encircling the watery brown iris. Tears spill over his sagging eyelids and trickle down the withered cheeks as his mouth struggles to voice some words. I bend down to hear him better and make out one syllable.

'*Low-low-low*—' It comes out like a harsh croak.

I look at her and she whispers, 'He is trying to say your name. He is trying to say Lotus.'

'*Low-low-low-tsss.*'

It is the last word he tries to say. His breathing soon becomes harsh and laboured and he starts Cheyne-Stoking.

When the ambulance arrives about fifteen minutes later they find me sitting on the floor cradling his body on my lap, Saroja sitting on a low stool near us, holding his hand.

The two men from the ambulance crew lay his body gently out on a stretcher and a young doctor examines him, checking his airway, his breathing, his pulse. His ABCs. There is nothing, of course. My grandfather had died in my arms before they arrived. They say that he probably had another stroke - a massive one - and ask whether there was anything that could have precipitated it - some unusual excitement or unaccustomed exertion perhaps. I say I don't know if there had been anything of the sort. His widow says nothing.

His son arrives shortly afterwards, and if he is surprised to see me there, he doesn't show it. He gazes at his father's body lying on the stretcher, then reaches down to touch the wrinkled forehead and smooths back the bushy white hair. He looks up and our eyes meet. There are unvoiced questions there, but they will be answered later. He turns to the young doctor and they converse in low voices.

Epilogue

My two fathers *(how strange that sounds!)* renewed their friendship and meet whenever my adoptive father is in town. This new relationship between us three is still very awkward and will take some getting used to. For instance, I'm not sure how I should address Dr Romesh Mendis – my biological father! He says I may call him by his first name but that's unthinkable. 'Uncle Romesh', maybe? That's slightly less weird. He continues his campaign to implement the registry for donors and the 'opt-out' system on driving licences in order to increase the availability of donor organs in the country. I still live with Aunty Sherine but I visit the Lotus Foundation frequently and have started to help out at the free clinic.

Anil Kumara's little sister Champa received a cochlear implant a few months later, paid for entirely by the Lotus Foundation. It was a state-of-the-art device – the very latest – and cost a cool two-and-a-half million rupees. She is now receiving rehabilitation and has to be trained to interpret the sounds she receives via the device. Her mother and Manoj's mother also accepted the down payment for the new flats, which they will move into in a few months' time. Sunil too, was rewarded for his role in the affair. He refused to accept money but agreed to the installation of a twenty-six-inch flat-screen LED television in his house. Lionel, the mortuary assistant, was gratified to hear that his suspicions about the missing kidneys proved to be true and had led to the uncovering of the organ-trafficking racket.

And the old man - the grandfather I was reunited with briefly - had a grand funeral two days after he died in my arms. Hundreds of mourners filed past the elaborate coffin to pay their respects, including many celebrities and dignitaries. I keep asking myself what kind of person would take an action like that - deprive a woman of her child just to satisfy another woman's maternal yearnings. Did he honestly believe that he was helping them both? Or did his fondness for his protégé completely overshadow his judgement? Did he ever regret deceiving my beloved mother Lakshmi, who died believing that the child she brought up was her own 'miracle baby?' I can't even begin to imagine how devastating the truth would have been to her, if it had been revealed during her lifetime. But perhaps *she* had, unknowingly, played the most vital role in the unfolding of recent events. If she had not named me 'Lotus', my curiosity would not have been piqued when I encountered my namesake - the Lotus Hospital - in my investigations into Anil's death. My father - my adoptive father, that is - told me later that when she was alive my grandfather had been a frequent visitor to our home, until he was struck down by illness. It was his image in the birthday photograph I had looked at, standing with my parents while I cut my birthday cake. I wonder whether it was the devastating strokes he suffered that effectively sealed the secret that he and Matron Yvonne shared. If he had the power of speech, would he have one day told any of us the truth? Would his son ever forgive him for his actions?

I don't know if I'll ever see Sonia again. I think of her constantly. The police had no success in locating her, either in this country or abroad, a fact which I secretly am glad about. Wherever she is, I hope she is happy. I know that Yvonne had attempted to communicate with her before she died. How frustrated Sonia must have been when she found out that the old matron had died before giving up her secret. Did she come back hoping to find out the truth? Did she suspect what had happened those long years ago? How much had Yvonne revealed to Sonia in the messages she had sent to her?

The doctors who were implicated in the organ-trafficking ring claimed that she was the mastermind behind it, but there was no doubt that the racket had been in place long before she joined the institution. And although the police didn't find any evidence linking her to the financial transactions behind the illegal kidney transplants, they seem convinced that she had been complicit in channelling foreign patients who needed kidney transplants to the Lotus Hospital.

I like to think that it was the tattooed man who was responsible for the attacks on the two young boys. But I can't help wondering, what was the actual extent of Sonia's involvement with the organ-traffickers? Had she really been instrumental in recruiting wealthy international clients? Had she benefitted financially from doing so? She didn't seem like a person who was interested in making money, judging by the clothes she wore and the battered little car that she drove.

If she suspected that some wrong had been done to her by the Mendis family, was this her way of getting back at the institution that they represented? Or was my biological mother inherently a crook who saw nothing wrong in exploiting vulnerable people for profit?

My father (Romesh) told me that they met when she joined the Lotus Nursing Home as a receptionist, and they had fallen deeply in love. She had been just twenty at the time. His parents suspected he was having an affair (he didn't reveal the identity of the girl to them, knowing that they would disapprove of her humble background) and had engineered a quick engagement to the daughter of a wealthy friend in England. His feelings for Sonia, which were still strong, led him to return home before his marriage, to seek her out, but by then she had left the country. Little knowing the drama that had been enacted in the nursing home in his absence, he returned to England broken-hearted, and married his fiancée. He didn't say if the marriage ended because he was still in love with Sonia – and I didn't ask. When Sonia first encountered him on her return two years ago she had made it clear to him that their relationship was to be strictly professional and nothing more.

My daydreams are now dominated by those moments when the three of us were together for a few seconds in time – descending in the lift the first time I visited the Lotus Hospital – unaware of the tie that linked us. I relish that moment, reliving it again and again. I know that it is extremely unlikely that we will ever be like that together again, like a family.

But that doesn't stop me from dreaming.

THANKS

To the members of The Wadiya Group and Poetry P'lau who first listened to the random medical anecdotes that were the precursor to this novel, and liked them and asked for more.

To my first readers who read various drafts of the manuscript and gave me valuable feedback.

To Professor Arjuna Parakrama – for reading the manuscript, suggesting improvements, and urging me to publish.

www.ingramcontent.com/pod-product-compliance
Lightning Source LLC
Chambersburg PA
CBHW032013150726
47990CB00005B/1949